C000068580

WINDS OF CHANGE

Further Titles in this series by Diana Bachmann

SOUNDS OF THUNDER

AN ELUSIVE FREEDOM

WINDS OF CHANGE

Diana Bachmann

The first world edition published in Great Britain 1998 by
SEVERN HOUSE PUBLISHERS LTD of
9–15 High Street, Sutton, Surrey SM1 1DF.
First published in the USA 1998 by
SEVERN HOUSE PUBLISHERS INC., of
595 Madison Avenue, New York, NY 10022.

Copyright © 1998 by Diana Bachmann.

All rights reserved.
The moral right of the author has been asserted.

British Library Cataloguing in Publication Data

Bachmann,   Diana
        Winds of change
        1.   Martel family (Fictitious characters) – Fiction
        2.   Gaudion family (Fictitious characters) – Fiction
        3.   Guernsey (Channel Islands) – Social life and customs - Fiction
        4.   Domestic fiction
        1.   Title
        823.9'14 [F]

        ISBN 0-7278-5351-1

All situations in this publication are fictitious and
any resemblance to living persons is purely coincidental.

Typeset by Palimpsest Book Production Limited,
Polmont, Stirlingshire, Scotland.
Printed and bound in Great Britain by
MPG Books Ltd, Bodmin, Cornwall.

NEWHAM LEISURE	LIBRARY SERVICE
BIB	501739
	98-142
COLL	0138476
CLASS	
LOC	CM

CONTENTS

CHAPTER   1. Children's Games
CHAPTER   2. Fledglings
CHAPTER   3. Generation Games
CHAPTER   4. Storm Clouds
CHAPTER   5. Attitudes
CHAPTER   6. Consultations
CHAPTER   7. Allegiances
CHAPTER   8. Balance of Power
CHAPTER   9. Veering with the Tide
CHAPTER 10. A United Family

I shall sleep, and move with the moving ships,
Change as the winds change, veer in the tide.

The Triumph of Time, Algernon Charles Swinburne

Chapter One

Children's Games

"Another shot like that and you'll smash Mum's greenhouse!" Debbie yelled.

"Eh? What? What did you say?" Sue spluttered.

"See! You've woken her again with your shouting," Roddy scolded.

"Can't you train one of your dogs to fetch the balls when they go out?" Justin frowned across at the Golden Retrievers who were lying at the foot of the verandah steps.

Troilus, who always knew when someone was talking about him, even when the person was rude enough not to use his name, raised his head to give the offender a critical glare and went back to sleep. Cressida, who never appeared to sleep, and had seen the ball sail over the netting, didn't move a muscle.

"Troilus would never do anything so demeaning," Debbie said, laughing, "And Cressida, who is ball mad, knows she mustn't touch one which has not been given to her as her own. I'll get it when this game is over."

Suzanne Martel yawned and sat up. "I find watching a tennis ball passing to and fro over a net quite hypnotic."

Aunt Filly moved slightly in the rocking chair and nodded. "Though frankly, I fall asleep after lunch almost daily."

"And so you should, at your age."

"Honestly, Sue! Do you think I'm that old?"

"You must be about the same age as Dad and he's been around forever, as far as I'm concerned." She was making a serious effort to keep her face straight.

Felicity Warwick's fading blonde curls flopped forwards as her plump figure trembled into giggles. "Beastly child!"

1

"You going to have a game, darling?" Stephen called to Sue as he came off the court.

"No thanks. I'm just about to go inside and put on the kettle. Who won?"

"Debbie and Justin, of course. They nearly always do."

"Why don't you have another couple of games? Tea won't be ready for twenty minutes."

Sue spread a cloth on the table on the verandah and left Aunt Filly to set out the plates and cups from the tray, while she prepared a pile of sandwiches and buttered the sliced gache. When she carried out the loaded plates, the older woman had wandered down the garden to search for another stray ball.

So she sat back on her deckchair to wait for them, shaded from the heat of the June sun by the verandah roof, smiling contentedly. Life was weird. How often, she wondered, casting her mind back to the war years, did things turn out the way one had planned? She would never forget longing for the home and family she had left behind at the time of the evacuation, even though she had been unable to remember what her parents looked like after a while. The excitement as the Allies fought their way back through France, Italy, Russia, Poland and finally Germany to defeat the Nazis. And afterwards the frustrating months of waiting to return to Guernsey, the joy of sailing into St Peter Port Harbour on the Fourth of August, 1945, and the mutual shock of reunion with Dad and Mum.

It had been so hard to understand, after five years in an emotional desert, that an essential ingredient of family life was the give and take, the accepting of responsibility towards the family unit. Mutual respect and understanding. And, unfortunately, Dad and Mum, in particular, having parted with a child of ten, took over the reins where they left off. Whilst she, having had sole charge of her own destiny for five years, had returned to the island a comparatively mature young woman, although only fifteen. The same age as her own daughter, Stephanie, was now.

Yes. And was their relationship any better than hers had been with her own parents? One could only work on it!

2

"Oh, beauty, Stephen! Lovely shot," Sue called as her husband powered a forehand drive down the tramlines past his stepdaughter. What a happy coincidence it was that, like Debbie, he was so keen on tennis: keen enough to be enthusiastic about buying this house with a court in the back garden.

Stephen hadn't tried to persuade her to sell the property overlooking Port Grat, the beautiful old family farmhouse that she and Jonathan had turned into a charming hotel. He had not needed to: the joy of its conversion had turned to such anguish after Jonathan's accident, which had changed his character almost overnight from the gregarious, loving man she had married into a morose bully. And although when he had learned he was terminally ill Jonathan reverted to the sweet, loving partner he had once been, nevertheless to live in a place filled with such memories would be too painful.

And anyway, Stephen wasn't an hotelier, he was an architect.

The estate agent had put a lunatic value on the hotel . . . and some lunatic promptly paid the asking price! She still hadn't got over their good fortune though she and Stephen had been married now for six years.

Aunt Filly waited till the current game ended before throwing the ball back over the wire, then she bounced back across the narrow strip of lawn to the house. "Debbie is phenomenally good,' she commented. 'Her timing is brilliant."

"Yes. That's what her coach says. Thank goodness we were able to find him: he's done wonders for her. Completely changed her grip for a start." Sue turned her head at the sound of footsteps scrunching on the gravel and waved a greeting as Justin's parents appeared round the side of the house. "Hello! Welcome. You're just in time for tea!"

"Hoped we'd judged it right. Got anymore of that gorgeous chocolate sponge?" Johnny Tetchworth guffawed. He was tall and pompous, adopting an unconvincing Oxford accent which became louder with the level of alcohol he consumed, lapsing into the vernacular more frequently. Sue

3

and Stephen found him hard to stomach at times, but the Tetchworth's were neighbours and Hilary, his wife, was genuinely upper crust, charming and unassuming. Sue had often speculated on how such a nice woman had ever come to marry Johnny. And stuck it out for so long. Justin was a first-class tennis player and despite the fact that Deborah was only fourteen, they made a splendid pair on court.

"Come and sit down." Sue indicated the empty chairs. "Afraid you will have to put up with a cream and jam sponge today, Johnny. Made this morning."

"I guess we'll survive. What?" he turned to Aunt Filly, hand extended. "So nice to see you again, Mrs Warwick."

The players left the court; Roddy and Debbie to sprawl on the verandah steps while Stephen handed out sandwiches and Sue poured tea.

Stephanie drifted in the front door and headed through the house to peer out of the dining room window at the assembled company. Only one person interested her – Justin. At almost twenty he was nearly five years her senior, which definitely added to his attraction, which was already considerable: blond wavy hair, intensely blue eyes which devoured one, he was the handsomest creature she had ever seen, and the sight of those long, tanned muscular legs lured her out to join the party.

Sue glanced up and smothered a sigh. If her own mother had still been alive she would undoubtedly have said that Stephanie was "asking for it!" Tall and skinny, the girl's soft amber eyes squinted through a long curtain of brown, wavy hair. The siren look. The tops of her thighs emerged from the pelmet which masquarded as a skirt. "Hello, dear. Are you joining us for tea?"

"That's why I'm here, Mother dear." The reply was as sarcastic as it was untrue.

Sue watched her sit beside Justin on the rail, and turned to glance at Debbie. Justin was the younger sister's idol.

Fortunately Debbie was occupied with fondling Troilus, nuzzling her short red curls into his neck. The dog grunted happily and rolled onto his back for more.

4

'Have you done your prep yet?' Roddy asked the younger girl.

"No. It's only history and geography revision. I'll do it in bed tonight."

Her brother frowned at her, sweeping the straight, platinum-blond hair off his forehead impatiently. "Really, Debs, you are hopeless. You don't give yourself a chance in the exams." Set in his thin, pallid face, his pale blue eyes were almost hidden under serious brows.

"And if you practised a bit you might be able to hit a tennis ball over the net occasionally," she snapped back. Deborah was really very fond of her siblings, but Roddy could be far too stuffy and intense at times.

"Anybody home?" a voice rang through the house.

"It's Richard!" Sue put down the teapot and jumped up to greet her brother and his wife Anne, Aunt Filly's daughter, and baby Derek. Sue grinned happily, always pleased to be surrounded by family and friends.

"Heard the news?" Richard demanded, emerging through the French windows. "Frank Chichester is nearly home with Gypsy Moth." He lived and breathed the sea. Boats were his business, his life, and he was totally awed by this senior citizen's achievement, the first yachtsman to sail single-handed around the world. "Don't forget to watch it on the early evening news. A huge flotilla will go out to meet him. Don't you just wish you could be there?"

"Not as much as you do," his brother-in-law commented.

"Are you into sailing?" Stephanie asked Justin, trying to draw his attention.

"Sure. As long as someone else does all the hard work. Though I do prefer power boating." He helped himself to another slice of gache, the local sweet bread full of mixed, dried fruits. "I never see you on the tennis court. Don't you play?"

"Far too energetic for me," the fifteen-year-old drawled, sweeping aside a lock of hair, with studied nonchalance.

"Want another game, Debs?" Justin asked.

Deborah crammed the last mouthful of sponge into her mouth and jumped up, eagerly.

Stephanie ground her teeth and drifted upstairs to her bedroom.

Built a short distance inland from L'Ancresse Common, La Rocquette de Bas was a very ordinary Edwardian house to which two or three generations of owners had done some extraordinary things: things which the authorities would doubtless ban, nowadays. The wooden verandah for example, which ran across the entire width of the rear of the building. And the miscellaneous wings either side that had probably begun life as garages or sheds. One was now an extension of the sitting room in the front while the rear was partitioned off as a study leading from the dining room. The other wing, through a door from the kitchen, served as both conservatory and utility. A simple family house built of plastered stone with a pantiled roof, it was painted white with black window frames and doors, and black chimney pots that made Sue think of housemaids' stockings. Not that people had housemaids any more. Just dailies.

Suzanne Martel had loved the house from the moment she first saw it, and had no difficulty in convincing Stephen it would be a perfect home for them and her children. With fresh paint and wallpaper, carpets and curtains they had imposed their own characters and lifestyle on the old place. And now they had a little boy between them, Bobbie, who was, at this moment, at a friend's birthday party. Sue glanced at the kitchen clock as she carried in the tea things: she would have to leave in ten minutes to collect him. Darling little chap, so like his Daddy.

Sue moved gracefully around the kitchen, putting the remains of the cake away in its old Quality Street Toffee tin, stacking the dishes in a plastic bowl of hot water in the sink. A tall woman of thirty-seven, she had inherited her mother's attractive high cheek-bones, and dark brown hair together with her father's sea-green eyes. They were lively, humorous eyes, full of fun and the laughter which often bubbled to the surface in solemn moments; overly serious people, pompous, full of self-image and importance, invariably sent her hastening for cover to hide her amusement and avoid offence. An accidental glance at Aunt Filly, or at Stephen, or Debbie, could set them off into gales of laughter. Never with Roderick of course: he found all matters in life very serious and toilsome. Even as a small child playing with his train set he tackled the layout of track and stations with an earnestness which sometimes troubled his mother.

As his sisters troubled him. Stephanie was an ardent fun-seeker: she surrounded herself with friends, at least half of them male, and squandered her considerable brain power on pop music and Beatlemania. And recently her clothes . . . ! He was sometimes so embarrassed he would pretend he didn't know her. Of course the feeling was mutual, but he couldn't help regarding her as a total let-down to the family. He was sure his father would not approve if he was alive today.

Roddy was very fond of his younger sister, Deborah. There was no doubt she was a brilliant tennis player for her age, for any age in fact, but he did wish she would work a bit harder at school. The trouble was she could not bear the mildest criticism; every time he suggested she study a bit more her grin would fade, often to be replaced by a sudden rage. A typical redhead's temper.

"Shall I fetch Bobbie?" Stephen asked from the door-way.

"Would you, my darling? It would be a great help if I could finish the washing up and get on with preparing supper."

He crossed the room to stand behind her at the sink, circle her waist with his arms and plant a kiss on the back of her neck. "Happy?" he asked.

She turned her face to rub her cheek against his. "You know I am."

Sue finished reading about Noddy and Big Ears and put the book down on Bobbie's bedside table. She was sure he was asleep, lying there with his small fist curled under his cheek. According to Stephen's mother, Julia, the child was the spitting image of his father at this age. She stroked the black hair from his forehead, kissed him and tiptoed to the door.

"Can we go on the beach tomorrow, Mummy?" a small, sleepy voice begged as she switched out the light.

"Depends on the weather, darling. The forecast isn't too good."

"Please, Mummy?"

"We'll have to wait and see if it's raining in the morning. We can't sit on the beach in the rain, can we?"

"We won't feel it if we're swimming." It seemed a perfectly logical argument to a six-year-old.

Sue could never remember it raining on L'Ancresse during her childhood: throughout the war years in North Wales her precious memories of L'Ancresse and Bordeaux beaches, of the sweet dry scent of purple common vetch and yellow meadow vetchling they called Lady's Slippers, which sprawled, short and stunted, over the mounds and hillocks of L'Ancresse Common, buffeted by sand on the salt breeze, never included a drop of rain. She'd recall only lying on hard, dry sandy tussocks, peering at the distance view made weird through the wavering heat haze. Strange how selective a child's memory could be. She mustn't forget to ask her father, sometime, if his memories of childhood were similar.

Greg Gaudion, Sue's father, watched his friend's second at the long fifteenth hole on L'Ancresse golf course skim low over the fairway, skirt the treacherous hollow on the left and finish nicely teed up fifteen yards short of the green. He hissed in disgust. "George, that was a real daisy-cutter, and just look where it's ended up!"

"Yes, I thought it best to aim for that mound," George said, loftily.

"Liar," Greg commented, wondering if his third shot would reach the green with a seven iron. He couldn't see any justice in this game. When they took up golf together six years ago, he had paid out a fortune in lessons. Tall, broad-shouldered and muscular despite his greying hair, he knew he was a natural sportsman, had been all his life, and he also knew he had a good swing, kept his head down and a straight left side . . . and yet his lifelong friend,

George Schmit, who had only ever had one lesson, held his driver like a axe, crouched and swung at the ball as though attempting to hack down a tree, and achieved far better score cards.

George, short, stout but rugged, fought to keep a straight face. "I repeat, I'm willing to give you some lessons any time, and I won't ask a penny for them."

"I hate to think of you wasting your valuable advice on me," Greg said sarcastically. "Why don't you make your offer to the pro. I'm sure he'd appreciate it."

"Greg, you're all heart. Oh dear," he stopped beside Greg's ball nestling in a hole, "You've put it in a divot."

Greg stooped to snatch up a few strands of vetch and tossed them into the wind, not that the information they gave would do him much good. "Gone round to the west, I see." He eyed the dark front filling the sky from the Atlantic. "Reckon we'll make it back to the club before that gets here?"

"Depends on how many more times you have to hit the ball." This time George couldn't prevent a grin speading over his weathered features.

"Fortunately L'Ancresse Common is one of my most favourite places on earth. Otherwise I'd never come out here with you, you old beggar!" Greg truly loved the place: the wildness of it, the winds you had to lean into at an angle to avoid being blown off your feet, the bracken and brambles, the old rocks and dolmen covered in lichen, the scent of gorse . . . sadly over-powered at the moment by the stench of oil on the beach from the Torry Canyon disaster.

"Beggar, possibly," George conceded. "But not old, surely?"

"They say you're only as old as you feel, and right this minute I feel ninety."

"I wonder how old Frank Chichester felt when he finished his trip? Wasn't that great?"

"Shows there's life in some old dogs."

"I've packed a picnic lunch, Steps. We are all going down to L'Ancresse for the day," Sue announced. It was a perfect

9

Sunday in August, only a slight heat haze softened the shadows cast by the sun and hid Alderney from view.

"Oh. But I don't have to come, do I?" Stephanie was lying draped across an armchair in the sitting room, legs dangling over one arm.

"The whole family are coming, darling."

"Well then you'll have lots of company. Couldn't you leave my sandwiches in the kitchen?"

Sue groaned inwardly. "Why don't you want to be with us? You used to love the beach."

"It's not that I don't want to be with you all," her fingers were crossed behind the straggling hair, "I just don't feel like going out." She wished her mother would leave her alone. She was old enough to make up her own mind what she wanted to do, and going on the beach and making sandcastles with Bobbie was not her first choice. Nor even her fiftieth choice.

Sue found it so difficult to understand her elder daughter sometimes. She was going through a very awkward phase at the moment. At least she prayed it was just a phase. Should she try to persuade the girl? It would be very easy to lure her along by saying that the Tetchworths were going to join them, but hardly fair. Justin was Debbie's friend, though of course that was all; just a friend. Neverthless, it would be a shame to distract him away from his tennis partner which would undoubtedly be Stephanie's intention. "You don't want to spend the whole day alone here. Would you like to invite Caroline along?" Caroline was an off and on friend, spoilt daughter of wealthy English settlers, who appeared only to want Step's company if nothing more interesting was on offer.

"She's going to Herm for the day on her father's boat." The girl sat up, tossing her magazine onto the floor. "I wish Uncle Stephen would get a boat." Though her three children were very young when her first husband died, Sue had never suggested they referred to Stephen as their father.

"Boats are too expensive to run, especially when you have a large family to support. Are you sure you don't want to come?"

"Absolutely."

Sue shrugged. "Very well. I'll leave your lunch on a plate in the fridge." In a way she was relieved: the irritation of watching Steps mooching around sulking all day would spoil the picnic for everyone.

"Are we walking across the common to the beach, or taking the car?" Stephen called from the utility when he heard her return to the kitchen. He was assembling rugs and towels.

"Let's take the car, we've far too much stuff to carry. Roddy and Debbie can cycle which will make a bit more room."

Debbie's red curls popped round the kitchen doorpost. "Okay if I go with Justin in his car? He's taking it so we can pop back for a set of tennis if we feel like it."

"Will there be room for me?" Roddy joined her.

"Well, it is only meant to be a two seater."

Her brother, who had not yet acquired four wheels although he was old enough to drive, looked disapproving. When he got a car it would not be some dangerous-looking sports job which could decapitate you if you rolled it at the speeds Justin enjoyed. "Perhaps, Mum, you wouldn't mind taking my bathing things in the car. I need a new saddlebag."

"Bobbie," Stephen called as he opened the car door for the prancing dogs, "Where's your shrimping net?"

"With my bucket," the little one replied from the garden.

"Well, put them by the car."

"I can't. I don't know where they are."

Debbie giggled. "I'll help him look for them."

Stephen wriggled down on the rug and lay his head in Sue's lap. "I'm absolutely stuffed," he murmured. "Those were gorgeous sandwiches. What was in them?"

Sue wrinkled her nose at him, making her sunglasses bounce. "Egg mayonnaise, ham, tongue, salad. You name it. I don't know which you had."

"Anything I could get into my mouth before Troilus willed me into sharing it."

11

Having checked the entire party for fallen titbits, the dog returned to his chosen rockpool where he lay in the cool, chin on a large boulder. Cressida stood over another pool, ears perked forwards, snout at the ready to pounce on passing cabous.

"Daddy! Do you want to come shrimping?" Bobbie asked.

Stephen groaned. "I'd love to," he lied, "But do you mind if I have a little nap first?"

"All right." The sun-tanned child stood in front of his father in a little red bathing suit, white cotton hat tugged on to his head, askew. "How long?" he sighed. "Five minutes?"

"Fifteen," Stephen bargained.

"Ten," Bobbie pleaded.

"Done."

There was a distinct huff from under the little sunhat. After all, ten minutes was nearly half the afternoon.

"Shall we take him shrimping?" Debbie whispered to Justin.

Shrimping was not Justin's scene. He rolled away from his tennis partner. "You take him. I need a snooze."

The tide was rising fast by the time they all returned to their picnic spot from their cricket match on the sand. Sue was feeling particularly proud of herself having caught Johnny Tetchworth off his third ball. Justin had clean bowled his mother after she had scored twenty-one runs – she had played cricket at her boarding school and was quite good. Aunt Filly stumped Roddy, quite by accident, but was delighted with all the praise from her team mates, and Debbie and her grandfather, Greg, were the top scoring partnership until hopeful enthusiasm had her run out, leaving Greg on twenty-nine not out and ankle deep in water.

"Let's move the gear on to a higher level and then swim off the corner rocks by the cabou pool as it fills," Stephen suggested. Everyone agreed and started to pack their things, except Bobbie who was shrimping again, and Troilus and Cressida who maintained a watching brief to ascertain whether the next action would be in the water, which they loved, or in line of food, which they loved even more.

A long path of pinkening sunlight shimmered across the bay to the group of swimmers, as the great orb sank towards supper time. Thin wisps of cloud were painted across its face, underlining the stillness of the evening, little birds were chirruping in the brambles above the beach, and far out on the rocky headland gulls were mewling.

Greg floated as though sitting in an armchair, with young Bobbie clinging to his shoulders. He was wishing that his beloved Sarah could have lived to enjoy this precious time with their grandchildren. Debbie watched her Adonis climb on to a rock, make an easy, shallow dive and swim towards her with lazy, effortless strokes.

Aunt Filly stood on a rocky outcrop to throw Cressida's ball into the water. The slim Golden Retriever bitch leapt from the rock to swim after it, grab it, and return to Filly for another throw. Filly slid into the water with a squeal of cold shock, hurled the ball as far as she could without ducking herself, then made for a distant rock where Hilary Tetchworth sat contemplating the evening sun.

The sunset was still warm on Sue's face. It had been a gorgeous day, one of those still hot days when one heard strange rumblings almost like distant thunder, together with tremors, known locally as *Les Canons des Isles*. A happy family day. Stephen was treading water beside her. Feeling his hands caress her skin, Sue was reminded of that other time, so many years ago, when they had first made love in the sea off the Buttes. Underwater, their legs entwined and, as his mouth sought hers, she hoped the gathering dusk would conceal their continuing lust for each other.

Afterwards, with jumpers pulled over their heads and huddled together for warmth, they pooled the remaining food and flasks of tea, while the tide lapped and turned just a few feet below them.

There was a faint, snoring sound. Bobbie was fast asleep, wrapped in his bathing towel between his parents.

Driving down the road towards La Rocquette de Bas, the

peace and tranquillity of the evening was shattered by the Beatles. Ringo Starr's drums reverberated through the neighbourhood from Stephanie's open window.

Sue shook her head. "I don't believe this," she muttered. "She'll waken the dead!"

"Who is going up to turn it off? You or me?" Stephen asked.

"You," Sue said very promptly. "She's going through a phase of ignoring anything I say. And anyway, I've got to put this little chap to bed." She smiled down at the child asleep on her lap.

Stephen was reluctant to enforce discipline on his step-children but knew he must back Sue, not duck his responsibilities towards her first brood. He strode upstairs and along the landing to the offending noise and knocked on the door. There was no response so he went in, straight to the turntable and switched it off.

"Hey!" Stephanie protested angrily, rolling off her bed. "What do you think you're doing?"

"What's more to the point is what do you think *YOU* are doing? That racket can be heard for miles. You really must show a little consideration for others."

"Like not charging into other people's rooms and interfering with their things."

"Don't take that tone with me, young lady!"

"Why not? You're not my father. I don't have to put up with this."

"I am *in loco parentis* and therefore you do have to put up with it."

Stephanie ignored him and replaced the needle.

"Very well, if that's your attitude you leave me with no alternative." Stephen switched off at the wall, removed the plug from it's socket and, with his penknife, cut through the wire, pocketing the plug.

A stream of tearful abuse followed him down the stairs.

"Do you think there's any chance she'll grow out of this phase?" Sue asked Sybil. She had always idolised her older cousin, was ecstatic that she had returned to live in the island,

and loved to pop in for tea and gossip whenever she could get away from her domestic scene at *La Rocquette de Bas*.

At forty-nine, Lady Sybil Banks remained enchantingly beautiful: shoulder-length blonde hair, fading only slightly, the Gaudion green eyes lively under thick honey lashes, while high cheek-bones and full lips, together with a statuesque figure, belied her age. Having joined the ATS at the beginning of the war and proved herself a competent driver, she had been assigned to Brigadier Gordon Banks as chauffeur . . . and eventually accepted his proposal of marriage. He rose to General, was duly knighted and when he retired they bought the old family home from the Gaudion estate, installed some overdue modern improvements and settled happily into island life. Although Gordon was more than twenty years her senior, Sybil sometimes found it hard to keep up with his almost youthful enthusiasm for life. He was a large man with a shock of white hair and bristling moustache, but was entertaining and unassuming company.

A wristful of narrow gold bangles tinkled as Sybil poured another cup of tea each. "Of course she will, providing you don't get your knickers in a twist every time she flexes her wing muscles," she laughed. "Don't get so uptight, Sue. Stephanie is preparing to fly the nest. It's a natural process that we've all been through."

"Have we?" Sue looked dubious.

"No. Come to think of it I don't suppose you did. You fell out of your nest at the tender age of ten."

The troubled mother laughed. "You can say that again! And went through agonies trying to scramble back in again after the war." She grimaced. "Failed miserably."

"Do you ever think back to how awful it must have been for your parents, losing you twice? They must have been shattered when their darling little girl returned and they realised she bore no resemblance to the one who had evacuated in 1940."

"The whole concept struck home quite forcibly when first Roddy, then Steps reached the age of ten. It must have been sheer hell for Mummy." Sue sipped her tea and gazed into

15

NEWHAM LIBRARY SERVICE

the flames in the grate. "But I had never thought about her losing me twice, till now when you mentioned it. You're right. It must have seemed like that to her. And to Dad in a way, though I always thought he was far more philosphical and understanding."

"Greg is a far more laid back character than Sarah was. Then most men are on emotional topics."

"Mmm." Sue nodded, thinking what a calming influence Stephen was. "Most of the time. But there was one almighty bust up a couple of months ago when Stephen finally gave up trying with Steph and cut the plug off her turntable."

It was Sybil's turn to laugh. "That must have reduced the pop volume, somewhat."

"Temporarily. Why they have to deafen themselves and everyone around them I cannot think. Much of it isn't music, anyway."

"To fill the void between their ears, I imagine. But it's the ghastly, Carnaby Street clothes that the kids are all wearing now that defeat me. They are so grossly and deliberately ugly."

"Who are you two gels tearing to pieces today?" demanded Sir Gordon from the sitting room doorway.

"Youth is the target. Modern youth." Sue told him.

"Ain't what it was in our day, huh?" He lowered his bulk into an armchair. "Any more tea in that pot?"

"Of course, darling. I brought in an extra cup in case you joined us." Sybil poured, then passed him the plate of tiny sandwiches.

"I've come over for a moan about my elder daughter, Stephanie," Sue explained.

"Roderick is the oldest, isn't he?" Gordon asked.

Sue nodded. "And Debbie the youngest."

"Then she's probably suffering from middle-child-itis."

"Is there such a thing?"

"Definitely. My mother used the term to my father to excuse my more appalling bouts of behaviour as a boy." He stared at her with a very serious expression. "I don't suppose you were aware that I ever was one."

Sue returned the stare. "We-ell, now you come to mention

16

it . . ." She tilted her head on one side, grinning. "Anyway, I can't imagine you behaving that badly."

"Huh!" Sybil snorted. "Why the devil do you think they shoved him into the army, if it wasn't a last ditch attempt to knock him into shape?"

"Really?" Sue brightened. "I wonder if that would work with Stephanie?"

The general shook his head. "Doesn't work with women," he teased, with a sly look at his wife. "There's the proof."

The subject of this discussion arrived home from school in a bad mood. Another bad mood. Miss Clarke had given her a Conduct Refusal for talking with Vanessa in class. Admittedly she had had three warnings, but that didn't mean it was fair to make her go back to school on Thursday afternoon. She had arranged to go for a walk with Tony – now someone else would snap him up. And he was *so-o* gorgeous. Together with a gang of her classmates, she had met him down at the bus terminus in Town. An insurance clerk sent to collect tickets from the airline offices on the South Esplanade, Tony was only too happy to chat up the bunch of girls in their attractively short gymslips. One girl who seemed to be older than the others – she was certainly the tallest – looked at him in a way that left him hopeful of making serious headway with her. When he asked her if she would like to go for a walk next Thursday she had not hesitated. They were to meet again at the terminus and walk down to the Bathing Places, if it wasn't raining or blowing an easterly gale. In which case there was always the back row of the cinema.

Stephanie tore off her uniform and slung it at the chair: it missed and fell in a heap on the floor where it would remain until next morning, unless Mum came in and made a fuss. But Mum was out at the moment. Good, it must be Bobbie's Cubs night. She rummaged in her schoolbag for the Beatles single that Caroline had lent her, put it on the turntable and turned the volume up to maximum.

She was eating a large sandwich in front of the television in the sitting room when her brother came in.

17

"What the hell are you doing?" Roddy shouted from the door.

"Eh? What's that?"

He strode angrily across the room to press the Off button.

His sister shrieked. "Put it on again, I'm watching!"

"You're welcome to watch when you've been upstairs and turned off that beastly racket. You cannot possible have both on at the same time."

"I most certainly can! Go away and mind your own business, Bossy Boots." She leapt out of her chair, barged him out of the way and switched on again.

Before she got back to her sandwich he had turned off again. "When the whole house is rocking with vibrations from your darned pop music, it is my business. I cannot concentrate on homework when I'm being deafened." He strained an ear towards the door. "Isn't that the phone?"

"I'll get it." The girl hurried to the door. "It's probably for me."

"You can bet your sweet life on that!"

"Hallo?"

"Stephanie?"

"Yes."

"Hilary Tetchworth. Could you possibly lower the volume, please? I've been trying to talk to my mother on the phone, she's in England you know, and I cannot hear a word she is saying." The voice was polite and moderated but the irritation was clearly evident.

"Oh! Sorry," was the curt answer, "I'll do it now," and the receiver was promptly replaced. "Silly old bag. Why didn't she close her windows." By the time Stephanie reached the top of the stairs *Paperback Writer* had been reduced several decibels . . . by Roddy. For once his sister didn't complain.

"I do wish there were some indoor tennis courts over here," Deborah moaned. "Whenever I get a chance to play in the winter it's always pouring with rain."

"Sod's Law," Stephanie explained, spreading her porridge evenly over the plate without actually eating.

"Why don't you play badminton during the winter season?" Roddy suggested.

"Because it would wreck my game. Totally different action."

"Oh." He turned over the page of English Political History without actually listening to the reply.

"Please don't read at the table, dear," Sue admonished. "Against the house rules."

"I suppose our conversation is not sufficiently intelligent for him." Stephanie pushed her plate aside.

"Yours certainly isn't!"

"What is the matter with you all this morning?" their mother demanded. "No one has made one pleasant remark yet!"

Deborah pushed back her chair to run and hug Sue from behind. "Darling Mumsie! Are we all being perfectly horrid?"

"Oh, spare us the mush!" her sister muttered.

"Anyone want a lift in to school?" Stephen got up from the table.

"Yes please!" Deborah pranced after him to the door.

Stephanie looked out at the October rain, debating whether to get soaked waiting at the bus stop or forego the possible pleasure of seeing David on the bus and arrive at school dry. Well, David wasn't that attractive anyway. "Yes, I'll come with you if you like."

Sue glanced up at Stephen to assess his reaction to the condescending offer. Apart from the suspicion of a wink, his expression didn't change. She smiled with relief. He was such a dear. And everything would be so marvellous if only Steph would be a bit nicer to everyone. And if Roddy wouldn't treat all life's little incidents like major disasters, and if Debbie would only take up some other sport in the winter instead of mooching round the house looking totally lost.

Still, they were just one, big, happy family.

Weren't they?

And so lucky. One never knew where tragedy would strike next: it was hard to believe a whole year had passed since

19

the Aberfan disaster last October. Even now her eyes would fill with tears when she recalled hearing it on the news – a whole generation of village children had died, one hundred and sixteen of them, crushed and suffocated to death under an avalanche of coal slag.

"Please help me get the extra leaves into the dining-table before you go off, dears." Sue poured milk over her corn-flakes, and waited.

There was no response.

"Well! Don't all shout at once!"

"I can't keep Justin waiting. He's coming round with some friends for tennis." Debbie grabbed her toast and pushed back her chair. "So if you'll excuse me . . . ?"

Roddy was frowning. "It won't take long, will it? I must get back to work."

Sue studied the dark rings under his eyes and his pallid complexion. "I really do think you should take Sundays off, darling. You're not getting enough rest."

"What do you need to expand the table for, anyway?" Stephanie asked.

"Lunch. Granpa, Richard and Anne are coming with little Derek. And Uncle John and Aunt Edna. So there will be ten of us."

"Nine," Stephanie corrected. "I'm going out."

"I'd like you to be here for the meal. Granpa does love to see you and you never go round to *Les Mouettes* to visit him."

"What we having for lunch, Mummy?" piped up the youngest breakfaster.

"Are you thinking of the next meal already!" his step-sister demanded. "You haven't finished this one yet!"

"I've got a lovely big sirloin, Bobbie. That's beef. And we'll have roast potatoes, Yorkshire pudding and veg-etables."

"Followed by your special apple crumble and custard?" Stephen said hopefully.

"Yes! Yes, please, Mummy," Bobbie put his vote behind his father's. "It's my favourite."

"Okay. Okay!" Sue held up her hands in surrender. "Now, may I make myself quite clear. I need help with the table, first thing, and I require everyone at the table, looking clean and respectable, at one o'clock."

"But Mum . . ."

"No buts!"

"That's not fair." Roddy exploded. "You don't need us all to do the table. I've got work to do. Steph does nothing all day except dress herself up like a tart."

"I do not! And you wouldn't know what a tart looks like. You're utterly sexless!"

Sue was about to boil over when she happened to catch Stephen's blank expression. His mouth was twitching and suddenly she saw the funny side, too.

"It's not funny, Mummy!" Stephanie said severely.

Which opened the floodgates, tears of laughter running down her mother's face. "You're not sitting where I am, my darling!"

"Hope I'm not late." Greg poked his head round the kitchen door.

"No, you're the first to arrive. Was Stephen still at the nineteenth when you left?"

"Yes. He and his fourball came into the clubhouse sometime after us. It was bitterly cold on the golf course today."

"Well, it is nearly the end of November. How Debbie and her friends can play tennis in this weather I cannot imagine."

"And where are the others?" He loved seeing his grandchildren growing up.

"Oh, they'll be here shortly." Sue prayed she was right. "I am afraid that Debbie has a double dose of your tennis bug. Look, you can see them out there on the court."

Greg stood watching through the window, across the kitchen sink, while Sue poured the Yorkshire pudding batter into a baking tray. "She has some magnificent ground strokes. Lucky girl to have had the opportunity of good tuition to start her off. Never had a lesson in my life so I was doomed to remain an also-ran."

"Daddy! You can't complain! You and Mummy had the most marvellous fun out of your social tennis."

"Yes. We had endless fun together." Which wasn't quite true. He sighed, because it had ended, far too soon. Sarah had died so young. Only in her fifties. Ten whole years ago, and still he grieved for her.

"Hallo, Granpa. Would you like me to show you my Spitfire?"

Greg rumpled Bobbie's dark hair. "I was hoping you would. Best aircraft ever invented, don't you think?"

"Absolutely," the six year old responded gravely, while he cleared a space on the kitchen table for a runway.

The front door knocker thumped and the door opened. "May we come in?"

"Hallo, Edna! Come through. Dad and I are in the kitchen." Sue whipped off her frilly apron and kissed her aunt. "Hallo, Uncle John, how are you?"

"Happy in anticipation of what's cooking! Smells delicious." John Ozanne, her mother's eldest sibling, was, like his brothers, short, fat and bald. It had been a great regret of his father's that the sons of the family had inherited their mother's stature while the girls had all been tall like himself. John's miserable first marriage had ended when his wife and children evacuated in 1940. Mary had been a depressing and depressed character who suddenly came to life in a munitions factory where she worked with her sister, and by the time the war ended she had no intention of returning. Meanwhile, released from her depressing influence, John's heart was touched by romance with Edna Quevatre who had a most uplifting effect on him. From being serious and morose he developed a great sense of humour, a love of life, not least due to Edna's excellent cooking, and as soon as he and Mary were divorced after the war, the lovers were wed. He reached up to kiss his tall niece, then grasped Greg's hand. "Good to see you, young feller. Been out on the golf course trying to catch pneumonia this morning?"

Greg punched him playfully in the stomach. "About time you thought of taking some exercise, old chap. Soon you'll be putting one arm and one leg in your trousers, one arm and one leg in your Guernsey, and no one will know the difference."

"Ah! He always was a cheeky young beggar," John told the women.

Richard and Anne arrived next, with baby Derek, who captivated his aunt and great-aunt with his laughter, until Anne settled him into his highchair and quietened him with a toy.

Sue opened the kitchen window. "Debbie!" she called. "I'm dishing up in ten minutes."

"This should be the last game," the bouncy redhead replied, her words carrying away on the wind.

Stephen came in. "Boy, that smells good."

Sue hurried to kiss him. "Have a good game, darling?"

"Terrible. I was on the beach at the third. Lost two balls in the water on the ninth and tenth . . . I was darned if I was wading in after them in this weather. Plus I found every divot on the course."

Sue laughed. "But the beer was good. I can smell it!"

"True. I'll just nip upstairs and change. Won't be more than two minutes."

"Tell Roddy and Steps to come on down, will you?"

Stephen raised his eyes to the ceiling. "I can but try."

There remained one empty place at the dining table when Stephen finished carving and everyone had been served with vegetables and crisp chunks of Yorkshire pudding.

"Shall I pop this into the oven for you to keep warm, Sue?" Edna pushed back her chair.

"Sweet of you, dear, but no thanks," Sue said firmly. "She should be here any moment."

Stephanie made her entrance ten minutes later, convinced that she was the ultimate fashion model.

Unfortunately none of her family agreed.

Greg's eyebrows shot up in amazement. "What on earth have you got on?" he asked, sure that she was in fancy dress.

"Oh, Granpa!" the girl sighed. "They're hot pants."

"They look like jolly cold pants to me."

"That's because you don't know anything about fashion," she told him severely.

"For goodness sake sit down, Steps, and hide that lot under the tablecloth," Roddy complained. "You're putting us all off our lunch."

"I didn't hear that. And I wish you'd stop calling me Steps. My name is Stephanie." She sat down, eyeing the gravy congealing on her plate.

"Your dinner is cold," Bobbie observed.

Stephanie picked up her fork and took a mouthful. "No it's not, it's just perfect," she lied.

Stephen decided on a diplomatic change of topic. "So, Dad, what do you reckon Callaghan is going to do about this financial crisis?"

Greg stroked his chin. "I have a horrible feeling he is going to have to devalue sterling."

"Lord forbid," John groaned.

"Why would that be such a bad thing, in the circumstances?" Stephen queried.

"It's all very well for young fellows like you. Your incomes will adjust. It's people of our generation, retirees living on their life's savings, that get hit below the belt."

"He won't do it, though," Richard chipped in. "He said only recently, and I quote, that 'devaluation was a flight into escapism'. Wilson can't keep him on as Chancellor of the Exchequer if he devalues the pound after making a public statement like that!"

Greg shrugged. "He will have to do what is best for the country, I suppose. Let's hope if it happened it will only be a small percentage."

Sue watched the gloom settling at that end of the table. She stood up. "More roast potatoes, anyone? Stephen, can you get a few more slices off that joint?"

"Sure," he got the message. "Roddy, be a good chap and top up the glasses, would you?"

The following Wednesday James Callaghan devalued the pound sterling by 14.3 percent.

Chapter Two

Fledglings

While glancing up at Miss Martin a few times, Stephanie's pencil was busy – but not in making notes on Medieval Fashions.

Vanessa leaned across the library table and twisted the notebook around. She snorted: the broken spectacles, scraggly grey ponytail and chinless face were unmistakably those of the teacher working at a bookcase the other side of the room.

The other two girls grabbed at the book and the quartet dissolved into muffled hysterics, hissing suggested additions for the cartoon.

The unsuspecting victim pulled the one-armed glasses down her nose sufficiently to peer over the top, frowned, held a forefinger to her lips and said "Sshh!" then turned back to her task.

The bell rang, Miss Martin glanced at her watch, replaced two books and hurried away.

"It's perfect," Karen shrieked.

"Steph, can't you do a full length one to include her skirt and those awful shoes?" Caroline laughed.

"I shan't do any more at all if you lot don't shut up! If that had been Miss Crabtree we'd all have been given Conduct Refusals. You know what she is."

"Yes. Sex starved!" Karen declared.

"Are you suggesting that in comparison old Martin gets a regular ration?"

"What bloke would want to do it with that animated beanpole?"

"What animation? Haven't noticed any myself."

"I distinctly saw her look at her watch, just now. Maybe she was calculating how much longer to her next fulfil-ment?" Vanessa giggled.

"Can one be fulfilled by school coffee at breaktime?" Stephanie asked, straightfaced. She waited till the next round of laughter subsided then announced, "I'm staying in here for break. It's bucketing down outside." She opened her bag and fished out a Crunchie. As upper fifth-formers they were allowed the freedom to organise their own work schedules . . . so called.

Karen drank from a plastic bottle of Ribena, Vanessa had an apple.

"Anyone want some crisps?" Caroline Patterson put three bags on the table between then, plus several bars of choc-olate. The poor little rich girl felt it was necessary to buy friendship to make up for her many other shortcomings.

Stephanie knew the score; she had been let down by the girl so many times, had had special outings cancelled when Caroline had a subsequent and more attractive diversion offered which did not include this particular friend. In a way she felt a degree of sympathy for the girl, whose parents treated her like a spare wheel, yet on the other hand she was half envious of the casual freedom Caroline had to do her own thing, of her clothes, her own horse . . .

Karen eyed the proffered feast. "Does your mother pack your lunch box?"

Caroline doubted if her mother knew she had one. "No, the maid does it."

"Mum always fusses about what is or is not good for me," Vanessa moaned. "Bad teeth, spots, obesity . . ."

"And despite her efforts you've got them all." Stephanie ducked as an empty, screwed up crisp bag was fired in her direction.

"You going on holiday with your parents this year, Caro?"

Caroline smiled brightly. "Of course. Dunno where, yet. They are talking of Cannes again." Not that she was feeling very bright about it. Flying south to join one's private yacht in the Med sounded all very exotic to her friends, but when

26

you'd done it several times, and been stuck with aged aunts and grandparents while Mum and Dad hit the town every night and spent most of each day sleeping it off, the novelty wears a bit thin. But it wouldn't do for the others to know that. "They're skiing at the moment," she added.

"So who's at home with you while they're away?"

"The maid."

"Then you've got the run of the house?" Karen asked.

"Yes. Why, do you think we should have a party?"

"Why not?"

"Well, it had better be this weekend. They'll be back the following week." Not for long, of course. Dad would be going up to London for a session of business meetings, and Mum would go with him to have her hair cut because she didn't think anyone in the island capable of doing it to her satisfaction. Sometimes Caroline wondered if she had been wise to make such a fuss against being sent off to boarding school; she didn't really see any more of her parents by being at a day school over here. Once, only once, she had allowed herself to wonder why they had bothered to have a child; maybe it was a desire to satisfy some natural instinct? Or the wanting to have something to cuddle, like some people who buy a puppy or kitten, or a teddy bear? But that whole line of thinking had been too painful to repeat. Anyway, she really couldn't complain: she was the envy of all her friends because she had everything she could possibly want. Everything, that was, that money could buy.

The four girls huddled over Stephanie's notebook, making lists. The list of boys was easy – all the decent ones they knew. The list of girls was more awkward: a matter of who to exclude lest they grab the best blokes.

A north-easterly wind was whistling through the boat sheds, rattling the corrugated iron doors and nearly tearing the roof off its bolts. But at least with the wind in that quadrant there was no rain. Not that it would have worried Richard Gaudion. The lunchtime concert on his radio was playing Beethoven's Fifth and he was humming along with it as he finished applying a second coat of varnish to the beautifully curved gunwale he had fitted onto the yacht's fibreglass hull. Cleaning his hands on a spirit-soaked rag, he stood back to admire his work, and smiled happily to himself. Job satisfaction, he decided, was one of the most precious gifts life had to offer. And he thought about Geoff. He often did think about his old schoolfriend, who had stayed on at school after Richard had left to start work in the yard. The boy had slogged his guts out, wrecked his eyesight, and finally got a place at university where he read mathematics and economics. He had some high-powered job in a London office, now, with about four times Richard's income, but for what? For a poky little terraced house on a suburban street, from which he commuted to and fro for three-quarters of an hour each end of the day to get to work. And for relaxation at the weekend he could choose between sitting in his garden, which was smaller than Richard's sitting-room, or taking his wife and family in their smart car to join a queue of traffic, all attempting to reach some moderately breathable air.

"How are you doing up there?" a voice called from the shed floor, twelve feet below.

"Fine, Uncle George. All the interior's finished and nearly everything up top. I just need to do the final coat on the hatchway and grab-rails this afternoon and when she's dried out we can put her outside."

"Good. There's some new people with a gin palace in the Albert Dock. They want her brought up and anti-fouled. And we are supposed to have the wiring fixed in the Patterson's yacht by the time they get back from Switzerland."

Richard swung a foot over the side of the hull and felt around for the top rung of the ladder, taking care to avoid touching any wet varnish. "They've got so many electrical gadgets on board it's a miracle their generator can keep up with them all," he commented as he clambered down to join his employer. "By the way, how are you and Dad getting on in the Swinburne?" A much coveted golf trophy played for annually.

"He's through to the next round, but I went out at the beginning. It was pouring with rain that day and blowing a gale and my arthritis was giving me gyp."

Richard gave him an old fashioned look; what golfer hadn't a good excuse for a bad round? "I'd better fill in my time-sheet before I go to lunch or I'll forget."

"I thought you'd been on it the whole morning."

"I was meant to be, but I can't charge this account with the half hour spent talking to some prospective customer about his problems. One of these people who don't know their bow from their stern but are determined to convince you they've been at sea all their lives. Pompous sort of chap by the name of Blaydon."

"Blaydon? That's the man I was just telling you about. The one with the gin palace," George Schmit laughed.

"A boat to fit the voice, then." Richard shrugged out of his overalls and pulled an old jacket on over his sweater. "I can't wait for the wind to back. This easterly cuts through you like a knife."

George walked out with him to the old Ford banger parked in the yard. "She's kept going well."

The owner patted the roof, fondly. "That's because I treat her well. They tell me cars are like women: they respond to TLC!"

"You're learning! See you after lunch!" George called, and headed towards his own midday meal, smiling to himself. It couldn't have worked out better, having Greg's boy working for him. Intelligent lad, and bright at school. He could have gone on to university and got himself a smart, pinstripe job if he'd wanted to. Yet he'd chosen the simple life; loved boats and the sea as much as George did himself, and his father-in-law before him. He'd never had any children of his own – his nearest young relative was his wife Gelly's nephew, Billy Smart, and he was bad news. Smart Alec, he called him. Of course he felt obliged to employ him for Gelly's sake, but the boy never did any solid work to justify his time-sheets. All he was interested in was dreaming up "deals" and impressing the girls and it was hard to decide which looked the shadiest. There was that business ten years or more ago when the boy was found to be selling goods to customers on the cheap, all pinched from each other's boats. Very awkward that had proved. Because

Billy had still been a teenager he had given him another chance. To do what, remained to be seen.

George could smell the lamb chops cooking before he reached the back door. Gelly looked round as he came in and quickly pulled the pan off the stove. George held open his jacket and she immediately slid her arms round him, underneath.

He was not a very religious man, but to be so very well blessed George reckoned there had to be a God in His heaven.

Richard's mind was working along similar lines as hugged his baby son while Anne turned the mackeral in the frying pan.

"There's a letter from Geoff on the table," she told him. "He and Rosemary intend coming over this summer with the children. They've booked into the Royal Hotel."

Richard put Derek onto the floor to leave his arms free for his wife. He nuzzled her neck and said, "Don't you wish you'd married him instead and could afford to stay at the Royal?"

Anne continued to tend the fish. "Well, I must admit I did find him rather attractive when we were playing the front and back ends of a horse in the GADOC pantomime one Christmas some years ago."

"Oh yes? And who was which end?"

"He was the head because he was taller. I had the enchanting job of clutching his rear every night. Quite exhilarating . . . Oh Richard, stop it! No, I can't bear it," she squealed as his fingers tickled her ribs.

He took the pan from her hand, put it onto the back of the stove and propelled her round so he could kiss her, thoroughly.

"Let's camp in Herm again this year," she suggested when he had finished.

"In our Royal Canvas Hotel?"

"Far more fun! Who wants to be all tarted up and breakfasting in a mausoleum when one can be sitting on Belvoir Bay watching the sunrise?"

"Did I ever tell you that I love you?"

"Not since you got out of bed this morning. You're slipping!"

Stephen yawned and looked at the little gilt carriage clock on the mantelpiece. "Ten thirty-five. What time did Richard and Anne say they'd be home?"

"About quarter to eleven. As soon as the film ends," Sue replied, adding, "I wish you'd stop yawning. It's so catching." She stretched her feet out towards the dying embers of the fire.

"I suppose Roddy will still be burning the midnight oil when we get back."

"Yes, and Debbie will be asleep. At least they won't be disturbed by Step's pop records tonight."

"True. Did she say she was staying tomorrow night with Caroline, as well as tonight?"

"Yes. One has to suppose that the Pattersons are reasonably responsible and won't allow the girls out till all hours." Sue had felt an inner reluctance about Stephanie accepting Caroline's invitation, but the girls were sixteen; you couldn't go on playing the fussing parent forever.

The noise of the front door opening heralded Richard's and Anne's return from their evening out. "Hello." Anne stuck her head round the door as she removed her coat. "Derek didn't wake up, did he?"

"Not a sound," Sue smiled. "I went in about half an hour after you'd gone and made sure the covers were over him. And Stephen peeped in an hour later and he'd hardly moved."

The two women talked babies for a few minutes while the men veered on to more masculine topics.

"Busy at the yard?" Stephen asked.

Richard laughed. "There are never enough hours in the day. I'm working on three boat at the same time right now. One is ours, which I'm fitting out to sell. There are some beautiful marine varnishes on the market at the moment," and he went into some detail on the different finishes to be achieved.

31

"What type are the other craft?"

"One is what Uncle George describes as a gin palace. A great tub of a thing belonging to some chap who plans to settle over here when he finds a suitable open market house." The island housing market was split into two groups: occupation of properties under a certain rateable value was restricted to people with local residential qualifications, and over that value was open to anyone, thus protecting the true Guernseymen from being outbid by wealthy English tax avoiders.

"And the other?"

"Another very upmarket job belonging to some people called Patterson who live in St Martin's. They're away at the moment, skiing, and they want a lot of extra electrical work doing before they get back next week. Why, what's the matter?"

Stephen was frowning. "Patterson? Have they got a daughter called Caroline?"

"Dunno. He is Simon and her name is . . . Millicent I believe. Why?"

"Nothing. Just that I believe they have a girl at school with Stephanie."

As soon as the car swung onto the road home Stephen asked Sue, "Do you know Caroline's parents' names?"

"Simon and Millicent. Why?"

"Richard is doing something to their boat. He says they're away till next week."

Sue swallowed hard. "Oh hell. And I suppose there is no chance that Steps didn't know that?"

"None, I imagine." He decelerated. "Want to go out there and see what's happening?"

"Tricky. Steps is touchy enough as it is. I mean, if it's just the two of them sitting up late watching telly I'm not too worried. Should we try telephoning first?"

"To be told what fairy story?" Stephen was trying to be realistic.

"But what possible excuse do we have for going out there at this time of night?"

"The truth. That we have just heard that Caroline's

parents are away and we wanted to be sure everything was okay."

"We could just drive up and see if the lights are still on. Couldn't we?"

"We're not likely to sleep if we don't do something."

"Oh, darling. I am sorry. But you did insist on marrying me warts and all."

"Your children are not warts! At least, not all the time!" He grinned at her in the darkness as he turned the car and set off in the direction of St Martin's.

"Do you think I give Steps too much licence?" Sue asked, watching the reflection of the lights of Town dancing on the water. "Roddy's always accusing me of being too soft with her. And Daddy gave me a roasting awhile back because I let her wear mini skirts. He said Mummy would be horrified if she was alive today."

"It's all very well for others to criticise, they don't have to deal with the problem on a daily basis. Come down too hard on the girl, try to make her into some fantasy dream of your own creation and you'll wind up alienating her completely. She has the need to conform to the current standard norm, whatever that might be."

"Whatever, indeed," Sue acknowledged.

They were left in no doubt that the Pattersons must certainly be out or away, and that no one had yet gone to bed: the heavy beat of pop music met them as they turned into the drive. The forecourt contained several cars and motorbikes, plus a young man with jeans and long hair depositing his supper and a good deal of alcohol in a flowerbed. The front door stood open so Sue and Stephen walked in to find a dimly lit scene. It took a few moments for their eyes to adjust, and Sue suppressed an instant urge to cough as she breathed in smoke from cigarettes and joss sticks. The noise emanated from a corner where a clutch of boys squabbled over a pile of records; some couples were gyrating opposite each other, others were gently swaying, draped round each others' necks. Round the sides of the sitting room the serious necking was under way on floor and sofas.

But it was none of this that really worried Sue. After all, she had considered herself seriously in love at the age of fifteen; it was the presence of alcohol which was her main concern. That, plus the drunken brawl going on in the kitchen.

And Caroline was undoubtedly the worse for drink. She had hiccups, which impaired her summoning of Stephanie. "Stepsanie! Hic! You'd better come up for air. It's your parents!"

Two pairs of legs disentangled on a settee and Stephanie's head emerged from under a black leather arm. "Mum? Mum! What are you doing here?"

"I was about to ask you the same question!" Sue found it difficult to keep her face straight; the whole situation was nigh *in flagrante delecto* and her daughter's expression was a picture. But to reveal her amusement would be to give the girl an open ticket. So she lowered her voice to a growl. "You'd better find your coat and come home with us."

Stephen and Suzanne were getting ready to go out; they were invited to the Banks for dinner.

"Any idea who will be there tonight?" Stephen asked, standing patiently while Sue threaded his cufflinks through the starched cuffs of his dress shirt.

"Just family, apparently. Gordon said he wanted to break away from the younger members, sometimes. They tend to make him feel far too old."

"He never strikes one as being old, he's so vigorous and full of fun. Any idea how old he really is?"

"There," Sue said, checking the nails on boths hands, "I've managed to get those beastly links in without breaking a fingernail, for once," adding, "Yes, let me think. Sybil must be fifty this year, which makes him seventy-one."

"Really! No one would ever believe it. But then it's hard to imagine that Sybil is fifty. She is so youthful."

"Yes. A wonderful head of hair, still, and her skin is perfect. I don't know how she does it."

"Want your zip done up yet?"

"If you can manage it. I'm putting on weight at the

rate of knots." It was a currently popular Victorian-style full length dinner dress, high-necked and long-sleeved in a printed, stiffened muslin with lace edging on the neck and cuffs. Sue was facing the mirror, watching Stephen grimace as he fought to bring the two sides of material together.

"I hope this denotes your joy and contentment, my love. At least it would make it worth this effort. Whew, got it!" He staged a gesture of wiping sweat from his brow. "But I suggest you stick to water and lettuce leaves tonight to avoid any embarrassing exposures."

"I guess I'll be safe so long as I don't breathe."

Maureen, Sybil's mother, and Greg, who both lived close by, were installed behind sherries when Sue and Stephen coincided on the doorstep with his parents, Ted and Julia Martel. Everyone stood round a charming antique rosewood cabinet, latest addition to the household, which Gordon now used to dispense drinks.

"Where did you get it?" Julia wanted to know, "It's beautiful."

"In a little shop up Mill Street," Sybil said, handing her a glass of Tio Pepe.

"Ah!" Ted nodded. "One can sometimes find a nice piece up in the old quarter of Town." As an architect he appreciated interior decor and furnishing, equally as much as exterior design.

Maureen caressed with one finger the smooth finish of an open door. Since her husband Andrew, Greg's brother, died, she had found more time to indulge her artistic inclinations and attended pottery and art classes. "Need a hand, dear?" she offered, seeing Sybil head towards the kitchen.

"No thanks. I have Mrs Marquis in the kitchen helping me out this evening." Sybil was wearing a simple long, black wool dress which set off the blonde, pageboy bob and diamond pendant earrings to perfection.

"How on earth does she manage to keep her figure?" Sue sighed enviously. It was more a statement than a question.

"Amazing," Maureen agreed, "Considering the number of dinner parties she gives or attends."

"Nothing amazing about it!" Gordon laughed. "Burns

it all up as fast as she eats. Always on the go. Never stops."

They were finishing their second round of sherries when they were summoned to the dining room. It was a deep crimson room; crimson patterned carpet, crimson walls and crimson and white curtains set off against white paintwork, picture lights illuminating gilt framed portraits and landscapes and gilt sconces either side of the mirror over the mantlepiece. Flames from the log fire and the table candlesticks were reflected in the crystal goblets on the white damask cloth and early hothouse flowers formed a centrepiece.

"I do love to see a reasonable degree of dignity maintained at dinner parties," Julia observed to her host on her left. "There is a sad trend nowadays to wear lounge suits or even blazers."

Sue, seated opposite on Gordon's left, glanced down the table at the other men all in dinner jackets and black ties. "I do agree, if for no other reason than it enhances a man's looks."

"You mean we look even more handsome and alluring?" Gordon grinned, though he noted her eyes were fixed appreciatively on Stephen.

She flashed him a flirtatious glance under lowered lashes. "Yes, if that were possible."

"Tut tut," Julia murmured with feigned disapproval, adding, "But seriously, I do think there is a steady decline in standards, generally. I mean, it's quite rare now for a schoolboy to remove his cap when speaking to a lady, or give up his seat on the bus."

"Really?" Gordon looked surprised.

"Well you wouldn't notice, would you. You never use a bus," Sue smiled. "And anyway, the class distinction and military etiquette you have lived with all these years has probably cocooned you against all that has been happening in society in the real world."

A pair of bristling eyebrows shot up under his white thatch. "Good grief! Do you think so?"

"Oh Lord! I hope I'm not blowing my welcome this early in the evening!" Sue grimaced.

"No, no. Not at all. In fact I'm sure you are absolutely right. One sees it so much on television. Decent manners and respect for other people has become *infra dig*. Everyone wants to be independent of everyone else."

"I agree," Julia nodded. "I think the nineteen sixties will go down in history as the decade of so-called independence."

"Yes," Sue said with feeling. "Children want independence from their parents . . ."

"The colonies want independence from the colonists . . ." from the General.

"This Labour Government encourages the workers to demand independence from their employers," Julia added.

"And the blacks want independence from the whites," Stephen joined in, "with which I wholly concur."

"They have certainly been grossly exploited," Greg chipped in from the far end of the table, "Particularly in South Africa."

"That's all very well and one accepts that," Maureen said sternly, "But aren't we drifting away from Julia's original point? I mean, the standard of speech and behaviour on television nowadays is quite appalling. What is it teaching the young?"

"That sex, nudity and foul language are in!" declared Sybil.

"Which leaves parents like ourselves with one hell of a problem," Sue groaned.

"Did you know this blasted Labour Government is planning to abolish stage censorship?" Stephen looked round the faces of his fellow diners. "You know, perhaps, that girls at the Windmill Theatre are allowed to pose nude providing they don't move a muscle? Well now some character is intending to stage a show called *"Hair"*, providing the censorship is lifted. There will be men in the show displaying full frontals."

"No!" his mother gasped.

Maureen closed her eyes with a deep sigh, shaking her head.

"Well," Sybil shrugged, "I don't see the point in paying

for the view of a male full frontal. Gordon wanders round the house starkers every morning."

Gordon cast a baleful eye in her direction. "I hope you are not offering to sell tickets, my love."

"Don't worry, Gordon old man," Ted announced with mock seriousness. "I shan't buy one."

"Frankly I wouldn't worry if you did. It's the ladies I don't wish to disillusion."

Greg smiled. World morality was busily moving the goalposts, but it was hard to believe that the sense of values on the island would change; not in little Guernsey, so well protected from the unpleasant influences of the English Labour Government, their attendant social workers and misguided do-gooders, by the sea.

"Weren't we lucky with the weather, yesterday?" Sue wrinkled her nose at the heavy drizzle running down the kitchen window. "Not much good for sunbathing today!"

"Just as well, I imagine," Stephen responded. "We all had a heavy ration of suntan on the boat."

Uncle George had invited Greg and all his family to join him and Gelly for a day-trip over to Herm – Sue's most favourite spot on the globe. The sun had shone all day, one of those brilliant, clear August days when the coast of France stands plainly visible on the horizon. Apart from the centre of the Little Russel, the main waterway between Herm and Guernsey where all the shipping sails to and from England, and where the tide surges in and out of the Bay of St Malo twice daily, the sea had been as smooth as a pane of glass. The separate households had converged at St Sampson's Harbour to load up their respective picnics into the ageing but immaculate craft, which George tended so lovingly every year. And once under way, Greg and George were easily persuaded to recount their adventure in this same boat when, in May 1940, they had dared to cross over to Dilette on the French coast to rescue Sue's Uncle William Ozanne and his wife and three small children, barely an hour ahead of the Nazi advance. Roddy and his sisters never tired of the tale, and Bobbie had peppered the elderly men with

38

numerous questions. They had pottered round The Humps, rocks north-east of the island, with mackerel lines over the stern. The catch was limited, but fun for Bobbie, and when George dropped the hook in Belvoir they had all swum together before lunch on the beach.

Away from her friends, even Stephanie had enjoyed ball games and bathing with her brothers and sister, and went so far as to take Bobbie off on to the rocks with his bucket, fishing for cabous. Aware that she needed to earn some Brownie points to counter-balance the debacle of Caroline's party, she continued to make a big effort. Much of the trouble at that party had been caused by gate-crashers who raided the Patterson's cocktail cabinet, broke glasses and succeeded in wrecking the sitting-room carpet. The Patterson's themselves were livid on their return, blamed the poor maid, who had been powerless to stop the invasion, and bought Caroline a splendid new large-screen TV to encourage her into more peaceful entertainment.

Sue had expected Stephanie to be furious that they had fetched her home, but after the initial shock of seeing them there, she said she didn't mind too much as she didn't really like the boy she was necking with that evening, anyway. Sue and Stephen had looked at each other with mouths hanging open.

"It's all right for you lot on holiday," Stephen said, grabbing an umbrella from the stand in the hall. "Some of us have to get back to work. What about you, Roddy? You did say you would like to come in to the office with me this week and try your hand on the drawing board."

"I'm ready." Roddy drained his cup and stood up. "Am I suitably dressed?" He was wearing his school grey flannels and jacket.

"Fine. Let's go." Both Sue and Stephen were delighted that Roddy was showing so much interest in architecture, seeming set to join the latter in the profession after leaving university. He was certainly an odd ball, had few friends, apparently being uninterested in socialising, and though he played a little golf and tennis he showed little aptitude in either. Although he was now seventeen, his frame remained slight, despite Sue's efforts to nourish him; he certainly didn't square up to Justin Tetchworth's stature, or even to the boys in Stephanie's circle of friends.

At the offices, Stephen left Roddy under the watchful eye of a kindly, older member of staff who had been with the firm forever, then went off to his own office to tackle his Monday morning desk. The mild sunburn of yesterday burned through the back of his shirt, a comforting feeling as he gazed through the haze of drizzle across the harbour towards the invisible Herm and Jethou islands.

There was a tap on his door which opened to admit his secretary. "Good morning, Mr Martel. Did you have a good weekend?"

"Hallo, Daphne. Yes, super. Went to Herm for the day. What about you?"

"We went down to Fermain and nearly got roasted alive. It was really too hot. Here, the post is early this morning." She deposited the pile of mail on his desk.

They discussed the anticipated workload for the day and she had only returned to her office two minutes when she called him on the phone. "I have an Englishman on the phone who insists he must speak to you only. Name of Blaydon."

"What is it about?"

"He won't say."

Stephen sighed. "You'd better put him through."

"Martel?"

"Speaking."

"I'm told you specialise in up-dating old Guernsey houses."

"Yes."

"I'm thinking of buying one. If I do I would like you to submit some plans along the lines I would give you, but I imagine it would be better for you to see the place to discuss feasibility before I go ahead. Could we make an appointment with the agent for later this morning?"

"I'm sorry but I have two interviews this morning plus a site meeting. Could we make it this afternoon?"

"I'd prefer this morning if you could rearrange your diary," Blaydon pressed.

Stephen didn't like his tone, but thought the work could be lucrative. "I might be able to change the timing of the interviews but I can do nothing about the site meeting. I have clients flying in especially. What's the time now, nine-fifteen. Shall we say nine-forty-five, providing I can make it. I can get my secretary to call you back within ten minutes."

"Hmm! Seems you're too busy to accommodate me!" There was a slight sneer in the voice.

Stephen was a mild, gentle man, never quick to rise to a baiting. But he was annoyed. "Sir, as I am sure you are aware, any professional man with an empty diary is a bankrupt. Happily I am not one of them. Nor, you will find, am I prepared to let down an established client on the strength of a phone call from a total stranger. However," he continued as Blaydon attempted to interrupt, "I should be delighted to accommodate you providing my secretary is able to adjust my appointments without inconveniencing anyone."

"Hmm! Well! I see," the newcomer blustered. "Then I'll wait to hear from you within five minutes."

"Better make it ten. Not always possible to get people immediately. I hope we may help you. Good-bye."

Ted Martel was standing in the doorway as Stephen replaced the receiver. "Hallo! Someone been ruffling your feathers this early in the day?" He walked across to the window and peered down at the harbour.

"Dammit, it's not as though we are anti these newcomers who come to settle on the island," the younger man growled. "But when they treat you like dirt and try ordering you about it really is a bit much."

"Some of them seem to think it's the price we must pay for the tax they pay into our economy. They seem to forget that they do so purely to dodge paying twice or three times as much in England." He sat on the window while Stephen asked Daphne to sort out his appointments. "Your mother's friend, Mary Phillips, has a dress shop in Mill Street," he went on. "She had a customer from Fort George the other day who spent an hour trying on just about every garment in the place." Fort George was the glorified millionaire's ghetto, the island's equivalent of London's Mayfair. "The woman finally made up her mind she wanted a dress, providing Mary knocked off a massive discount. Mary refused, the woman argued, and finally Mary said, very quietly, 'Can you please explain to me how you, with your obvious wealth, can justify trying to force me, with my fractional comparative income, into giving you money for nothing?' Well, this was going on in front of other customers and the woman felt an absolute fool. She turned tomato red, said something about it being worth a try, wrote a cheque and left."

Stephen laughed. "The big question is, did the cheque bounce?"

"I haven't heard that it did. But it certainly wouldn't be the first to do so written by these big spenders!"

Daphne knocked and came in. "I've been able to change those appointments for you. I'll adjust the times in your diary."

"Mum? Can I have a word with you?"

Sue, on her knees weeding along the border below the verandah, smiled up at Stephanie, happy the girl sought to discuss anything with her. "Of course. What's on your mind?"

"A holiday with my friends." Stephanie sat down on the parched lawn near her mother, obviously conjuring up the best words to frame her request.

Sue's heart sank. "What sort of holiday?"

"Camping."

"Go on."

"Well, Vanessa and Karen were wondering if I could join them in Alderney for a week."

"Just the three of you?"

"Well, no. Karen's brother and two of his friends are going, too."

Sue tipped back off her heels to sit beside her. "You are asking me for permission to go off and sleep in a tent with three boys?"

"No. They have got their own tent. Karen and Vanessa are going to be there, I told you."

"And you can give a one hundred percent guarantee that the boys will remain in their tent exclusively, while you girls remain in yours?" Sue shook her head, holding up a hand. "No! Don't answer that. You cannot possibly give me a satisfactory answer without fibbing. Can you?"

Stephanie scowled at her. "Mum, I am sixteen now! Of course we would socialise with the boys and have our meals together."

Sue reached out her hand. "Yes, darling, you are sixteen. And surely you are old enough to realise at least some of the problems that could arise." She grasped Stephanie's arm affectionately. "Therefore you do understand that I couldn't possibly agree to you going."

Stephanie snatched her arm away. "No I do not! You are just proving that you don't trust me. You treat me like a baby!"

"Oh, Steps, you know that's not true," Sue pleaded.

"It is true. And please stop calling me Steps. My name is Stephanie, and funnily enough I like it!" She got up and stomped onto the verandah. "You might at least have said you'd think about it!" she called over her shoulder.

Sue had picked up the weed basket to take down to the bonfire, when Roddy came round the corner of the house on his bike. "What's up with you, Mum? You look bushwacked."

"I feel bushwacked. I've just had another set-to with your sister."

"Oh, not again!" He leaned the bike against the wall.

"Tell me. You were at school with her friend Karen's brother, weren't you?"

"Yes?"

"What is he like? Him and his friends."

Roddy shrugged. "I don't know. In what way do you mean?"

"Well, do you reckon there is any harm in them? As far as girls are concerned?"

"Oh, I see. Well they're not bad. As far as I know they

43

are just as harmless as any randy sixteen or seventeen year olds."

Sue couldn't help smiling. "Like you, you mean?"

"I'm eighteen, in case you've forgotten. And girls take to me just about as much as cats take to water." He made a moué. "So what's this all about?"

Sue told him. "Steps was so cross when I said no, she made me feel totally unreasonable," she added. "Do you think I'm being too strict?"

"I've never thought you were strict enough. You've always let her get away with murder."

"Oh, Roddy! Now you've got me completely confused."

"Don't see why. I mean, she knows all about sex, and either she's going ahead, or she won't. Stopping her going camping won't make any difference. And as for the boys, they may take what's offered but I don't imagine they'd force the issue."

"Even if they got themselves drunk?" Sue said doubtfully.

"Ah! That's another matter."

The girls met at the end of the Albert Pier in Town, overlooking the harbour, and settled themselves on a bench seat to chat. They were discussing their respective parents' reactions to the camping idea, and Stephanie was bemoaning the fact that hers were the most old-fashioned, narrow-minded of the lot.

"I suppose your mother visualises you having sex morning, noon and night," Karen remarked.

"What about you?" Vanessa accused.

"Have you gone all the way?" Stephanie asked Karen.

"Yes, of course."

"I didn't know you had. What's it like?"

"A bit of a bore, really."

"How many times?" Vanessa wanted to know.

"Oh, four or five," Karen bragged. "Can't actually remember."

"If it is such a bore, then why did you go on doing it again and again?" Stephanie clearly didn't believe her. It was not that she hadn't entertained the idea herself. She had had the urge to go on a couple of times, then lost her courage. But the idea that her friend, Karen, whom she thought she knew so well, had done it several times without telling, was hard to believe. "Do you think Caroline has done it?" she asked the others.

"Yes."

"No."

They continued to speculate about all their mutual acquaintances, male and female, before moving on to the school teachers and anyone else they could think of until they ran out of subjects. Then they went into the café for ice cream cones.

"Do you think you could face going up to the Richmond for drinks with some new clients of mine?" Stephen asked at supper.

"When?" Sue was making a mental note to get more fish with her next order, not really concentrating.

"They suggested after Christmas. They'll be in London till the New Year."

"What are they like?"

"Not too bad, once you get to know them."

"Are they formal or informal?"

"Informal. Just wear a frock or something."

"Men! So you want me to meet some strangers sometime next year, wearing a frock?"

"I do love you when you are being vague. You are all soft and cuddly."

"Oh, Uncle Stephen, must you?" Debbie complained. "We are trying to eat our supper!"

"What's their name?"

"Blaydon."

"I thought that was the name of the man with the tarty wife. You said they were awful."

"Yes. But like I say, they improve with knowing."

"Sounds like one mighty exhilarating evening coming up!" Stephanie commented.

*　　*　　*

"Steps, have you ever been in love?" Debbie was using her sister for tennis practice and wishing she had chosen the side wall of the house instead; at least the ball would keep coming back.

"Don't call me Steps or I won't help you practice." She thought she was doing her kid sister a great kindness. "Yes and no. Yes, I like necking, but no I've never fallen mind, body and soul for one bloke. How much longer do I have to keep this up?"

"We can pack it in now if you like. Tell me, have you ever done it?"

"Mind your own business," Stephanie retorted, adding, after a moment's thought, "Why do you ask? Are you in love with Justin?"

"Yes."

"Can't be at your age. It's just infatuation."

"Come off it! You're only one year older than I am!"

Stephanie ignored the comment and finished collecting up the practice balls.

Chapter Three

Generation Games

A peroxide blonde with huge earrings and a voice and bosom to match, opened the door. "Oh, hi! Are you the, um . . . Martels?"

"Yes. Are Mr and Mrs Blaydon in?" Sue responded, wondering who on earth this creature could be, while Stephen mentally kicked himself for not forewarning her.

"We certainly are. That's me, Carol Blaydon. You'll have to excuse Cyril for the moment, he's on the phone to one of his brokers. Come on in."

The suite in the Richmond Hotel would have been charming, but for the litter of clothes, papers and empty glasses strewn everywhere. Stephen and Sue followed their hostess across a bedroom and through an intervening door to another which was furnished as a sitting-room with a small dining table in the window, overlooking the lights of the harbour.

Their intended host was sitting with his back to them at a small desk, rocking on the back legs of a dining chair, no doubt doing it untold damage. A telephone receiver was clamped between his shoulder and ear, a damp cigar was clamped in his teeth, in his right hand was a gold pen with which he was scribbling indecipherables on the blotter, while the fat fingers of his left hand waved, acknowledging their arrival before returning to drum impatiently on the desk. "Yes, yes, Giles old chap. So forget about the gilts for now and only sell those others if they go over four quid. I reckon that's where they'll peak. Now I must go, I've got some people arrived to see me. Cheerio." And having disposed of the phone and the pen, he got up and extended a podgy hand towards Sue. "You have to be Suzy, Stevie's gorgeous wife I've been hearing so much about." He squeezed her hand unpleasantly tight. "I'm Cyril Blaydon," he announced with pride, adding graciously, "Call me Cy."

Sue's reaction to the pain in her knuckles and offence at being called Suzy, which she hated, was hidden behind a polite mask.

Stephen, who had never been called "Stevie" in his life, was trying to recall ever having mentioned Sue's name to the man.

"Cy" lifted the phone again. "Bollinger and four glasses, as quick as you like. And plenty of nuts and crisps."

Sue watched him, wondering how this funny little fat man with coarse features and ill-manners had come by his money. He was virtually hairless, not only on his head, which he regularly polished with a sweaty hand gleaming with a large, diamond signet ring, but he was noticibly lacking in eyebrows and lashes. Only his nose sprouted verdant growth. "So, have you seen any more interesting properties recently?" she asked. Stephen had told her that the Island Beauties Committee had turned down all the gross alterations his prospective clients demanded him to make to the lovely old Guernsey granite houses they had wanted to buy.

"I've made an offer on a house which isn't strictly on the market. The old couple don't really want to move, but" he gave a smug grin "everything on this earth has a price."

Sue couldn't resist grinning back at him, saying, "Except in Guernsey, you may find."

Stephen coughed and Sue got the message.

"Do you have family with you?" she changed the subject, addressing Carol.

"Two of the girl's are here. Amanda and Coralie. They should be back soon. Neal is—"

"My son," Cy interrupted, "is in business with me. He's an accountant. And my daughter, Victoria, is a career girl in the City."

"You understand that Coralie and Amanda are my daughters," Carol explained, seeing Sue's bemused expression, "and Neal and Victoria are Cy's. By our previous marriages."

48

The barman arrived with a tray of champagne, nibbles and glasses, expertly removed the cork without sound or spillage, and poured.

"You say your girls are coming in soon?" Blaydon asked his wife. When she nodded he told the barman, "You'd better bring up another bottle and two more glasses, then."

"Certainly, sir," the Italian replied, accepting the generous tip for the lack of a "please" or "thank you". And when he opened the door a young woman was standing there, waiting to enter.

Amanda Smith was very obviously her mother's daughter – not so much in looks as in style. In Sue's eyes the very high heels, microscopic black leather mini-skirt and see-through blouse, topped by Rita Hayworth-length curls over her shoulders and film-set make-up, denoted a second generation vamp. Introductions made, Amanda gave her champagne glass a liberal smearing of lipstick and clawed at the crisps with red talons. She made no contribution to the conversation.

When her sister arrived the visitors, anticipating more of the same, were silenced by the difference: Coralie was as skinny and flat-chested as Amanda and her mother were well-endowed, plain and sexless. She had a strangely faded look as though someone had washed all the colour out of her thin, short hair and pale blue eyes.

"Coralie is mad on horses," Carol said, as though she felt some explanation was needed. "And she's just finished an advanced course in flower arrangements."

Sue failed to see a connection between the two. "Which do you prefer?"

"Flowers," said Coralie, who loved horses but was scared stiff of riding them. "I'm hoping to start up a business over here. I particularly like dried flowers. Don't you?"

Sue didn't but offered a polite reply. She had a constant urge to look at her watch, wondering how much longer she and Stephen would be obliged to stay. "And what about you, Amanda? What are your interests?" Apart from men! Sue thought tartly.

"Acting. I'm resting at present but have a couple of auditions coming up soon." She didn't mention that the possible parts were as film extras, and fortunately Sue didn't ask.

Eventually Stephen saved Sue's sanity. "Good Lord! Look at the time! We really must be getting back to the family." It was only seven-thirty but though the family had absolutely no need of them, he too had had enough.

"I thought you said they improved with knowing," Sue accused on the way home.

"Well, he does. She's his second wife and he's her third husband. One has to wonder what on earth his first wife could have been like for him to have swapped her for this one!"

"I imagine it more likely that she was the one who decided to swap!"

A freezing north-easterly wind was delaying the advance of spring: the soft green fingers of compound leaves on the horse chestnut tree in the front garden were regretting emerging so early from their buds, the last of the camellias were torn from their beds and tossed face-down on to the ground and the black-stocking chimney-pots on *Les Rocquettes de Bas* streamed smoke. Indoors, Troilus and Cressida lay on their hairy hearthrug in front of the fire where Stephanie had joined them.

She adored the dogs; the dogs adored her. They loved the feel of her fingers combing through their coats and scratching round their necks and ears, prompting her with wet-nosed nudges if she stopped. But, perhaps even more important, they showed no resentment when she absented herself for hours, when she returned just allowing her to resume where she left off. They seemed totally indifferent to what she was wearing or the state of her hair, never criticised the chaos in her bedroom and only once objected to one of the boyfriends she brought home, chiefly because he happened to own, and smell of, a boxer. Troilus and Cressida could not stand boxers.

Stephanie was lying stretched on the rug between the Golden Retrievers, propped on one elbow, hair strewn over her heavily made-up face, half woman, half child. "Who's a daft old fellow, then?" she crooned at Troilus. Cressida raised her head and nudged a beloved tennis ball into the girl's back. Stephanie reached over, grabbed the ball, pretended to throw it and, whilst the excited bitch dashed to retrieve it, she hid it under the rug. Troilus watched the game for a while as his mate hunted round the furniture, and eventually dragged himself to his feet, fetched the ball from where he had seen it placed, and lay with it conspicuously visible between his paws. When Cressida saw it she bounced up and was brought up short by the dog's playful growl: he had no intention of relinquishing it till he became bored with the game.

"Troilus, you old spoil-sport!" Stephanie gave him a shove, which he ignored.

Sue was in her armchair, supposedly knitting, but in reality the half-finished navy-blue sleeve lay in her lap while she watched her daughter with the pets. Strange, how relaxed and natural the girl could be at times: with animals, with young Bobbie and with strangers; with her friends, male and female, one could hear them laughing and joking together. With people who did not make her feel threatened. Threatened? Who was threatening her for heaven's sake? Sue picked up the knitting, focusing her eyes on the wool and needles, trying to hide her disappointment and hurt that her daughter could not share the same laughter and intimacy with herself. She felt so cut off: a mother amputated from her daughter's feelings.

Had her own mother felt like this, she wondered? Had the intimacy and understanding they shared shortly before Sarah died made up for the terrible gap in their relationship after the war? And had the war really been to blame? Or was this perhaps a common phenomenon across the generations?

Sue felt a constant need to discuss the situation with someone. Sybil? She was a dear but one got the feeling of being a dreadful bore repeatedly raising the problems of one's relationship with one's children with her, especially as she and Gordon had no children of their own. Aunt Filly had often proved a staunch ally in the past, but being of her mother's generation she was too far removed from current mores amongst the young. Of course it was Stephen's ear she most wanted. But he was so busy nowadays . . .

"You do understand, don't you," Stephen said for the umpteenth time, "that if you want to extend the kitchen out this way, instead, we have to draft a whole new set of plans to submit to the States for approval and licences? That can take months more of delays."

"Shuddup, Carol. The bloody kitchen is perfectly okay as it is and if you don't like it after agreeing it was fine earlier, then hard bloody cheese! You can bloody well lump it!" Cyril Blaydon left his wife sulking in the back of their Daimler while he led Stephen by the elbow back to the lovely old house he had had virtually gutted. "No good listening to women, they'll always whinge that something is wrong. Never bloody satisfied. Now," he examined the footings where part of the extensions would rise, "Tell me again why this inspector bloke won't play ball."

Counting to ten, Stephen took a deep breath and went through the entire problem for the third time, hoping that his client could finally assimilate the details. At least when he got home tonight he would be able to reveal to Sue just how this character had made his fortune: war surplus and scrap metal, primarily, plus a lucky choice of business partners thereafter. They supplied the brains while he supplied the brass. And Blaydon had hung on to his share till his partners bought him out, expensively.

Sue would love to hear the story, providing he could stay awake long enought to tell it.

"You still having problems with the Blaydon's boat?" George asked.

"It's all these modern gadgets they want. The first lot they ordered wouldn't fit, not without carving up the saloon. So I'm still waiting for the more sensible replacements to arrive." Richard laughed, rubbing his forehead with an oily hand. "The ones I suggested they have in the first place."

"Never mind. The delays in our yard are no worse than those on the QE II. Her maiden voyage has been delayed for months," George remarked.

"And she'll be out of date, anyway, when they've got this Concorde plane in service. They say she'll cross the Atlantic in three and a half hours! Quicker than the speed of sound!"

"There's one thing sure: you'll never get me on one of those things. Never for all the tea in China!" George Schmit stomped away, shaking his head.

"How did it go today, Steps?"

Stephanie slammed the front door and came into the sitting-room, throwing her school bag onto the settee before flopping onto the floor with the dogs.

"Tell me then, dear!" Sue snapped, irritated at being ignored.

"Certainly, when you stop calling me Steps! The best thing you ever gave me was my name, and for some reason you keep ruining it."

Sue hissed. "Very well. How did you get on in your exam, *Stephanie!*"

"I haven't the faintest idea, Mother!" The girl rolled over onto her back, arms folded under her head. "It was one of those papers that give you a choice of three subjects in each section, on which to expound. Whether my expounding will appeal to the examiner will doubtless depend entirely on what he or she, or it, has had for breakfast that morning." She really wasn't terribly interested in comparing seventeenth-century English history with that of France and Spain, anyway.

"Yes, you're probably right. Those sort of papers depend so much on the personal opinion of the examiners. By the way," Sue said as sweetly as she could, "don't you think you ought to get up, dear? Your uniform is getting covered in dog hairs."

Stephanie rolled on to her knees to scowl at her mother

before snatching up her bag and disappearing off to her bedroom.

Damn, I seem to have done it again! Sue thought. Should I have worded it differently? Or said nothing and waited till she'd changed into mufti, then collected her uniform and brushed it all down? Because sure as God made little apples, there is no way Stephanie would brush her clothes herself!

Still, it could be worse. Just imagine having two daughters like Amanda and Coralie Blaydon . . . no, not Blaydon. What were their surnames? Smith and Brown, but she couldn't remember which was which. And maybe Steps . . . Stephanie . . . was no worse than she herself had been at that age. Sue smiled, remembering how untidy she had been, how she had drifted through days on end so madly in love with David Morgan that she could think of little else. I wonder what has happened to him. Is he some business tycoon in Canada, now? At least Stephanie didn't imagine she was in love with anyone, apart from hugging herself with glee when a particularly attractive male star appeared on the TV screen, and freely admitting "getting the hots" for various boys from time to time. If only she was a little bit more co-operative at home, showed a bit more respect for her elders and concern for family matters. If only she would dress with respect for herself, instead of getting herself up to look like a tart . . . well, at least not quite as much so as the Amanda creature.

She looked at the clock. Time to be getting the evening meal prepared. Stephen would soon be home. And Debbie? She was late again today. But thank goodness she, at least, was sweet and stable and co-operative. Debbie was developing into a real beauty; those green eyes were fascinating, sparkling. Particularly when Justin was with her? Well, that was just girlish fantasy: he was years older than she was. Six years, in fact.

"I've changed my mind about going on to university, Mummy." Debbie announced.

"Why?" Sue's heart sank into her sandals as she wandered

along L'Ancresse beach with her daughter and the dogs. "We thought you had your heart set on a career in sport."

"I know. I had. But I've been thinking about it a lot lately and it seems to me that as I don't know if I'll ever be good enough to do well on the amateur tennis circuit, I would be much better to get an ordinary job on the island to cover my expenses while I play local and Hampshire county tennis, perhaps even regional, till we can see how I shape up. Don't you agree? I really don't want to finish up teaching beginners in a girls' school." She gave her mother a hopeful glance, praying for a favourable reaction. "Quality of life and all that, you know."

No, Sue did not agree . . . but how to say it without upsetting the girl? Without putting a barrier between them, like she had with Steps. Debbie was terribly sensitive. "Darling, I don't know what to say. This does come as a bit of a shock. I mean, what sort of a job had you in mind?"

Debbie picked up Cressida's tennis ball and threw it across the wet sand. "I don't know, really. Anything that comes along. I have no great career ambitions and I'm not artistically talented like Stephanie."

"Your great talent has always been your sport. You are so very athletic. But you would be bored stiff doing just any job. Surely you would need something to stretch your mind a bit. Something that needs advance training?"

"It hardly seems worth it, Mum. All I really want to be is a good tennis player and a good wife."

"You'd need to find a husband for that!"

"I already have. You surely know that Justin and I have an understanding."

Sue stood and stared at Debbie's retreating back. "You have! Since when?"

"Oh, Mummy! For years! Forever!" Debbie turned to walk back to her. "I can't believe you didn't know!"

Yes, of course I knew you were infatuated with the latterday Adonis with the great tennis talent, Sue admitted to herself, but I tried not to believe it because he is so much older and . . . unsuitable? "I could see you liked Justin a lot . . ."

"We were obviously made for each other, weren't we?"

Sue watched sheer joy transform her pretty daughter into an ethereal beauty; not even the splash of summer freckles could detract from the huge, dreamy green eyes, small, perfect nose and wide, pearly smile while, highlighted by the late afternoon sun, her soft, red curls formed a halo round the heart-shaped face. "Perhaps. Time will tell, dear."

Not a satisfactory response, as far as Debbie was concerned, but at least her mother wasn't showing any antagonism.

They walk on towards the Pembroke end of the bay in silence, Sue horribly aware she should be using this opportunity to get through to Debbie, get her back on track to her original plan of higher education. But how? When one thing was quite abundantly clear: Justin was the reason the girl didn't want university. She simply did not intend to be separated from him.

It was fortunate for the sake of Sue's troubled confusion that she didn't know what Debbie had really wanted to ask her this afternoon before she finally lost the courage.

"This is spectacular!" Greg whispered to Sue as they watched the balls skim to and fro, low over the net. "Quite phenomenal! I had no idea she had come on so well."

"Well, we think she is exceptionally good, but the English coach who was over here recently said there were several flaws in her game that needed attention. Unfortunately, he didn't pull his punches at all and Debbie was awfully upset."

"Reckon you've talked her back into going to college?"

"No. She is hopelessly infatuated with that boy and won't consider being separated from him." Sue indicated Debbie's handsome opponent.

"He's a good player, too," Greg noted, "But his shots tend to be lazy. Needs to crispen up that forehand cross-court shot, it's too loose."

"I have a feeling that's the story of his life. But for heaven's sake don't repeat that to Debbie – she'd never forgive me!"

"What does he do for a living?"

"Nothing, yet. He has just finished at university and shows little career ambition, other than tennis. Not that one can imagine him doing anything as humble as club coaching. He flits over to London quite frequently for the high life. Loves boating and has asked his father for an aeroplane for Christmas."

Greg removed his panama and fanned his face. "Oh yes? And what did Daddy say?"

"That he should find someone else and they could go halves."

Her father shook his head slowly. "I don't know. What is the world coming to?"

The young couple came off the court to join them.

"Hello, Granpa!" Debbie bent over to kiss Greg's cheek. "You should have come earlier and we could have played mixed doubles with Mum."

Justin shook his hand. "Evening, sir. Yes, pity. We could have had a game." He did not look too disappointed.

"I won't be in for a meal, tonight, Mum. Justin and I are going out to dinner with friends. Okay?" Debbie looked at her watch. "In fact I must fly or I won't be ready by the time you get back to collect me," she smiled adoringly at Justin.

"Get going, then," he ordered, adding formally, "I may see you later, Mrs Martel. Good-bye sir."

An hour later Sue watched him roar away with her daughter in his Triumph Spitfire.

It was not a good car for necking in, so Justin took a rug out of the boot, kept there for the purpose, and the pair hurried down the grass bank, through waist-high bracken to their usual clearing.

"What on earth are you wearing?" Justin asked, wrestling with her buckle.

"It's a jumpsuit. Blouse top and trousers all in one."

"Good grief. If I'd known before we left the pub I'd have stayed for another drink."

"Justin, darling! I didn't know we'd be coming out here

57

tonight or I'd have worn something else." Debbie nuzzled against his cheek and fell back onto the rug under his kisses. Life was bliss. Justin was bliss. And she was so lucky. Lucky that the most gorgeously attractive male she had ever seen, even in films, was in love with her. "I do love you so much, my dearest," she whispered as they broke for air. And he was such a brilliant tennis player, too.

"And I love you, too, my little doll," he whispered back as he negotiated the blouse buttons. "Mmmm."

Debbie squirmed with pleasure; the sensations he sent running through her lithe young body made her dizzy. Frantic for more . . . Yet a worry was itching at the back of her mind. She was acutely aware of the hard lump pressed into her thigh and knew what it meant. He was desperately wanting something she had not yet dared to give.

He voiced what was on both their minds. "What about the pill? Are you on it yet?"

"No. I haven't been able to ask Mummy, yet. But I will, soon, I promise."

"You've been saying that for weeks."

"I wish we could wait until we are officially engaged. It would make it so much easier to broach the subject."

Justin had never officially proposed. But in the interests of advancing their necking he had referred to "when they were married they would not have to hide out in the bracken to make love" several times, and it had never failed to relax her inhibitions. On the other hand, of course, he didn't want to get her in pod. "We cannot get engaged till you are older. Your parents wouldn't dream of giving permission."

"I'd have thought it more likely to get permission for that than for the pill!"

"But lots of girls your age are on the pill, nowadays. You really must make the effort, Debs. Honestly, I can't wait forever." Abruptly he rolled away from her and started to tug at the rug. "Come on, let's go before I explode."

Summer ended with sudden thunderstorms and endless rain.

At first Sue hoped that the weather would clear, giving

them a lovely, soft Indian summer, late into October. But it never happened. The temperature plummeted and she was soon lighting coal fires, trying to raise their spirits as much as anything. The cold and damp were so depressing.

So, too, were the expressions on the faces of her children. Roddy didn't appear to be worrying about anything in particular; he simply continued to carry the cares of the world on his shoulders, as ever. He was so serious, worked too hard even during the vacations, and soon he would return to university without appearing to have relaxed and enjoyed his holiday at all. Sue suggested he might like to invite a university friend over to stay, but he said he preferred just to be with the family. There were times when he threw back his head and bellowed with laughter, teased Stephanie, played tennis with Debs and really looked happy but those times seemed all too brief, and she would find him leaning over a book on the dining table, straight blond hair flopped over his eyes as they peered through thick-lensed glasses. Perhaps, because his father was dead and Stephen, however much he might try, could never replace him, Roddy felt an additional weight of responsibility . . . *in loco parentis.*

So different from Stephanie, who wouldn't allow such thoughts to cross her mind. She hated responsibility: her bedroom looked like a bombsite and she would wail in frustration when she couldn't find a clean garment, although she had not put so much as a dirty sock in the linen basket. She gave every appearance of being fond of her siblings, especially Bobbie, but would react angrily if asked to feed or look after any of them. She would laugh and play with them, watch children's TV on the settee with her step-brother, but seldom with her mother or step-father.

And that hurt. Sue adored her, and watching her with the others Sue longed to feel the warmth of Stephanie's affection, too, share a knowing smile. Touch. Occasionally it happened, but not often enough to salve the sores of repeated rebuffs.

Being the baby of the original family was possibly the reason for Debbie's softness and affectionate nature; she looked for Sue's company . . . when she arrived home from school or from a game of tennis, or when she came downstairs from her room. If Sue was in the kitchen preparing a meal, Debbie was at her side stirring the contents of a saucepan, chopping onions or simply talking over the day's events. Of course she was by far the most sensitive of the three, needing lots of encouragement and reassurance. She was easily hurt and became very despondent when she was off her game. Being the youngest she had scarcely any memories of her real father and allowed Stephen to fill the vacant role far more than Stephanie and Roddy had done. And what was more, she adored her little step-brother. She loved to take him to the beach, shrimping and swimming, or walking the dogs on the sand. And naturally she loved teaching him tennis, to which he was responding with remarkable success for his eight and a half years.

So, when Sue was feeling glum about her latest failure to communicate with Stephanie or Roddy, doubting her ability as a parent, it was invariably Debbie who lifted her spirits.

Actually, Stephanie loved everyone, including her mother, the day she received her A-level results in August, and the euphoria had carried her along on cloud nine right up till her departure to university in October. Art and design had always been her goal, and now she was away to the college of her choice, away from the strictures and suffocations of family life.

She was free as air.

It was one of those continuous parties which start at about eleven in the morning and drift on all day.

"Mummy, can I help, please?" Bobbie's face was smeared with chocolate, his shirt was half out of his pants and he had discarded his shoes.

Sue stopped herself before saying, '*may* I, not *can* I', remembering how it used to irritate her when her mother corrected her years ago. "That would be marvellous, dear. I need someone to pass round the crisps and nibbly bits . . . not eat any, of course," she added. "Come here," she grabbed the dish cloth, "Let's get rid of some of this mess."

"Pooh! No," the boy spluttered, ducking away as the wet cloth wiped across his face. "You've been doing something with raw onions!"

"What time are people asked for, Mum?" Roddy asked. "Eleven."

"Are you sure you got the day right? It's ten past and there's no one here yet."

"You only seem happy when you've found something to worry about," Sue laughed. "I told them any time after eleven. Debbie, he'll arrive whether or not you stand waiting at the back door," referring to Justin. "Until he does, could you carry on scrubbing those jacket potatoes?"

"Do you think this will be enough punch?" Stephen was stirring the dark, pungent liquid in Sue's jam-making *bashin*.

"You've plenty more wine to top it up, haven't you? And there are more cloves and cinnamon sticks in the spice rack." Sue finished arranging the Coronation Chicken on its serving dishes and placed it on a shelf in the pantry.

"Cooee! Anyone home?"

"Come in, Aunt Filly! Happy Christmas! You lot haven't had your pressies, yet. Quick, before anyone else arrives." Sue led them all into the sitting-room, which looked bare with the furniture either removed or pushed back to the walls.

Troilus and Cressida were very excited and insisted on helping to carry the Warwick's parcels.

Christmas paper was still being torn when the Tetchworths arrived, en masse. Everyone was kissing, shaking hands and spilling punch on the carpet, but nobody cared.

Stephanie was the last to arrive, making her grand entrance down the stairs in long, flowered Indian ethnic garments, and various strings of beads, dangling earrings and bits of leather tied round her neck, wrists and ankles.

Roddy hissed his disapproval; Sue swallowed while Stephen slid his free arm round her in sympathy.

Caroline cheered. "Here she is!"

"Well, what have we here?" roared Johnny Tetchworth

in his pseudo Oxford accent. "The harem comes to little Guernsey!"

The unfortunate Hilary Tetchworth was standing near her husband as, having glanced sadly at the ceiling, Stephanie walked towards her saying in a very loud stage whisper, "Dear Mrs Tetchworth, please accept my most sincere sympathy. He is so very gauche, isn't he?"

The remark was tempered with such a wide smile that Hilary was unsure how to take it.

Vanessa, Karen and Caroline, who were standing nearby with a group of young men, were in no doubt and burst into gales of laughter.

Johnny flushed angrily, and so did Sue who headed for the kitchen for a tray of hot cocktail sausages; Steps had asked for it, dressing up in such weird gear, and Johnny had been out of line, but Steps had no right to speak to a senior guest like that. The moment passed and was forgotten by everyone except Debbie who was deeply hurt on Justin's behalf.

The invitation had been very open and casual and Sue wondered how many people would leave before lunch, but nobody did, leaving her calculating wildly about slicing the remaining ham, and bringing out the leftover chippolatas from yesterday. Luckily, the canapés eventually took the edge off most appetites, and after the main course slabs of cheese, bowls of trifle and loads of fruit salad and cream filled any remaining voids.

Everyone seemed relaxed and happy, even Roddy. The mildly inebriated young took themselves off into the sitting – room to play soft, moody pop, leaving Richard's little Derek asleep, Bobbie playing with his Christmas presents and the older generations chatting and dozing round the debris on the dining room table.

The sound of "Gentle on my Mind" drifted across the hallway through the open door.

"That has to be one of the better hits of the year," Greg observed.

"Really, Dad! I didn't know you were into pop!" Sue laughed.

"If you can't beat 'em, join 'em!" he grunted.

"Incredible to think of The Rolling Stones wowing them all in Madison Square Gardens." Gordon helped himself to another glass of port.

"Haven't we done well with our British films this year?" from Maureen. "Have you seen Richard Attenborough's *'Oh What a Lovely War!'*?"

"Yes," Anne said, "We both loved it but I must say I preferred *'Women in Love'.*"

"That was because she was knocked sideways by Oliver Reed wrestling in the nude," her husband teased. "Which was your favorite, Sybil?"

"*'The Prime of Miss Jean Brodie',*" was the prompt answer, "But I suppose the vote from the other room would be for *'Easy Rider'.*"

Sue stifled a yawn. She had been up since seven preparing food, added to which the wine was making it almost impossible to keep her eyes open. "I'm going to make a pot of tea. How many takers?"

Apart from Richard, Johnny and Gordon who were still circulating the port between them, everyone agreed.

"No!" Sue said sternly as willing hands began collecting up dishes. "If any of this stuff goes into the kitchen I won't be able to move in there! Please leave it all and go and join the kids."

No one argued.

Debbie had a job as sales assistant in a sports shop in Town – not what Sue and Stephen had had in mind for her, but the girl was so happy, so sweet and cheerful a member of the household, that her parents withheld their opinions.

However there were odd moments when she seemed strangely moody. "I can't make her out," Sue told Stephen one night early in the New Year. "She gives the impression she has the weight of the world on her mind, and I ask her if she has a problem."

"And . . ."

"We-ell, judging by her immediate reaction, I'd say she wanted to unload a whole heap of problems, but she always shakes her head and says 'no'."

"You're sure she's not pregnant?"

"Stephen! Don't even think about it!" Sue huddled under the bedclothes and into his arms, adding. "She and Justin don't sleep together. And anyway, she doesn't look pregnant."

Three weeks later, when Sue was sitting alone by the fire knitting one evening and Stephen was in his study, Debbie joined her, and after a while the subject of love and marriage came up.

"When did you and Uncle Stephen fall in love, Mum?"

Sue had never told any of the children of the affair she had had with Stephen while their father, Jonathan, was still alive, thinking it would be better all round for them not to know. And better for her, too. On the other hand, she was more than ever convinced that Debbie was worried about something and surely, if she confided the truth to the girl and begged for her understanding, it would encourage Debbie to do the same. She launched gingerly into the tale, choosing her words very carefully.

Debbie listened intently to the details, the reasons and excuses, watching the guilt in her mother's eyes. And when Sue finished she stretched out her hand to grasp her mother's arm. "No need to worry, Mum. We all realised that Uncle Stephen was extra special to you. I don't remember very much about Daddy, but Stephanie and Roddy say he was very cross and grumpy most of the time."

Sue gulped. "He didn't used to be, not when we fell in love and got married. Not until after his terrible accident."

"You mean, not until he couldn't have sex any more?"

The knitting needles stopped clicking and three stitches were dropped. "That was certainly part of the reason he was so . . . so angry with life. And with me."

"Why with you? It wasn't your fault!"

"No. But I think it helped him to have someone close at whom he could direct his anger."

"Do you think all men get angry about things that seem unreasonable to us?"

Oh-oh! Was Debbie's problem about to surface? "Men

and women often seem to see things differently, in a lot of ways."

"But Uncle Stephen doesn't, does he?"

"Uncle Stephen is a most exceptionally gentle man. But then I suppose he needed to be to take on you lot!"

"How did you know when you were in love, Mum?"

Sue grinned. "Guess work!" she shook her head, "It's so difficult to say. There are so many reasons for believing we are in love."

"Like what?"

"Like reaching a stage when one feels the need of a mate. So you meet someone who seems passably suitable and fix your sights on him. That's the way I was with my first boyfriend and I honestly and truly thought I was in love."

"And weren't you?"

"When I fell in love with your father I realised it couldn't have been the real thing. I mean, you can't be truly in love with more than one person, can you?"

"Oh no! Absolutely not!"

"Some people have a special friendship with a boy," Sue went on, hoping this wasn't going to sound too obvious, "and are so desperate to hang on to it they imagine they are in love. But," she added quickly, not wanting to linger on that one, "I think the most difficult reason to sort out in one's mind is lust."

Debbie's eyebrows shot up and her jaw dropped: this was not the terminology she expected from her mother. But she didn't interrupt.

"When our sex glands are fully developed," Sue continued, desperately hoping she was making sense, "and respond to the sexual attraction of one boy in particular for possibly no better reason than that he happens to be around at the right time, one is inclined to imagine that this is *it* . . . with a capital 'I'."

"What's difficult about that?"

"The fact that he may be totally unsuitable. Wrong background. Not the sort of person you would easily make friends with, but for the lust. Wrong type of thinking to match your own."

65

"But a few minutes ago you said that men think differently from women. How can they ever match?"

Sue wondered whether she wasn't digging herself a very deep pit. "Well, there are many various areas of thinking. If it is only a matter of simple details like whether to spread one's marmalade on the toast or put a little on for each bite, no problem. But when you have totally opposing attitudes on moral values, on what is right or wrong, then the relationship can run into trouble. You see, sexual attraction alone doesn't last. Friendship and mutual respect do."

Debbie stared at her, frowning. "Hmm. But you still haven't told me how you know when you're in love."

Sue nibbled the end of her knitting needle, thinking hard. "When you know you've got all three at the same time for the same person."

"Friendship, respect and sexual attraction?"

"Yes."

Debbie sat for a long time fondling one of Cressida's ears while staring into the fire, watching the wavering flames send thin spirals of smoke up the chimney. Eventually she looked up and gave her mother a relaxed, happy smile. "I'm so glad we've had this chat, it really has cleared my mind." She sighed and gave herself a little hug. "Mummy, please may I go on the pill?"

Chapter Four

Storm Clouds

April showers had been delayed till May, bringing a miserable morass of mud mingling with the building materials.

Hunched in fisherman's waterproofs, with rain trickling down his neck, Stephen trod carefully in his wellingtons to avoid slipping and falling full length in the mess. There was no sign of any workmen outside. Or inside. He walked through from room to room of the old part of the building, trying to avoid loose planks of wood, pipes and miscellaneous wiring, calling out "Anyone there?" but no one answered.

Back at the car Cyril Blaydon was fuming. "Didn't I tell you? Your bloody island builders are too damn work-shy to turn up. What's the matter with them?"

Stephen had given up counting to ten, months ago. "They know they can't do blockwork in this weather; the mortar would wash away before it had time to set."

"Then they should cover it up, dammit!"

"You decided against erecting tented scaffolding."

"Total waste of money in this supposed climate. I was told we were coming to live in sunny Guernsey."

Stephen laughed politely at the little joke.

"Well, there is plenty for them to do in the old part," Cy grumbled. "What's happening in there?"

"The painters and decorators can't move in till the electricians and plumbers are finished," Stephen explained yet again. He had been saying the same thing over and over for the past three months.

"Why aren't they finished in that part? Off on some other job, kidding some other poor sucker along." Cy was in a

67

filthy mood, not least because the hotel manager had told him that morning that other guests were complaining about the volume of Amanda's music. When he told her off she wailed to her mother, and Carol had flown into a paddy which could have been heard down at the harbour. The sooner they were in their own place the better, but the date of moving in was receding by the hour.

"They can't complete the ducting till the extensions are complete or the ducts won't marry." Stephen didn't add that no matter where taps and radiators and electric sockets were sited, Carol would undoubtedly decide to have them moved, adding to the chaos and delay. "You know, one really doesn't want to finalise details till one has the overall picture," he said diplomatically.

"Hrmph!" Cy growled. "Take me to a pub, I need a drink!"

It was still quite early and the bar at the Rockmount hadn't filled up yet. The two men sat at a table with their pints, Cy glaring out of the window at the driving rain.

"Are you beginning to regret coming to live in Guernsey?" Stephen said with a grin, trying to lighten his client's mood.

"I may well if this doesn't let up, soon. I imagine the view out there must be pretty good on a decent day."

"Yes. Cobo is spectacularly beautiful. A very popular beach and fishing harborage. Holidaymakers love it."

"When it's not raining, you mean?" his heavy jowls managed a smile. "Now look here, Stevie," he was the only person to abbreviate the name since Stephen had left school, "I've got my son and his wife coming over for a week at the end of next month, and I want you to meet them. We had hoped, when he booked the date, that we would be in the house. As it is he'll have to use hotel accommodation. Thought we might all get together. Will you have family over?"

"Yes, indeed. The two at university should be home by then. The other two live here, anyway." While he was talking, Stephen was doing some quick thinking. Would Sue kill him if he asked the Blaydon's down to *La Rocquette de*

Bas? But Blaydon had so worded his desire to get together, that he really had no option. "Why don't you all come down to our place?"

"Splendid idea! Let's make a date."

"I'll have a word with my wife when I get home, and ask her to phone you. Nearer the time, perhaps." Who knows, something might crop up to delay the arrangement . . . indefinitely? Chance would be a fine thing, though he had to admit that apart from the times when Cy Blaydon was losing his rag, he was quite good, entertaining company. Pity about the wife and daughters, though.

After dropping his client back at the hotel, Stephen drove down to the office wondering how he was going to broach the subject with Sue. Darling Sue. She really was his most precious and prized possession, but no one could deny she had a spirited temper when roused. Would she really be mad as hell at him? And there was something else on his mind which he felt a need to discuss with her. Roddy.

Strictly speaking, Roddy was his second cousin as well as his stepson. Jonathan, the boy's father, had been his first cousin, and although Stephen had known Sue when they were still at school and had adored her even then from a distance, Jonathan, the dashing ex-RAF wartime pilot had been any girl's obvious choice of mate. Their marriage had nearly broken Stephen's heart. Roddy, with his very blond hair and blue eyes, looked so like his father, was so unlike himself, that after Jonathan's death, when Sue had finally turned to him for love and marriage, it had been difficult to see the boy as a son, though he was very fond of him. So not unnaturally, he was rather worried that Roddy was not showing quite the interest he, Stephen, felt he should in his chosen career as an architect. Up to a year ago, or even more recently, Roddy had seemed so enthusiastic about the subject, studied hard and gone on to university to read the subject before coming back to the island to work in the firm which bore his family name. But during the Easter vacation there had been a subtle change in the boy's attitude. He still worked hard, paid attention . . . and gave the subject due lip service? For that was the way he was beginning to sound.

* * *

"You are joking, of course," was Sue's immediate reaction to the suggestion of entertaining the Blaydons. "Who on earth could we dilute them with? Uhtred and Tilly?"

Stephen looked bashful and took her in his arms. "No! Definitely not Uhtred and Tilly. Nor Frank and Christine. But I tell who would cope with them beautifully – Sir Gordon and Lady Sybil!"

Sue giggled. "Yes. Gordon would sort him out in no uncertain terms!"

"And Sybil would make the wife look like a decorated carthorse, ready for the North Show!"

"You realise we are being horrid?"

"Yes. And you realise I cannot possibly turn them down without causing deep offence?"

Sue hugged him. "I know you can't, my darling. So you want me to ring that awful woman and make a date?"

"Yes." Stephen kissed her nose. The crisis point had passed without injury, but he elected to say nothing at the moment about Roddy.

Which seemed, later, to have been a wise decision. In fact when Roderick, as he now preferred to be called, returned for the summer vacation having completed his second year at university, and settled down to some seriously hard draught work which he completed with precision and care, Stephen decided he had dreamed up the doubts he had felt at Easter.

"Sir? Do you think that by facing this corner and the archway at the side in granite we tend to marry the extension into the theme of the old building, here, or does it make it look pseud?" Roderick stood back from the elevation on the drawing board, waiting for Stephen's comments.

"Pseud, as it stands. But once you've added the odd tree or Virginia creeper to this stretch of blank wall I think it will all blend in as though it had been there for a hundred years or more." The work that the twenty-year-old had done was exquisite. Perfect in every detail. "That is a splendid job. Our clients will be delighted. But, Roderick, old man, do stop calling me sir, or Uncle. I

70

think the time has come for you to call me Stephen, don't you?"

A flood of red climbed up Roderick's neck. "If that's all right with you . . . Stephen?"

"Fine. Now shall we go out to the Blaydon place and see how the carpenters and decorators are getting on?"

"You mean you want me to come with you?"

"Yes. I'd like to get your angle on the interior design."

"I'm not much into decor and furnishings, if that's what you mean."

"Have you touched on the subject at university?"

"Not really. It's been far more a matter of calculating loadbearing strengths for wall and girders, and making buildings blend into local environments. We've also covered a lot of detail on soil and subsoil in relation to foundations, and aspects regarding sunlight and the quality of plaster facings. But we've yet to open the book on interiors."

"That's understandable, I suppose," Stephen nodded, though personally he thought interiors of prime importance in regard to dwellings. People lived inside their houses, not outside, and sat looking at the four walls of their living space.

They left the office together and went out to Stephen's car.

Sue was pleased to have Bobbie with her at home: with Roderick and Stephanie away at their respective universities and now Debbie doing the junior tennis circuit in England, the house seemed so quiet and empty, even when Stephen was at home. The latter tended to spend too much time in his study doing extra work brought home from the office.

"Can't get the drawings out on time when one has to spend so many hours a day on site," he'd explain.

"Then why don't you take on extra draughtsmen?" Sue kept asking.

"Simply a matter of economics, darling," he would reply.

But at least he was there, in the house and not out every evening following some sport or hobby. So she didn't complain too much. And Bobbie filled the vacancy very well. Now nine years old, he was an intelligent kid, good at modelling aircraft and warships and increasingly keen on tennis. Sue spent at least an hour a day on the court with him throughout the summer and already she felt he should have more professional coaching. Plus, with Stephen's encouragement, he was learning to play the piano. However, not even Bobbie could distract Sue's mind from the other three – not completely. She missed them so much: found herself listening for Stephanie to rock the house with pop music, or for the *pluck!* of tennis balls out on the court. Throughout her middle childhood and teenage years she had longed for the family life she had been denied by the war. She had married young to fullfil that need and found herself trapped in an almost macabre shell of wedlock, tied to a man who, after his disabling car accident, gave every indication of despising her. Fortunately, before her mother died the two women had repaired their relationship, severed by the war, and when Sarah succumbed to cancer aged only fifty-six, no one could ever replace her in Sue's affections. Aunt Filly was a wonderful confidante, as was Sybil, but that wasn't quite the same as the mother and daughter intimacy Sue and Sarah shared in the latter's final years. It still hurt so dreadfully that Sarah was not around to watch her grandchildren growing up. Families were so important.

Sue often thought, now, how marvellous it would be to have Debbie lean on the kitchen counter, chatting, while she prepared dinner, though she hadn't recovered yet from the shock of the girl's request for the pill. That had come right out of the blue, leaving Sue speechless, helpless to think of the right words to say, how to stall this turn of events.

Of course she had had to accede: Debbie had said quite plainly that she and Justin were going to sleep together anyway, with or without the pill, so it had seemed the lesser of the two evils. And now, with her parents' blessing, Debbie was off on tour with her beloved Justin, gloriously happy and contented and enjoying phoning home whenever she had the chance for a cosy chat with her mother.

Right at this moment, Bobbie was at his piano lesson;

he and Stephen and Roderick would not be in for another hour and a half and the family house was full of oppressive silence. Even Stephanie's aggressive glares would have been welcome.

The phone startled Sue out of her misery. "Hallo?"

"Mum! It's me." Stephanie's voice.

"Hallo, darling. I was just thinking how much I was missing you. How are you? When are you getting back here?"

"Fine. Look, don't expect me back yet awhile. A crowd of us are planning to go to a Rock Festival next weekend. It's going to be a total wow and I couldn't possibly bear to miss it. The only thing is, I'm running a bit low on funds at the moment. Do you think you could spare me a bit of housekeeping?"

The disappointment dropped into Sue's stomach like a lump of lead. "How much longer will you be away?"

"Another week or so, I imagine. I'll phone again as soon as I know."

"Karen is back. I saw her in Town yesterday."

"Really? Well she had to get back to help out in their shop for the summer." There was a pause. "So what about the lolly, Mum?"

Sue put her hand over the mouthpiece as she sighed. Mustn't upset the girl or she wouldn't even bother to phone. "How much do you want?"

Stephanie laughed. "How much can you spare?"

"Thirty pounds?"

Another pause. "Couldn't you make it fifty?"

"I suppose so. Where do I send the cheque? Are you still at college?"

"No. I'm staying with my friend Margaret, in London. This is her address. Got a pen?"

Sue wrote it down. "Where is this Festival?"

"Look, Mum, I mustn't chat. I'm running up Margaret's phone bill. I'll speak to you again soon."

"Oh, all right. But why don't you reverse the charges next time so we have a chance to talk?"

"Sure. As long as you don't mind. Cheers. Bye!"

"Bye, bye, darling. Take care of yourself . . ." But the line had already gone dead.

"How did she take it?"

"Not with overwhelming enthusiasm," Stephanie said with a laugh. She was sitting with a bunch of students, some of whom might be described as friends, in Margaret Sedgewicks's flat. They were drinking coffee with powdered milk and eating their way through two packets of Digestive biscuits. "The money should arrive in a couple of days."

"Meanwhile, how do we eat?"

"Isn't your rich friend Caroline due to join us sometime soon?" asked Marcus, of the long sideboards and shoulder-length hair.

"Yes!" Margaret brightened. "She'll be good for a few Indian takeaways."

Anthony, his curls tied back by a strip of cloth, stood up. "I'm going to the park. Anyone coming?"

One by one the crew drifted after him. They were a motley band, the boys sprouting beards, and wearing loose waistcoats and tabards over collarless shirts and jeans, the girls long-skirted and sandalled, their hair threaded with ribbons. Two people carried guitars and Melanie had a flute in her Mexican bag.

After much debate, Sue and Stephen decided that a Sunday lunch was best for entertaining the Blaydons, when they could be diluted with as many members of family as could be rallied.

"Pity Debs and Stephanie can't be here," Stephen began as he and Sue arranged outdoor furniture on the lawn.

"Just as well," Sue countered, "Debs could find herself faced with the choice of playing patball with those girls or wiping them off the court completely. And one never knows what sort of impression Stephanie may elect to make on the spur of the moment. I find her so unpredictable nowadays."

"Well, it will be up to Roderick to amuse them, I fear."

"I think I must offer my apologies on the grounds of a previous engagement," Roderick appeared on the verandah.

"You dare! You'll get no supper for a week," his mother threatened.

"Sounds as though it may be worth it," he mused.

Sue threw a raffia tablemat at his head, and missed.

The Bankses were there, plus Richard and Anne with little Derek; Roderick was on the tennis court with young Bobbie, and the baked ham was dished up and ready to carve when the Blaydons turned up in their Rolls half an hour late, without apology.

Sue was not amused and Stephen felt guilty for having invited them, but he put on his best smile as he welcomed the guests and made introductions. "Our sons are still on the court and I'm afraid our daughters are away in England," he explained, "But meet Sue's brother Richard and his wife Anne. That's their boy, Derek, playing with the dogs."

"Oh, aren't they sweet!" Coralie exclaimed, throwing herself onto the grass to stroke Troilus and Cressida, and ignoring the toddler.

Amanda hung onto Richard's hand far longer than necessary, mentally dissecting him. She was in a very tight cotton print, backless dress with not a lot more attempting to cover her front; her lipstick was drawn over her face far wider than the extent of her mouth and her mascara-laden lids made her look tired rather than sultry. "Hi!" she drawled, "Do you live here in little Guernsey?"

"And this is my boy, Neal," Cy announced with pride, "and his wife, Annabel." A totally mismatched pair, physically. Neal was a perfect replica of his father, round and bald, though happily considerably taller; happily, because Annabel was exceptionally tall. Even on this sultry day, and despite being on holiday, she arrived dressed for a boardroom meeting rather than an alfresco meal, and gave every appearance of tension and boredom.

"Do you have any children?" Stephen asked.

"No. I'm afraid we have both been so tied up in business so far that there doesn't seem to have been time yet," replied the prospective, loving mother.

And you'd find them too tedious to have around, Stephen thought, imagining the effect of sticky fingers on her immaculate outfit.

Lady Sybil, meanwhile, was gazing down at Cy with sympathy. The look rather indicated that he was suffering the ultimate family burden, with which, as far as his step-daughters were concerned, he would have agreed had he been able to interpret accurately. Unfortunately, his inability in that direction led him to believe he had made an immediate hit, a belief from which Sybil longed to disillusion him.

Gordon, sitting on the arm of a chair, found himself on eye level with Carol's impressive cleavage.

"Everyone to table, please," Sue called, "or lunch will be spoiled."

Fortunately the sun continued to shine, only a gentle breeze shaking the table parasols and scattering the pathway with cascades of Albertine rose petals from the west wall of the house. At this moment Sue was happy – she usually was when entertaining, when the guests were all smiling and conversation flowed freely over the table. Afterwards, Anne helped her to clear the dishes and glasses into the kitchen while everyone else played an argumentative game of croquet, excepting for Annabel who half sat on the verandah rail, watching, and Coralie who played ball with Cressida while Troilus eyed them with disdain.

"Thank heavens for dishwashers," Sue gasped as the last surface was cleared.

"Yes, I envy you," Anne said. "But I don't see us getting one in the near future. A new washing machine is the next priority."

Through the kitchen window Sue could see the croquet game coming to an end. "I suppose we had better lay on some tea. They don't look as though they intend leaving yet. Thank goodness you brought that fruit cake, Anne. My sponge won't go far with this crowd."

When they manoeuvred the tea trolley outside, Richard and Roderick were partnering Amanda and Coralie on the tennis court, having borrowed sports shoes from the locker in the utility. Neither of the girls appeared to have played before, but Amanda was obviously enjoying being taught by Richard.

"So what do you do over here to keep yourself amused, Gordon?" Cy spoke through his teeth which were clenched on a fat cigar.

"Oh, I remain in touch with Whitehall, ye know, in an advisory capacity. Pop up to Town quite frequently."

"He runs a local cricket team," Sybil cut in, "which takes up far too much of his time when I need him in the garden. What sports do you play?" guessing quite accurately that Cy gave sport little if any of his time.

"Poker. Best sport there is. And most lucrative."

"Ha! Only if you have a poker face," declared Gordon. "Knew a chappie years ago in Poona who looked permanently as miserable as a bloodhound and won two thousand pounds before shipping back to Blighty. He was known as Happy Carruthers in the regiment."

"If Cy could win that sorta money it would make his prolonged sessions worthwhile," Carol groaned. "Goes off for days on end then says I can't have another spending spree in Harrods. I love Harrods, don't you Lady Sybil?" She couldn't quite bring herself to drop the 'Lady'.

Cy ignored her. "Well, old chap, I reckon there will be fewer defence cuts now the Tories are back in government. Your lot must have had rather a thin time under Labour."

"Don't you worry," Gordon responded vigorously, "We soon showed 'em who was boss. Hadn't got a clue, that lot. Only hope Edward Heath can do better. Tell me, how did the previous government affect your business?"

They had affected Blaydon's business very nicely, more cuts meaning more Army surplus to be disposed of, but somehow he felt it might not be wise to say so. "Same as they affected most businesses. Hadn't a clue about money, financing. I only hope we've got rid of 'em in time." A strange answer, one might think, coming from a lifelong, ardent Labour supporter . . . given the right company.

By the time the scrap-iron millionaire and his family drove off in their Rolls, Richard realised he had been talked into taking Amanda out in his boat. He did not anticipate the trip with any noticable enthusiasm.

"These digs are awful," Justin complained. "Couldn't you find anything better?"

"Yes, but far too expensive. I can't afford to splash out too much or I won't be able to complete the tour."

The room was pretty shabby: the thin curtains had lost much of their floral colour and their hooks, the cheap, worn brown carpet was stained and the painted furniture badly chipped, but Debbie loved it because it was their little love nest, however humble.

"Well, why won't you agree to sharing digs with me? I seem to spend most of my time in yours, anyway."

"You know my reasons," Debbie sighed. It was one thing to get her mother to agree to her going on the pill, but quite another to actually, deliberately live in sin.

"I still can't believe your mother is that old fashioned. Lots of people share digs nowadays." She was such an attractive little piece, lovely body and good legs, he felt the need to have her within reach on a more regular and easier basis. "Makes far more sense," he added forcefully, "than all this extra expense and coming and going night and morning."

He was right, of course. Debbie softened. "Do you think we could work it *pretending* we had separate addresses?"

"If that will keep your mother happy." He took her in his arms, relieved that he seemed finally to have made a breakthrough.

Debbie still wasn't completely sure. Quite apart from her mother's attitude, she wanted to be sure of Justin's. He was certainly subject to some strange mood-swings . . . but then maybe he'd feel better once they had a more solid relationship. There was no doubt about her own feelings: she simply adored Justin to bits. He was her whole life. More so even than tennis.

Not that they didn't both hurt her from time to time. Some of the criticisms of her game were very cruel: destructively so. She hated the bad sportsmanship on the circuit. It was one thing to have someone try to help by advising her to alter the angle of her racquet head for her forehand drive, or throw the ball higher for her first service. But after an off day, to be told by the parent of another player, or even on a couple of occasions by an official, that she was so hopeless it was pointless for her to be playing the circuit . . . that was devastating. Justin could be so kind and helpful at such moments: put a comforting arm round her and tell her to ignore the stupid old duffer or jealous witch. But occasionally he would simply disappear off to London in his car, not saying why he was going, nor when he'd be back, leaving her feeling deeply dejected. A dark cloud of depression would then descend to envelop her for hours, sometimes for days on end. Her fingernails suffered badly.

Debbie's life did have it ups, though. When she reached the semi-finals of the Hampshire Championships she was over the moon, and not even her defeat in the next round could suppress her sense of achievement. Likewise, she did well in Gloucestershire, and Suffolk, and she was thrilled for Justin who defeated a strong opponent in the first round of the Surrey matches.

Two weeks later they motored north to Harrogate, and Debbie wore a gold band on her wedding finger as they signed into an upmarket guest house. It was the start of a very happy fortnight for them both.

The Tetchworths were invited to join the family party going over to Herm one Sunday. Richard was taking the party over in George Schmit's boat; the latter was always happy for the competent young man to use her when he wasn't taking her out fishing. Sue, Anne and Hilary compared notes about the picnic food on Friday morning, each keen to provide different items.

"Johnny suggests we buy two or three ready-cooked chickens," Hilary told Sue.

"I usually roast them myself. And I've got a ham to boil. Why don't you do a couple of bowls of different salads, instead?" The very idea of buying pre-cooked stuff detracted from the ambience of picnicking, in Sue's mind.

"If you're sure that will be enough." Hilary was only worried about Johnny's reaction: he did so love 'pushing the boat out'. But she'd suggest he bring some wine. That should pacify him. "I'll get some French loaves, too."

"I'll do a couple of big flasks of homemade ice-cream to have with the strawberries," Anne offered. "And I've made some scones for tea."

They set out from St Sampson's Harbour at ten-thirty in the morning, Richard at the helm, Stephen and Roderick busy with warps and fenders while Johnny, carefully attired in a traditional, oiled navy wool "fisherman's Guernsey" and red bandanna tied round his neck, hurried to and fro getting in their way. Bobby had brought a school friend and the two of them, in lifejackets, settled themselves up on the foredeck in prime position. The ladies busied themselves in the cabin, stowing the endless bags of food and bathing things, watched by Jane, Justin's rather colourless sister, now nineteen years old.

The wind was in the west – good for dropping anchor in Belvoir Bay, but not so good for the diesel fumes curling up the transom to the cockpit and blowing over the seafarers. Johnny's popularity rating was not improved by comments about modern, speedier boats out-running the fumes, and asking when George was going to swop this old thing for something more convenient and up-to-date.

Richard's response was abrupt and to the point. "Who on earth would want to exchange a classic craft for some flashy bit of fibreglass?"

"Lot of French yachts around this weekend," Stephen observed, tactfully. "I wonder if there is a race on?"

"I do love to see all those colourful spinnakers." Hilary appreciated the change of subject. Then added *sotto voce* to Sue, "I would so love us to take up yachting but I'm afraid we would never agree on the type of boat. Would we?"

Sue winked at her and said nothing.

It was decided to eat aboard, anchored in the bay, but most people wanted to swim ashore beforehand, some for ice creams, others just to take a walk.

Bobbie and his friend jumped overboard feet first, holding

their noses, Anne and the men dived in while Sue and Hilary climbed down the transom ladder in more dignified fashion, passing little Derek to his mother in his rubber ring.

Roderick did not find Jane Tetchworth a very attractive female at first. They went off for a walk together, just for something to do, and stopped to see St Tugual's chapel. "Do you know how they managed to build these arched roofs, all those centuries ago?" Roderick asked, prepared to impress her with his knowledge.

"Yes. They built the walls then packed ground within them, mounding it up to support the stones as they arched them into position until the stones met in the centre when the wedge-shaped keystones were locked in." She smiled shyly at him. "Then they dug all the ground out again through the doorway."

Eyebrows raised, Roderick nodded appreciatively. "You have been doing your homework!"

"I love old buildings. When we lived in England Mummy and I would go off together for the day to explore castles, or an abbey or cathedral. Sometimes Mummy would take her paints and do a watercolour. I'm hopeless with a brush. I enjoy pen and ink so much more." Suddenly she blushed and changed the subject. "Do you know anything about this saint?"

"No. No one even seems to know if St Tugual was a man or a woman. The chapel was built of imported granite and dedicated to the saint by Catholic monks. Lovely to think that it has been so beautifully restored and is still in regular use."

They went on to discuss buildings in general, and Roderick was moderately impressed with her intelligence.

Jane, on the other hand, though pleased that he seemed happy in her company, thought he was a bit pompous. Rather like her father.

By the time they returned to the beach, all the others were aboard and lunch was being laid out on the saloon table and in the cockpit. "We'd better swim out to the boat," Roderick said, striding down the steeply shelving shingle.

Jane's eyes were big as saucers. "The tide's come up a lot. It looks a jolly long way."

Roderick suppressed a sigh. "Do you want me to fetch the dinghy? Or will you feel safe enough swimming alongside me? You can always hang on if you get tired." Compared with his sisters this girl seemed rather feeble.

Reading his reaction only too clearly, Jane felt awful. "I'm game to give it a try," she said bravely.

Roderick was a fairly good swimmer, but he doubted if he could cope if she panicked halfway across. "I'll get the dinghy. You wait here. It won't take me long." He plunged into the next wave and struck out.

The Rock Festival had been a weekend affair, starting on Friday evening and continuing all day Saturday with different groups and soloists taking turns on the scaffolding stage. Stephanie hadn't been sure what to expect; three or four of the gang had been to other such gatherings before and described their impressions, which had proved very confusing as they were all so different. She had looked around at the litter of bodies, standing, sitting, lying; walking, talking, laughing, sleeping. Everyone doing their own thing. And there were thousands of them. Many, like her own crowd, were in jeans, shirts and jumpers, with some of the girls in ethnic cottons, others were dressed up really weird with wigs, feathers and top hats. Beads, earrings and pendants were in for both men and women. They had brought groundsheets, rugs, sleeping-bags, and plastic carriers of food and drink. There were food stalls and beer tents round the edge of the field, though most of the gathering were wary of inflated prices. Toilet facilities were hopelessly inadequate and it didn't do to get downwind of them.

Stephanie had shivered when dusk and dew were falling, one stage better than rain, but a chill breeze had blown across the open meadows from the west.

"Why don't you put this rug round your shoulders?" Tony suggested, unrolling it and placing it over her cardigan. He had come, ostensibly, as Melanie's partner, but hoping to

82

make it with this luscious art student before the weekend was over.

Seeing the gesture, Marcus had known only too well what was in Tony's mind and had every intention of beating him to it. He sat on her other side, unzipped his sleeping bag and suggested she put her frozen feet in it, sandals and all. Stephanie smiled at them both and thought how sweet, kind and friendly everyone was.

Melanie took out her flute and played a haunting, James Galway type piece.

Caroline Patterson sat up in her smart new sleeping-bag, dug her teeth into a large piece of pork pie which she had no intention of sharing with anyone, and wished she hadn't come.

A dark-skinned, leather-clad chap in a group nearby plucked at his guitar, in tune with Melanie's flute, and soon his friend with the dreadlocks had joined in, too. It was a pleasant sound and everyone in the vicinity began to hum and sway.

Marcus produced some bottles of beer. "Here, have one of these, Stephanie."

She took the bottle and drank deeply from the neck. She didn't much like the taste but she knew the effect would be good if she got enough of it.

With darkness had come the lights, flaming torches round the perimeter, and psychedelic, flashing electric spots round the stage powered by the distant generators. Then the serious music started, thumping like the rhythm of heartbeats. Several people got up to dance; lively, jerky movements, bodies lurching back and forth.

Stephanie's party had danced together, no one partnering anyone in particular, all united by the obsessive beat which took command of their senses, drove all thought out of their minds.

When the performing group took a break to rapturous applause and the dancers flopped to the ground for refreshments, someone passed round a thin cigarette.

Stephanie had developed a deep love of God, of the world and of all the people in it.

*   *   *

In Guernsey everyone is either someone's old schoolfriend or their cousin. Everyone knows everything about everybody, going back generations. Islanders knew their family history was public knowledge, but few cared, because for every skeleton known to be in your cupboard, you knew of equal skeletons in everyone else's.

William Smart was Geraldine Schmit's nephew, and Geraldine, usually known as Gelly, was an old school friend of Sue's mother Sarah, and of Aunt Filly, and was George Schmit's second wife. And everyone knew her sister Louise had had the misfortune to marry a "Bad Lot", a shotgun marriage when she was five months gone, and had endured a miserable life of hardship and abuse until she finished up in the Castel Hospital with a mental breakdown, only three months before the "Bad Lot" fell under a bus in a drunken stupor.

William, young Billy, the only outcome of this unhappy union, never shone at school, left when he was sixteen, and Uncle George had kindly agreed to take him on in the boatyard, where he shone even less. This was largely due to the fact that his agile mind was constantly preoccupied with schemes for accumulating the maximum amount of money for the minimum amount of work. Years ago, he had involved an unwitting Richard in a blatantly dishonest venture from which they were extricated only by a great deal of goodwill and repentant promises. Although, as George variously swore to his friend, Richard's father Greg, he didn't believe 'a leopard could change its spots', and 'what is bred in the bone will come out in the blood', nevertheless, he continued to employ the boy for Gelly's sake. And now, at thirty-four years of age, Billy continued to dream and scheme and leave most of the hard work to Richard.

"I promise you I've got a winner this time," he told Richard that August. "There's this firm in France who buy up bankrupt boats and sell them on cheap to yards all over the continent. I can pick up a really nice motor cruiser for five thousand quid, bring her back here where we put five thousand's worth of gear in her, plus pretty her up, then flog her off for twenty-five or thirty. It can't miss."

"And who is going to buy it?" Richard asked, not really paying much attention as he wrestled with a propeller shaft bent by a speeding owner on a sharp rock.

"There are yacht-brokers springing up all over the island now, selling to business people in Birmingham who register and berth their boats here to dodge English taxes. Do you realise they can fly here for a weekend's sailing far quicker than they could motor down to a marina on the south coast? Those are our customers."

"You mean they would be our customers if we had ten thou lying around waiting to be invested in your scheme."

"Well, that needn't be a problem. If we put the figures to your father and to Uncle George, either of them could cough up that amount without blinking."

"How little you know my father or Uncle George," Richard snorted. "Neither would cough up a bean without losing sleep. Here, pass me that hammer, will you?"

Richard didn't give the matter another thought until he was on his way home that night. Then it occurred to him that Billy's idea might not be such a bad one, providing one had that much capital to invest. He might just mention it to Dad next time he saw him.

It was a warm September day. Bees were collecting the last dustings of pollen from the asters and Michaelmas daisies below the verandah, a collar dove was cooing a monotonously boring song out of sight in one of the conifers; Cressida was scratching her back on the stunted, dry grass on the lawn watched by Troilus, who was lying nearby with his chin on his paws waiting for something sufficiently interesting to happen to make it worth his while getting up.

Sue sat in her deckchair, an open book on her lap, listening. But there was no "*pluck*" of tennis balls on the court, no din of pop music coming through an upstairs window. No one called "hallo" as the front door slammed, or scrunched the gravel with cycle tyres. Bobbie was back at school, Debbie had flitted over and gone back again to England to finish the tennis season, Stephen was at work, and Roderick had gone off to see some English cathedrals before returning to university. As for Stephanie, well, she hadn't come back all summer and Sue could only hope she would be going back to college eventually. Sue had begged and pleaded with her on the phone and had the receiver slammed down on her ear for her trouble. She had wept, written letters which were returned *"Gone away, address not known"* and now she knew she could only try not to think about her daughter at all, because the thoughts made her so miserable she was depressing everyone else round her. It wasn't fair on Stephen and Bobbie, or on Roderick and Debs when they happened to be around. She had asked herself "why?" a million times but no answer seemed to make any sense. What had she done to cause the girl to reject her, reject home and family? Where had she gone wrong? Or was this God's punishment for some unwitting transgression? Oh no, not that line of thinking again; she had gone down that track after Jonathan's accident, worrying that it was some form of retribution for having thrown David Morgan over to marry Jonathan. So was she really to imagine that once again she was being punished, this time for having had an adulterous relationship with Stephen while Stephanie's father was still alive? Rubbish! She had decided long ago that God had sent Stephen to her at that time to keep her sane . . . for the sake of the children if for no other reason.

So forget it. Forget Stephanie. The girl would come back when she was good and ready. She had her reasons, however obscure they might seem to an older woman. To her mother.

And in the meantime, the sun was shining, the bees buzzing and the birds singing and . . . she was bloody lonely and miserable.

Sue looked at her watch again. There was tons of time to take the dogs across the common to the beach and back again before Bobbie came home from school. She pushed herself out of her chair and immediately Troilus's head came up, ears forward in expectation. "Come on then, you two."

On impulse she grabbed her swimsuit and towel from the utility before heading out to the gate. There would be sufficient wind out there to build up some boisterous breakers in the bay. A bit of belly surfing would do her good.

It did. She loved it, and so did the dogs. In calmer seas they would love to swim out with her, but they did not enjoy being rolled in the breakers, so while she waded out into the surf, Troilus and Cressida paddled in the marbled backwash, pouncing triumphantly on pieces of *vraic* torn from the sea bed. As she sped into the shallows on her stomach the dogs would hurl themselves on her, licking her face and prancing around till she waded out again. Sometimes she would mis-time her leap forward with the curling breaker, and find herself upended, rolled over and over, gasping for breath until she was released to fight for her footing against the undertow. It was desperately exhilarating, so absorbing one never got cold however freezing the wind, and anyway the water was always so warm in September.

Sue was fighting to maintain some degree of modesty as she dragged on her clothes under a towel held together in her teeth, when her cousin's voice shouted, "Hi there! What's it like in?" She grabbed the towel with one hand and yanked her trousers up to her waist with the other. "Sybil! Gordon! You must go in, it's gorgeous. Very warm." She zipped up and dropped the towel. "What's the time?" She fished her watch out of her pocket. "Oh hell! I was in for nearly an hour and Bobbie will be home wondering where on earth I am. Would you like to pop in for a cup of tea after your dip?"

"We'd love to. See you later."

Bobbie was watching television and didn't seem to have noticed her absence. And the phone was ringing.

"Hallo?"

"Mum?" It was Stephanie.

"Hallo, darling. How are you?"

"Fine, thanks."

"Where are you. Back at college yet?"

"No, I'm at Margaret's in London."

"What date do you go back?"

87

"That's what I'm ringing about. I've decided not to go back."

Sue gasped.

"Mum? Are you there?"

"Yes."

"Well, aren't you going to say something?"

What does she want me to say? "What are you going to do instead?"

"I've got a job as a waitress, at the moment. A bunch of us have all made the same decision and we are going off to Wales next month to rent a house for the winter and do some painting."

"But what will you live on?"

"We'll grow most of our own food and some of us will have jobs."

"Listen, darling. Why don't you come home for two or three weeks . . ."

"No!"

"Why not?"

"Because you'll spend the whole time trying to talk me out of it."

True.

"I've made up my mind. This is what I want to do. We are all artists. Some are sculptors, some potters and others are musicians. We all get on so well together and are so very happy. I want you to be pleased for me."

"I might be if I knew more about it. When did you say you going?"

"Soon. I'll send you our address as soon as we arrive. I must go now. This is costing a bomb."

"All right, darling. Write soon."

There was a brief pause, then Stephanie said, "I do love you, Mum."

Sue tried to swallow the lump in her throat. It was the first time Stephanie had said that for years. "And I love you too, very much."

"Bye for now."

"Look after yourself."

The line went dead.

"Why are you crying, Mummy?" Bobbie asked.

Sue had no idea how long she had sat there with the buzzing receiver in her hand. "I'm not crying. I went for a long swim in the breakers and got a lot of salt in my eyes."

"Oh. I see. What time is tea?"

Chapter Five

Attitudes

Coralie had persuaded her stepfather to put up the funds for her to open a flower shop in St Peter Port. Situated up Mill Street in the old quarter of the town, it was unlikely to attract much passing trade other than tourists, but collected a small clique of faithful clientele, sufficient for the venture to break even by the middle of its second year.

Coralie herself could only be described as drab. Her shapeless skirts and dresses were of pale, Liberty printed cottons in summer, and donkey-brown and mulberry wools for winter. She seldom bothered to wear make-up to add colour to her face and her straight, mousey hair was cut short, without shape or style. Yet she was a nice girl. In her shy, quiet way she went about her work creating beautifully artistic arrangements with both fresh and dried flowers, painted imaginative flowerpots and plant stands and sold several macramé pot holders which she worked at home as a hobby in the evenings. In her solemn way she appeared to be perfectly happy and fulfilled, though her stepfather frequently remarked that the money involved in the shop could be earning a far better return if invested elsewhere.

Edward Heath's government was not flourishing. The death and destruction wrought by the IRA in Northern Ireland had spread to the British mainland and the fact that, despite the Government's failure to settle the problem there or the currently growing disruption caused by militant union workers in industry, the Prime Minister elected to skipper his yacht *Morning Cloud* in the Admiral's Cup, climaxing with the 605-mile Fastnet Race, did little to help his popularity rating in the country.

Even Richard, yachting's most ardent enthusiast, condemned him. "The man has to be an idiot if he imagines his team's success will improve his standing in public opinion! Just to contemplate going off on a jolly at a time like this, when people are being blown to pieces on the streets and industry is being throttled by picketing violence, has to be an act of crass stupidity." Which for the mildly spoken and easy-going Richard, was quite a statement.

Guernsey was wallowing in a property boom: a property magnet with a British passport and a foreign name, had taken the island market by storm, was traversing each parish from end to end offering phenomenal and irresistible sums for hotels, guest houses and private homes and then reselling them before the ink had dried. Prices soared overnight creating a mini-boom in trade economy.

Coralie was happy, busy supplying plants and flower arrangements to newly wealthy homes and offices, so much so that she needed to take on an assistant to mind the shop while she was out on her rounds.

Debbie had had modestly successful tennis tours in 1970 and 1971, but was feeling very deflated by both the bad sportsmanship amongst some of the the players, their coaches and supporters, and by some of the adverse criticism of her game.

"Why bother what this man Beechy says about your service, dear?" Sue counselled as she kneaded dough on a floured board on the kitchen table. "He is of no importance whatsoever to anyone but the players in his own stable."

"But he is one of the top coaches . . ."

"Trying to undermine your confidence in favour of his own girls."

"Oh, Mummy! Do you think a man of his standing would play such a rotten trick!"

"You think I'm inventing nasty thoughts about him, I suppose. Just to make you feel better." Sue shook her head. Really, one did dig holes for oneself when bringing up children. One spent the first ten or fifteen years of the children's lives trying to convince them that there were no such things as nasty Bogeymen, and the next ten or fifteen years warning them against them.

"I don't think I will ever be strong enough, mentally, to be classified as a seriously good player."

"Debbie! That is so negative."

"No. Just realistic. There has always been such profound sense of fair play in our family. What Granpa calls good sportsmanship. You know how he often says things like 'better to be a good loser than a bad winner', and 'the game's the thing', and so on. Well, honestly, Mum, that attitude doesn't exist on the tour. You can hear your opponent's coach or parents hissing at you to 'miss it!' and actually laughing if you have a double fault. Players are not supposed to receive any help or advice during matches, yet it is happening all the time. When you go on court you discover you are not playing against a single person, you are taking on their entire team."

Sue scratched her head. "How disgusting! That's cheating! And you've had to put up with that for how long?"

"Two seasons."

"Why haven't you ever said anything about it before?"

Debbie shrugged and gave a wry smile. "Because I thought I would sound unsporting. You always warned us not to whine when we were losing, or make excuses."

"I suppose bringing paid professionals into the game has changed it from a sport into a business," Sue reflected sadly.

"The players were certainly divided into the 'haves' and the 'have nots'. Some of the more successful ones were staying in smart hotels and driving round in jazzy cars while the rest of us were riding borrowed bikes to and from our digs. Except for Justin, of course."

"And which do you reckon came first: the success or the money?"

Debbie pondered that one for a bit. "At the risk of sounding bitchy, I'd say the money. Mind you, a player put on tour by backers has to work his or her butt off. Practice morning noon and night with coaches shouting the odds. Justin coaches me and sometimes gets cross, but nothing like some of those others. Mum?" she waited till Sue looked up at her. "Will you mind very much, me giving it up? I do enjoy being a strong club player and hope to go on playing for the island for a few years, but I don't think I can face trying to take it any further than that." Debbie hated even thinking it, let alone saying it; but the snide comments and back-biting on the circuit were too painful and demoralising to bear.

Visualising the necks of her daughter's persecutors, Sue twisted off chunks of dough, kneaded and shaped them and dumped them into bread tins. "What do you plan to do instead? Tennis has been your whole life for so long."

"Coralie has offered me a job working for her in the flower shop. That's what I'd like to do, but I said I'd talk to you, first." With her forefinger, Debbie pressed three indentations into each lump of dough.

"You really want to do that?" Sue paused to peer closely at her younger daughter's expression.

Debbie nodded, biting a fingernail. "Just until we get married."

Sue said nothing. She put the six bread tins on a tray and carried them away to the airing cupboard to rise. There was nothing she could say: certainly she couldn't speak the thoughts going on in her mind. Thoughts, feelings, that Justin was playing Debbie along in a dead-end relationship. She longed to relay the sound of warning bells in her brain, confide her thoughts and feelings on the subject to this gentle, vulnerable child, but she knew that far from helping, she would simply be creating distance between herself and Debbie. "The flower shop sounds like a lovely idea, darling. And if something else more interesting crops up at a later date, there is nothing to say you couldn't make a move. Coralie seems a nice girl: do you get on with her?"

"Oh yes, she's a sweetie. Terribly kind and thoughtful. I find it hard to believe she has a sister like Amanda!" Debbie kissed Sue's cheek. "I'll go and give her a call to say I'll take the job."

When she had gone, Sue flicked on the electric kettle and flopped on to the kitchen stool, crisis temporarily averted.

The relationship between a mother and daughter had the potential for great confidence and intimacy, yet seemed so fragile. Unlike the relationship with one's sons who tended always to hold one at a distance. Normally the females of any species including cats, dogs and horses, were much more affectionate and loving. Yet look how her relationship with Stephanie had collapsed! Hopelessly. And she still didn't have a clue why.

She warmed the teapot and measured in the leaves before the kettle switched itself off, poured and waited, thinking back to the strained relationship she had had with her own mother, Sarah.

Over the years she had developed a guilt complex about it, starting in Denbigh during the war when, with no photographic reminders, she had forgotten what her parents looked like. She knew she missed them, longed to return to them, to be one of the family again, daily loved by and loving the people around her.

The guilt was magnified dramatically when, after five long years, the great day of reunion dawned . . . and she had felt nothing! Armed with a man-sized handkerchief for the emotion of their meeting, she had carried her battered suitcase along the dockside towards two vaguely familiar strangers: her tall, handsome father now gaunt and grey, her beautiful mother prematurely aged and shrunk. The fact that these people, however changed from the pre-war photographs of them all sent to her after Liberation Day, were the parents she had longed to see again, made her drop the suitcase and rush impulsively to hug and kiss them, hang on to them, reclaim them as her long-lost family. But there was no deep-seated stirring, no special sense of loving. Just a blank. As though Sarah was a distant aunt, Daddy an old family friend.

So what was the matter with her? Had she become some cold, unnatural freak? True, Mummy hadn't helped, trying to boss her around, treat her like the ten-year-old she had been when she was evacuated from the island with her school, just days before the Germans had landed. As a streetwise fifteen-year-old, oh how she had resented that. But it had been no excuse for the vacuum in her soul, her lack of feeling, particularly for her mother. She had hoped that maybe, after a few months or even a year, the fractured relationship would heal, but when it did not, so the guilt grew. Thank God a new kind of loving had developed between them a year or so before Mummy died.

Sue suddenly remembered the tea, poured herself a cup and took a biscuit out of the tin.

The guilt had remained until quite recently when, after visiting Stephanie in her commune in Wales – a heart-wrenching experience – she had boarded a train in Rhyl bound for Euston, London, and found herself sitting opposite a plump, middle-aged woman whose face seemed very vaguely familiar. She had glanced at her several times and found the woman staring at her.

"Suzanne Gaudion?" the woman said, suddenly.

Sue stared back, memory stirred. "Angele Phillips?"

The old, wartime schoolfriends had both laughed, shaken hands and asked a thousand questions.

"Where do you live?"

"What happened to you when you left school?"

"Have you a husband? Children?"

Sue told her story, briefly, leaving out the gory details.

Angele's tale followed. Then she added that she had had a wonderful billet throughout the war with a couple who treated her like their own daughter. The heartache at parting after the Liberation of the island was only matched by the total void that had existed between her and her real parents after their reunion. She had born a painfully strained and guilt-ridden relationship with the latter until leaving school, going to England for training and then being free to return to North Wales to take a job near her dear foster-parents in Denbigh. She had married a Welsh boy, raised a family, and lived in Wales ever since. And now, still feeling guilty for failing to maintain a love for her real parents, she was hurrying back to Guernsey for her father's funeral.

The train journey to London had taken over five hours. Five hours of open-hearted confessions and memories which,

95

for them both, swept away a twenty-six year long burden of guilt.

Sue poured another cup of tea. Yes, mother and daughter relationships were very fragile, so easily broken. And while praying she wrong, she had a quite frightening feeling that the bouncey, bubbly, loving and super-sensitive Debbie was going to need to have their relationship intact in the not too distant future.

"She's a real peach, Richard!"

"How is she rigged, ketch?"

"No, sloop. She'll need some of the rigging replacing, mind, but that shouldn't be a problem," Billy enthused.

"I thought you said she'd only be a hull. How come if she's needing so little, she's going so cheap?" Richard emerged up the companionway sticking his head and shoulders through the hatch of a battered-looking Westerly.

"The galley's a bit of a mess, all the charts are missing and she'll need to have radar installed." Billy took a packet of Silk Cut out of his breast pocket, offered one to Richard who shook his head, and lit up. "She should have all new cushion covers and curtains in the cabins and saloon, too. Freshen her up."

"And you are absolutely sure the hull is sound?"

"Guaranteed. Though she could do with a coat of anti-fouling."

"Well, let's see what Uncle George and my father think about it."

There were two visits Sue had wanted to make in England in the summer of 1972: one, with Stephen, to see the Tutankhamen Exhibition in London, and the other to Stephanie in Wales again. It was decide that she should see her daughter first and Stephen would join her at the Strand Palace on her return to London. The choice of gifts for Stephanie was not difficult: food and money. Packets of dried fruits, soups and cake mixes seemed to be both manageable as luggage and could easily be stored by Stephanie. Sue wondered about clothes, but couldn't make up her mind what sort. New ones would seem a waste of time and money in the commune setting, yet her own cast-offs, which should fit the girl, would be laughably out of place.

The widower father of a London art student called Griffith Evans had died in 1970, leaving his very rundown and dilapidated farm in Wales to his only child. Friendly with Marcus and Tony, Griffith was equally cheesed off with the demands of his degree course and was keen to drop out of university. And so the group had moved into the farm with great determination and enthusiasm for healthy living and self-sufficiency, agreeing to pool their funds and resources. Unfortunately, neither had lasted very long – only the stubborn determination 'to make it work' remained, along with a reluctance to return to a "bourgeois" lifestyle and nine-to-five jobs. Artists are not particularly practical people: they make pots and pictures and "interesting" collages, but when it comes to repairing a broken window or hole in the roof they often prove exceptionally inept. When the members of the group had not been involved in "creative" works, the girls had been obliged to learn manual skills while the boys strummed their guitars and composed love songs.

Sue checked into a guest house in the town nearest to the farm, and from there she took a long taxi ride. She had written to Stephanie that she was coming but was unsure of the exact time she would arrive, finally turning up unannounced.

"Stephanie's outside, I think," said the dreamy-eyed girl who answered the door. "Probably over there beyond that wall, in the vegetable plot."

Wales was obviously having a damp summer. Sue picked her way around the worst of the mud in the yard and peered over a grey stone wall to where a plump girl was bent over a row of greenery. "Excuse me!" she called. "Can you tell me if . . ." The girl stood up and Sue gasped. "Stephanie!"

She was largely pregnant.

"Hello Mum! What are you doing here?"

"Didn't you get my letter?"

"The one about Debs working in a flower shop?"

"No, later than that. It should have arrived last week."

"The postmen don't deliver here anymore. Not since one got bitten by one of our dogs." She stretched her back to ease some discomfort.

"You didn't tell me about the baby," Sue remarked.

"Didn't think you'd want to know. Can you wait a minute while I finish pulling these carrots?"

"Of course. Have you grown them?"

"Yes. My only success. Everything else I've tried always gets eaten by slugs or rabbits before it's ready to pick." She pulled half a dozen more and put them in a plastic bag.

"I haven't seen any dogs." It was just something to say.

"They're probably with the boys who have gone fishing. And in answer to your next question, no, I'm not married."

"I wasn't going to ask," Sue assured her. "Who is the father?"

Stephanie hesitated before saying "Does it matter?"

Sue tried to smile. "Where will you have the baby?"

"Here. Melanie had her's here; a midwife came up from the town. It was fine."

Sue attempted to sound open-minded. "You could always come home to have it if you want to."

"No thanks."

"Or I could come here to help out till you feel, well, you know . . ."

"Don't worry, Mum. I'll be okay. Truly."

How can you say that? How do you know? Supposing it is a difficult birth and you end up with a string of stitches and can't walk for a week? Sue felt quite panicky as the thoughts raced through her mind, but she resisted the temptation to voice any of them, asking instead, "Is Caroline Patterson still here with you?" At least she was another Guernsey girl and might call if Stephanie needed help.

"No. She left ages ago for the fleshpots of the Mediterranean." They reached the farmhouse door. "Is this your bag?"

"Yes. I've brought some things I thought might be useful. Mainly food."

"That was clever of you. Very useful. Come on in." The place smelled of animals: cats, dogs and goats. "Sorry about the pong. Marcus has been trying to make goat cheese. He's not very good at it."

The rooms were a shambles. Clothes and rugs and cooking pots were scattered amongst books and papers. A bunch of wild flowers had died a natural death in a vase, some weeks earlier. Dirty mugs and overflowing ashtrays littered the tables, miscellaneous cats littered the chairs. Every room appeared to be used for a multitude of purposes, excepting for the kitchen which was comparatively tidy.

"This is my domain," Stephanie announced. "Here I reign supreme, mainly because no one else wants to cook. Not, Mummy dear, that I want the role of chief cook and bottle washer. But I do like to eat." She gave a rare smile. "In fact right now I could eat a horse, if it was well cooked."

"Why don't you keep me company for dinner tonight?" Sue suggested. The girl might have a large appetite but she didn't look as though she was eating much. "The taxi is coming back for me in an hour. You could come with me and return when we have eaten." The outlay in fares would be astronomical, but so what?

Stephanie frowned and bit her lip. "Oh, I don't know, Mum. I don't think I'd better. The boys will be wanting a meal when they get back. I might have to cook fish, if they've caught any."

The temptation was to argue but Stephanie was being quite nice and friendly at the moment, not at all her old aggressive self, and Sue did not want to upset her. Spoil the atmosphere. "It's up to you, darling. Now let's get these things out of my bag."

That evening in her room, Sue starting scratching, first a leg, them her stomach. Armed with a cake of damp soap she undressed very carefully, caught the flea on the soap and crushed it between her fingernails. Then cried herself to sleep.

Next day, when the initial shock had worn off, Sue felt a bit better. She and Stephanie spent the whole day together, talking quite normally, as though the girl's weird, drop-out lifestyle was not an insurmountable barrier between them.

But of course it was, and Sue spent the whole journey back to London trying to compose herself so that her despondency didn't spoilt the next few days with Stephen.

They both enjoyed the Tutankhamen Exhibition enormously. It was exquisite, exciting, exhilarating and they both exceeded their budgets on souvenirs.

Stephen was aware that Sue had something on her mind, but it was not till they were back home in Guernsey that she told him about Stephanie's baby.

"Hallo, Dad. Have a good game?" Sue reached up to kiss Greg's cheek.

"No. Had a disaster every time I took a wood out of my bag. Finished up using an iron off every tee." He sagged into an armchair. "Dunno why I go on playing. Getting too old."

"Better not let Uncle George hear you. He'll crow for a week."

"He wasn't much better. Said he was going home to bury his putter six feet deep in his potato patch."

They both laughed.

"Lunch won't be long. Stephen has just taken Bobbie to stay with his friend for the weekend. Will you have a drink?"

"Yes. A G and T would be nice. Tell me, do you hear much from young Stephanie?"

Sue poured them both an aperitif. "Yes indeed. In fact, strangely enough, she seems to be writing a lot more frequently than last year. Why do you ask?"

Greg stared up at her as she passed him his glass. "I worry about her. One hears things about these communes."

"Like what?" Sue asked, though she guessed what was coming.

"Drugs. And people sharing each other's beds in haphazard fashion. Flower power and all that." He raised his glass. "Cheers."

"Cheers. Though you certainly don't sound very cheerful."

"I can't help thinking what your mother would say about it all, if she was alive today."

Sue moved over to the window. "I hope she doesn't know, Dad."

"Makes me so sad. Is there nothing we can do?"

"Not a thing. You know I've been to see her three times. I've tried desperately hard not to show my disapproval, or ask her to come home. She knows how we all feel without me saying anything."

"Do you think she's happy?"

Sue didn't answer immediately, wondering whether or not to add to his misery by telling him the whole truth. That Stephanie had given birth to a beautiful baby daughter and either wouldn't or couldn't name the father. That the girl was looking thin and ill; thoroughly under-nourished. And that behind her false calm she looked restless and unhappy. "Hard to say, Dad. She seems to take life very seriously. She has done some beautiful art work. They all do, there, and sell some of it in tourist shops."

Greg watched the tonic bubbles in his glass. "And what about her sister? Such a shame she has given up her ambitions re tennis."

"I thought so at first. But maybe she just wasn't mentally cut out to drive herself through all the stress and strain. And the unsporting attitudes were getting her down, badly."

"How do you mean?"

Sue told him of her conversation on the subject with Debbie.

Greg screwed up his face in horror. "Well those cheats and thugs don't behave like that for honour and glory! It's all money. That's the effect that money has on people . . . and on sport." Sue had seldom seen her placid, easy-going father get so heated. "It destroys the whole meaning of sport! Unfortunately it seems to be happening more and more in every walk of life. Moral standards have dropped out of sight. Politics and business were the first to go."

"Come on, Dad! That's as ever was, right back to ancient

Egypt!" She remembered the relevant history she had learned on her trip with Stephen to the Tutankhamen Exhibition.

"But we are supposed to be a modern and civilised society," Greg argued.

"That doesn't alter the nature of *Homo sapiens*, does it? It just means he is that much craftier and more devious."

"Things weren't like that when your mother and I were young. Anyone caught cheating at sport was ostracised for life! Did that apply only in Guernsey? Or did the same standards exist in England, then?" Suddenly he looked up at her. "By the way, What is her relationship with that young man?"

"You mean Justin?" Sue shrugged. "They appear very fond of each other."

"Yes. But that's been going on a long time. Isn't he going to propose?"

She turned to her father, feigning horror. "Debbie is only nineteen, Dad! There is plenty of time."

Greg gave her an old-fashioned look. "Not unless she is acceding to his requirements, I imagine."

Sue flushed. It was so unlike her father to refer to such matters! "Well stop imagining, Dad. It won't do you a ha'p'orth of good! Now I'd better go and put the carrots on." And she escaped to the kitchen. It was bad enough worrying one's self sick about one's children, without the older generation putting their oar in as well.

While at university, Roderick had had a nodding acquaintanceship with a young man named Alex Grolinski who was reading Economics and Social Sciences. Roderick, with his career clearly mapped out before going to college, had no idea what Alex meant to do when and if he got his degree, but then neither had Alex himself. Until he came to Guernsey.

One day Roderick received a telephone call from Alex. "I've come to work over here," he announced.

"Doing what?"

"Real estate."

"Oh! How long have you been doing that?"

"I haven't, over here. I start on Monday. Meanwhile, I wondered if we might meet up for a drink."

Roderick chose the upstairs bar at the Kosy Korner during the lunch hour because it was reasonably close to the office and easy for Alex to find following his directions.

The latter was there first. "What will you have?"

"Er . . ." Roderick did not normally drink during working days and seldom went into a pub, "What are you drinking?"

"Whisky dry."

"Er . . . no thanks. I'll have a half of mild."

"So, tell me what you've been doing with yourself since graduating," Alex demanded when he returned to the table with the beer.

"What I always planned to do. Architecture."

"Go on."

Roderick elaborated for a few minutes then asked, "What about you?"

"My father wanted me to go into the business with him."

"What sort of business?"

"Producing farm machinery. But you know what these family businesses are," Alex smote his forehead dramatically. "Degree or no degree, it is decided that you know nothing and must start at the very bottom, on a pittance of course, and work your way very slowly to the top by the age of sixty."

Roderick laughed. "I know what you mean. We have some firms like that here in the island."

"And do they go broke and get sold up through lack of modernisation?"

"Most of them, yes! So how long did you stick it out?"

"Nearly six months. Then Dad asked me to deliver some heavy machinery to a firm in Nassau, in the Bahamas. Marvellous place. Met some super people and sent Dad a telegram giving him my notice with immediate effect."

"Crickey! So what did you live on?"

"Not a lot! But as you may remember I had done a fair amount of yachting. One of these people I met needed to

103

have a sloop delivered to a Miami broker's yard and its replacement brought back to the island. He couldn't go himself and offered me a handsome sum to do it for him."

Roderick gave him a sidelong glance. "Are you sure it was only the ketch you were delivering?"

"No, in retrospect. At the time I was totally innocent about the drug-running activities between the islands and Florida. Wasn't until I delivered a third boat, for one of his 'friends', and was handed a briefcase full of cash by way of payment on delivery that I finally smelled a rat. Never went back! Boxed up the money and sent it to the bloke by courier and got on the first flight back to London. Didn't draw a decent breath till I was home!"

"So then what?"

"I had a serious chat with an uncle of mine in the real estate business in the south of England and have been working for him for three months. Boy, that's where the money is."

"You can say that again! There is a hell of a boom in the market over here at the moment."

"I know. That's why I'm here. And that's what I want to talk to you about. You see, uncle has the basic know-how and wants me to be his agent over here, but I have no local knowledge. Now there are three options. One, you and I could set up business together working for uncle. Two, I would open up under my own steam and pay you a consultancy fee. Three, you can tell me to bugger off and forget it."

Walking back up High Street towards the office, Roddy couldn't stop grinning to himself. Of all the wild, impetuous propositions in the world, this had to be the most audacious. Dammit, he hardly knew the guy! And for that matter the guy hardly knew him! Of course he hadn't wanted to be rude so he'd told Alex he would think about it . . . but naturally there was no way he'd give it a second thought. The only decision he had to make was how to tell him he was taking the third option!

Throughout the afternoon as he leaned over sets of plans his mind drifted back to the lunchtime conversation . . .

and recalled the fact that he had thought about the property market several times, as an alternative to the much harder work and less lucrative job of architecting. He had accepted the status quo most of his life, but there had been times, especially more recently, when he had felt the urge for more and better. He hoped that within the next five years or so he would meet a girl he would want to marry. But what were the prospects? Years of saving up for a down payment for a mortgage, followed by twenty or more years trying to pay off the darned thing. Twenty years of counting every penny, whilst raising a family. Restricting the size of family to what they hoped they could afford. What standard of home could he hope for? What kind of lifestyle? No doubt Mum and Stephen would want to help a bit, financially, but they could do no more for him than they could afford to do for for the other three as well. Stephen and his father paid him a decent salary, and no doubt his prospects in the firm were excellent, but he never saw himself becoming . . . rich, or even well off.

By the time he and Stephen headed home that evening, Roderick had calculated that if he sold one hundred thousand pounds worth of real estate in a week at two percent commission, he could make one hundred thousand pounds in a year . . . allowing for taking two weeks holiday off.

Next morning Roderick made a telephone call to Alex Grolinski, suggesting they have another drink at lunchtime at the Kosy Korner.

Piped jazz greeted the guests as they drove up to Cy and Carol Blaydon's new place, jarring with the otherwise peaceful ambience of the old granite house.

"Maybe the noise is in keeping with the grosser garden ornaments," Sue suggested to Stephen, as they got out of the car. It was not her first visit, but it was still hard to resist comparing the end result with the way it might have been had she been in charge. She thanked Heaven she was not in Stephen's shoes, being paid to design the alterations and then forced to accede to such fearful examples of bad taste. But this was to be a garden party and, apart from the addition of gnomes, frogs and other plaster and stone *object d'art* the hosts had shown little interest in the layout of the garden, leaving it to hired professionals.

"Stevie, boy!" Cy called as they crossed the lawn to the gathering. "Suzy! So nice to see you. Hey you," he turned to a temporary barman, "give these people a drink," and he wandered off to greet more newcomers.

"Oh look, there's Richard," Sue noted. "But I don't see Anne anywhere."

"She's at home with the children," Richard explained. "She thinks little George has measles. Derek is just recovering from it. His whole class went down with it at school."

Amanda, yards of thigh emerging from microscopic short-pants which failed to cover the curves of her bottom, pranced up on very high heels which served well for aereating the lawn. "There you are, Dickie. Come on, I want to introduce you to some friends who are staying with us. Excuse us, won't you?" she smiled sweetly at his sister, slid a possessive arm through his and dragged him away.

Stephen and Sue watched in amazement. "What an incongruous pair!" the latter exclaimed.

Roderick joined them. "I still think Richard was crazy not to go on to university. You know, he really does have a brain."

"He is so happy doing what he does," Sue argued. "He loves his life."

"But he could have so much more. That house of theirs is so tiny, and his car is totally delapidated. He could have a decent job . . ."

"I wouldn't say as much to him if I were you," Stephen suggested. "I've never seen a man happier in his work."

"I already have," Roderick grinned sheepishly.

"What did he say?" Sue asked.

"He enquired whether I thought sitting at a desk throughout the daylight hours, looking out at the sun you can't feel, might be better."

"That boy has his priorities right," Stephen said with feeling.

Roderick stared at his stepfather in surprise. Then shrugged and wandered off.

"Superb food," Sue remarked on the way home.

"And good wine. Too good, really, for alfresco eating."

"Alfresco! Sitting at tables laid with white linen and cut glass! You have to be joking!"

Stephen patted her knee and laughed. "Okay. I'm joking. Now tell me why weren't the Tetchworth's there?"

"They're in England."

"Oh. I wondered if there had been a grand falling out."

"No." Sue shook her head. "Well certainly not with the young. Amanda and Coralie seem to get on very well with Jane. They are often at the Tetchworth's place. I didn't know very many of the people there. Did you?"

"No. I think most of them were English newcomers."

"Who don't fraternise too much with the natives?"

"I think they're somewhat put off by the fact that the locals are so appallingly unimpressed by ostentatious wealth."

"Oh come on! Not all the newcomers are like that. Some of them are charming."

"Yes. I've just acquired a new pair of clients whom I think are very nice. You must meet them. They're keen on tennis and want a court."

"What are their names?"

"Martin and Sheila Gillespie."

"Where's dinner?"

"In the oven."

"Can't eat it in there. Can I get it out?" Tony asked.

"It won't be ready for another half hour."

"Why not! I'm starving!"

"No you're not, just greedy!" Stephanie snapped. "And what's more, if it wasn't for my efforts we would all be well and truly starving!" She stomped out of the kitchen, cradling the baby on her hip.

"What's got into her?" Tony asked Melanie as he followed her through to the living room.

Melanie shrugged, smiling. "We all have the right to our

moods, don't we?" she took the cigarette from Marcus, inhaled, and passed it on to Tony.

He took a couple of drags and handed it to Stephanie who was standing by the sideboard, taking out a miscellany of mismatched, chipped and cracked plates. "No thanks."

"Take it," he ordered. "You need it."

"I said no thanks! I do not need it."

Aggressively, he stuck it between her lips.

Furious, she spat it onto the floor and ground it into the carpet with her heel.

Tony's hand shot out and hit her across the ear before she could duck.

She screamed.

So did the baby.

"For Crissake, Tony!" Marcus drawled. "Leave her alone, unless you want to take over as cook!"

Stephanie fled upstairs. These altercations were beginning to happen more frequently, and she suspected it was because Tony had starting sniffing some hard stuff. It made him behave very oddly at times. He never used to get rough. She was thankful her mother hadn't met him; his odd behaviour might have surfaced and . . . and what? And nothing. Mum would have done nothing, because she, Stephanie, wanted her to do nothing.

It was very tempting to taking a lungful of smoke, stop the worrying, stop minding about the occasional swipe from Tony. Stop wondering about what sort of life baby Sarah was going to have . . . her darling little daughter named after her great grandmother.

Richard and Anne were invited to La Fregate Hotel for dinner with Richard's old school friend and his wife, Geoffrey and Rosemary Duggan. The Duggans hadn't been over to the island for two years but as Geoffrey's mother was ailing they decided to come for a long weekend.

Walking down the carpeted stairs to the restaurant, Anne was very self-conscious about her dress. She had put on quite a bit of weight since George was born and this was the only respectable garment she could still get into. Just. The trouble was that the buttons down the front were straining too much over her bust and she was terrified one would pop open during the meal.

"Does it look all right?" she whispered to Richard.

"Fine. You always look stunning. And I promise that as soon as we've replaced the living room window you will have a new dress. Hopefully by Christmas!" He put an arm round her waist to give her a reassuring hug, just as a waiter came to take her wrap.

Geoff and Rosemary were waiting in the bar, looking as prosperous and self-assured as ever.

"Splendid to see you again, Richard. How are you, Anne?" the London businessman shook hands and kissed cheeks with accomplished ease. "Will you have a spot of bubbly? Anne, do sit here by me. How are your boys?"

Once in the dining room and the meal progressed Richard found himself able to relax a little more, though he remained very conscious of the difference in their lifestyles. Rosemary produced photos of their home in Surrey, large with lawns and a waterfall. The pair talked of their annual skiing trips, and their cruises. Anne said they loved the islands so much they stayed at home for holidays, taking lots of trips to Herm and Sark.

Afterwards, on the way home, Richard was very quiet.

"What's up, darling?" Anne asked.

"Just thinking about something Roderick said the other day."

"What?"

"That if you go on to university and get a degree you have the world at your feet. You can get a job in anything you like, climb the ladder to success . . ."

"What as?"

"Anything. Doesn't matter what the subject. Providing you have flexed your mental muscles sufficiently you can become a leader in business, finance, you name it." He patted her knee. "Doesn't it get to you, sometimes, that people like the Duggans have so much and yet we have so little by comparison?"

"Depends on your priorities. I would hate to be like her,

109

having to employ someone else to bring up my children while I go out to work for money for fine holidays. And look at you. Would you like to leave home every morning at half-seven and be gone for twelve hours?" she leaned across the gear lever and handbrake so she could lay her head on his shoulder. "I like having my husband coming home for lunch every day, and seeing him play with the little ones in the evening before they go to bed."

Richard grinned into the darkness. Sometimes, just sometimes he fell into the trap of thinking the other man's grass was greener. But Anne could be relied upon to set the record straight.

And of course there was always a chance that Billy Smart's scheme for doing up secondhand boats might work out . . . put a little extra into the coffers.

Debbie came home with a fresh lot of photos she had just collected from being developed. They included snaps of a seriously fun beach party last month, just before the weather turned nasty, when people were darting around in bathing suits playing cricket in the shallows. They had built a fire in the rocks and burnt sausages and chicken thighs, and she had taken a lovely shot of Justin washing his bit of chicken in the sea, after dropping it in the sand. And there was another one of Peter wearing Sophie's sunhat.

She showed them to Sue in the kitchen. "When you've finished going through them I'll pop across to show them to Justin before we have supper."

"That's a naughty one of someone wrestling with a bathing suit under his towel!" Sue laughed as she handed them back.

"That's Don Bainbridge. His towel is only the size of a handkerchief. Right, I'll away. Back soon," and she skipped out of the door.

Stephen and his neighbours had been persuaded long ago to cut a hole in the hedge dividing the two properties and put a gate in, to save Debbie and Justin the bother of going all the way round via the road. She slipped through the gate quickly before the dogs could follow, much to their

110

disgust, and went to the Tetchworth's kitchen door, looking for Hilary.

"Cooee?" she called.

No reply.

She remembered that Hilary's car wasn't in the drive, but Justin's was. She peered into the sitting room. It was empty. So Justin must be in his room reading or listening to records. Upstairs the music was louder. She rapped briefly on his door before swinging it open . . . then gasped, swayed and leaned against the doorpost.

Justin and Amanda Blaydon, were on the bed together, stark naked, locked in passionate embrace.

Chapter Six

Consultations

Sue pushed the large Pyrex dish of macaroni cheese to the centre of the oven shelf, closed the door and returned the ovencloth to its hook. There was a little mirror on the wall near the kitchen window: she glanced into it as she brushed a wisp of stray hair away from her eyes. She raised her eyebrows in an attempt to get rid of the crow's feet, grinned to examine her teeth . . . then shrugged and gave up; at forty-two what could one expect. Age was definitely catching up. A change of skirt, a comb through her hair and a fresh dash of lipstick might improve things, she decided as she moved away past the window.

It was only by chance that her eye was caught by something, someone outside, standing by the wire netting round the tennis court. The evenings were drawing in and her eyes narrowed as they pierced the gloom. She opened the back door for a better view, then frowned. "Debbie? Is that you? Are you all right?"

There was no reply, but the shoulders hunched a little more and the head flopped sideways against the wire.

"Debbie!" Sue darted across the path and the wet grass. "What is it? What is the matter?"

Debbie's fingers were locked into the wire for support. She stared at her mother. Then squeezed her eyes closed very tightly. Opened them to stare again, her mouth opening and shutting involuntarily.

Sue put her arms round the girl. "Darling! Come into the house, you're shivering."

But Debbie either couldn't or wouldn't unlock her fingers from the wire.

112

They both heard the click of the side-gate latch and saw Justin leap up on to the verandah.

"No! Oh no, please no," Debbie gasped and shook her head. "I don't want to see him."

Justin heard her voice. "Debs? Is that you?" he came across the grass towards them, then saw Sue. "Oh, hallo. I suppose she's told you. Well it's her own fault! She shouldn't have come bursting in like that . . ." he began to back away.

"Like what? Bursting in on what?"

From beyond the fence came the sound of a car ignition, an engine engaged, wheels churning gravel and a gear lever grinding as the machine drew away.

Justin turned towards the noise and uttered a strangled, "Oh God, my gearbox!"

Sue's brain was doing overtime. Someone was over there with Justin when Debbie walked in . . . ?

"Amanda . . ." Debbie whispered.

"Look, she's gone," Justin said sharply.

"Amanda Blaydon?" Sue exclaimed.

The young man glared at her. "Do you mind leaving us, please? I need to speak to Debs."

"No!" the girl wailed, turning her face away.

"You heard her," Sue snapped. "Out!" She pointed at the gate, repeating "Out!" as he hesitated.

Justin retreated with a couple of "Huh!"'s.

When the gate slammed behind him Debbie gave a long shudder of relief, released her hold on the wire netting and allowed Sue to lead her indoors and up to her bedroom. Sue undid Debbie's wet shoes and slipped them off, then swung the girl's legs up onto the bed under the eiderdown. "I'll fix you a hottie," she said. When she came back from the bathroom, Debbie was lying on her back, staring at the ceiling.

"He was with Amanda?"

The girl nodded, accepting the hot water bottle.

"Upstairs?"

Another nod.

"In bed?"

The questioning had the desired effect. At last, with a huge, shuddering gasp, the floodgates opened. Clutching the hottie, Debbie rolled onto her side, buried her head in her pillow, and wept.

"She caught him in bed with Amanda Blaydon," Sue explained to Stephen at supper.

"What?" Stephen threw his fork onto his plate. "Seriously?" but he could see by her expression it was true. "The bounder! The dirty, rotten cad!" He pushed back his chair. He pushed away his plate of slightly burnt macaroni. "You can put that in the oven. I'm going over there to give the rotten little sod—"

"You will do no such thing!" Sue ordered sharply. "There is nothing you can tell him that he does not already know. And if he doesn't, he never will."

"But—"

"Like me, all you want to do is let off your own fury at the boy. Which would certainly make us both feel a lot better, but will do nothing whatever to help the situation."

Stephen was puce with unquenched anger, but he sat down. "Where is Bobbie?"

"Watching TV. He had his meal early."

"And Roderick?"

"I've no idea. Out clinching another deal I suppose."

"What about Debbie? Isn't she going to eat?"

"The bottom has just fallen out of her world, darling. Macaroni cheese is hardly the best foundation on which to rebuild her life." Sue toyed with a forkful in front of her mouth.

"I still have an urgent desire to go and shoot that bastard."

"Then try to overcome it," Sue snapped irritably. "I must go up to Debbie again, but I don't want to leave you alone if you are going over there as soon as my back is turned to make more mayhem."

He shook his head. "Don't worry, I won't. But tell me, did you ever suspect he was getting up to this?"

"In a sub-conscious sort of way, yes. I suspected for a long time that his feelings weren't sincere."

114

"What made you suspicious?"

Sue shrugged. "Feminine intuition? Anyway, I'll nip up with a glass of milk and see how she is."

The door closed behind their late-evening client, and his footsteps could be heard retreating down the hallway to the stairs. Alex and Roderick looked at each other, questioning with their eyebrows.

Then Alex grinned. "Can't be bad?"

His partner could only manage half a smile. "Almost too good to be true."

"How do you mean?"

"Can he really come up with this sort of money?"

"He has written deposit cheques on at least half a dozen properties placed with other people, to my knowledge. I haven't heard of one bouncing, yet."

Roderick ran slim fingers through his long, blond hair, sweeping it back from his forehead. "Yet. But how long can he keep this up?"

"Don't you trust him?"

"It's not that. I just don't like him. He's so slick . . . smarmy . . ."

". . . and foreign? There are some honest foreigners around, you know. Anyway, what does it matter? The deal is straightforward enough and if his money is good then we've nothing to worry about." Alex eyed him speculatively. It wasn't the first time he had questioned his own decision to take his straight-laced, solemn-faced old friend into partnership. Roderick had some very old-fashioned ideas on business, almost like his own father. Heaven forbid!

In fact Roderick had cursed several times the impetuous impulse that made him telephone Alex back for further discussion on the idea of them working together. His step-father, Stephen, had been appalled when he told him he was resigning, and spent a month trying to dissuade him. So he had only himself to blame. Yet there was no questioning the fact that, financially, the venture had proved an outstanding success . . . though not least due to the extraordinary activities of this same man with his foreign name and

115

accent, boosting the property market with fantastic offers, island-wide. Roderick had to admit he admired Alex for his confidence and daring; he had bought an open market flat, meaning that as a non-islander he was allowed to occupy it, and much of the bank loan involved had already been paid off in the first year. So Roderick himself was now looking at local market cottages before the prices went up any further. He could certainly afford one. G & M Properties Ltd. was a very profitable concern.

"The only problem," Alex went on, "Is finding enough people willing to sell to keep this beggar happy."

"Yes. And that is the amazing thing. It can't have missed your attention, that he doesn't often complete a conveyance until he has a market for the resale."

Alex laughed again. "Nothing if not crafty!"

"Hm. One day he may find he has a hell of a lot of money tied up in properties he cannot sell. Then he's up the creek."

"Of course. But in the meantime, let's cream the system."

"Then what?"

"Sit back and wait for the market to restabilise. Dammit, we are moving places with other clients besides him. Several local market ones, too."

Roderick went to the window and looked down into the parking lot where his orange MGB GT stood under the lamplight, so out of character with his previous image. Yes, he smiled, the business was perfectly healthy, even without the weird foreigner.

"I haven't seen Debbie over at our place, lately," Hilary remarked as she stretched her legs towards Sue's kitchen Aga and sipped her cup of tea.

Sue tipped a baking tray of fresh-baked scones onto the wire cooling tray. "I thought Justin was away?" She hadn't expected Hilary to pop in and was unsure how she wanted to tell her the news which Justin had obviously failed to mention.

"He is. And that's odd, too. He suddenly announced the

116

other day at breakfast that he was sick of the island, and walked out. I cannot think what is going on."

"Like a scone while it's hot?"

"Yes please!"

Sue put butter and homemade strawberry jam on the table. "Help yourself."

"Suzanne Martel! You're withholding something from me! What has happened?"

Sue plonked herself down on a kitchen chair, began buttering a scone, and said, "The kids have split up."

"Oh, no!" Hilary leaned back in her chair. "Why?"

Sue took a deep breath. "Because Debbie marched into your house one day, uninvited, and found Justin in bed with Amanda Blaydon."

Hilary's eyes closed, deep furrows between them. "Oh dear. Oh dear, oh dear, oh dear." Then she gazed sadly across the table. "Oh Sue, my dear, I am so very sorry. I did so hope he would not turn out like his father."

Sue looked startled.

"Oh sorry, didn't you know? I thought everyone knew that Johnny chases everything that moves in a skirt."

Sue rubbed a floury hand across her forehead. "Then it's my turn to say how sorry I am."

"Oh, don't worry. I have become used to it over the years. It used to hurt like hell, in the beginning. But not any more. At least he doesn't fall madly in love and go off with them."

Sue thought that was probably because Hilary held the purse strings, but she didn't say so.

"Poor little Debbie. How is she?"

"Pretty grim, I think. She walks round like a zombie. Doesn't eat enough to keep a fly alive, and goes off to work every morning as though her life depended on it."

"Perhaps it does."

Sue sighed. "Perhaps."

Debbie wrote the little card, attached it to the bouquet and laid it in a cardboard delivery box. The phone rang and she answered it, pen in hand, no longer fearful that Justin

117

might be on the other end. She placed the order note in the tray, picked up the next instruction and moved round the shop selecting flowers from buckets and display vases. Debbie wasn't smiling, but then nor was she crying: she was simply going through the everyday motions of living . . . trying not to feel.

"Everything going all right?" Coralie asked in a matter-of-fact voice as she staggered in behind a huge cardboard box.

"Fine. No problems," was the colourless reply.

Coralie deposited the box in the middle of the floor, enabling her to peer at her friend over the top. "And what about you? Did you eat those sandwiches I bought you?"

"I had some of them." Debbie omitted to add that she had only managed a couple of bites of one ham and tomato before hiding the rest away in her handbag.

But Coralie guessed. "Honey, you just have to eat or you are going to make yourself seriously ill. I still can't believe my bloody sister has done this to you." Strong words from one who normally avoided saying 'damn'.

"Don't worry about Amanda. I gather from the gossip flying round that she wasn't the first. Look," she held up a stem of golden lilies, "do you think these would look right in the Harvey's centre piece for their dinner party?"

Coralie put her head on one side and considered. "No. Too tall for diners to talk across. Try cutting the stems down on these lovely, flat zinnias."

The subject of Justin's infidelity was dropped, temporarily.

"Mrs Harris has made a lovely job of those cushions," George said through the hatchway. "Who chose the material?"

"Anne did," Richard replied, fixing a bottlescrew into place. "Like the colour?"

"Turquoise is my favorite. And it matches the curtains and the decoration on the plastic cups and plates. Very smart. Almost makes me feel our asking price is too low. What do you think?"

"I'm more interested in the hull and the engine. That's what should sell the boat. They are in good nick but still secondhand. I think we've set a fair price."

"I don't." Billy was listening from the floor of the workshop. "We could have asked another three thou."

"That would give us a disproportionate amount of profit," George said severely.

"Only because I got such a good deal on the hull in the first place," his step-nephew grumbled.

"But she wasn't just a hull. She was virtually a fully-equipped motor sailer."

"So I knocked 'em down. Why not?"

George presumed the previous owners must have been hard up and had to sell – or they were mentally retarded, and the brokers who bought her couldn't wait to get rid of her. But he didn't pursue the argument. "We'll advertise her while she is still up. Prospective buyers prefer the chance to inspect the hull."

Richard climbed down over the spanking new dodgers, patting the freshly painted boot-topping appreciatively as he passed. "Definitely. You are so right, Uncle George." Though George Schmit was not really an uncle, because he was his father's longtime friend, the younger man continued to give him the courtesy title.

"Are you ready to start work on that one, yet?" Billy asked, indicating a barnacle-clad hull blocked up on a trailer at the far end of the workshop.

"No. We have to finish the work on a couple of local boats, first," George replied, leaning over the trim.

"Don't know why you bother," Billy remarked. "We only get peanuts for labour."

"We! You should try putting in a bit of labour yourself, sometime. Then there might be a few more peanuts all round." George was always irritated by the young man's reluctance to work with anything but his mouth.

"I'm cutting off home now. I have to drop in at Sue's on the way with a bag of stuff Anne borrowed," Richard said on the way to the corrugated iron gable door. "See you after lunch."

119

He drove off along the Bordeaux coast road, glancing repeatedly across the grass and rocks to the Little Russel. With the westerly wind against tide, white caps were charging down past the Brehon Tower between Guernsey, and Herm and Jethou, buffeting the rocks at the entrance to the little harbour and setting all the small fishing boats dancing on their moorings. He smiled, thinking about Geoff Duggan. "Who'd want to live and work in a city?" he asked himself out loud.

Sue was on the phone when he walked into the kitchen. "Fine, I'll see you tomorrow at about three-thirty. 'Bye!" She replaced the receiver. "Hi, little brother! Haven't seen you for weeks. How are you all?"

"Derek's been off school with a cold, but otherwise we are all fit. What about you lot? Saw Debbie the other day and thought she looked very peaky."

"She isn't feeling too good yet. You know she and Justin have broken up?"

"No! Good grief! I thought they were all set to get married. What happened?"

Sue grimaced and told him and was surprised at his reaction.

"That tart! She had a go at me once, back along. Gave every indication of wanting to roll me in the hay."

Sue had to laugh. "No! When?"

"Remember that party her folk gave in their garden in the summer? Well, there she was, dolled up to the nines and as Mum would have said, 'Asking for it', following me round to every group of people I spoke to, in a tiny little pair of shorts that showed off virtually everything she has."

Sue nodded. "I remember them well."

"Who wouldn't? And next thing I know she links her arm through mine and is rubbing her thigh up against me, quite deliberately."

"Charming!"

"If you like that sort of thing and your wife enjoys sharing your favours. Anne does not. I was fool enough to tell her when I got home. She was not amused and accused me of encouraging the painted witch."

120

"Poor Anne! She must have felt very upset at the thought of it going on in front of all those people."

It was Richard's turn to laugh. "Poor Anne nothing! You may remember she was carrying quite a bit of extra weight after having baby George, well apparently Amanda's behaviour decided her to look to her laurels. She started dieting like mad and now says she needs a complete new wardrobe!"

"Well done Anne!" Sue exclaimed. Adding, "but it's not fair to blame Amanda entirely for Debbie's misery. Since the break up, people have felt free to relay gossip over all Justin's other infidelities. It seems that even while they were on tennis tours in England, he would go off to London or elsewhere to meet up with various *amours*. Debbie never suspected a thing."

"Just as well she is rid of a type like that before getting hitched."

"True, in a sense. The pity is she ever fell for him in the first place. She really believed that her whole future was mapped out with him as husband and father of her children to be. Now, the bottom has fallen out of her world. It's worse than a bereavement. At least if he'd died she could cherish his memory. As it is, she cannot even think of him without hurting."

"Tell her her Uncle Richard says she is well rid of the louse," he growled.

"The court is quite playable after this dry spell, Debs. Would you like to pull on a sweater and come out for a knock?" Sue was worried to find the girl still shut away in her bedroom as lunchtime approached one Sunday. January was very chilly but they might still work up a steam.

Debbie looked up from the magazine she wan't reading, green eyes unnaturally large and pale in their dark circles, set in a pinched little face. Compared with the bouncing, bubbling character of a year ago who had been so full of enthusiasm for life, this was a pathetic ghost.

Sue's heart plummeted. She wanted to weep.

"It's very sweet of you, Mummy darling, but I think I'd

121

rather go for a walk along the shoreline with you and the dogs. After lunch?"

"Of course, sweetheart, if that's what you'd prefer." Sue sat on the edge of the bed with a sigh. "What can I do to help?"

Debbie reached out to pat her hand. "You are helping, Mum. Just by being there."

"But that doesn't seem like enough. You are not getting over this. You look worse as every week, every month passes. Talk to me. Tell me what is going on in your mind and we can discuss the thing through."

"I don't see how we can. Or how it could help. I mean, without being rude, how can anyone your age know how I feel?"

Sue managed not to laugh but couldn't avoid a wry smile. "My age? Do you imagine that the teens and twenties have exclusive claim to all feelings of love and sexual desire?"

A faint grin and pale flush crept into the girl's face, but she said nothing.

"Do you think I cannot remember my first love? And my second? Not to mention my third. Do you think I didn't grieve for the man I married when your father's accident robbed him of his love for me? Turned that love into cruel aggression, almost hatred? Do you imagine I didn't weep into my pillow for years at the daily reminders of what once had been? Do you think I don't know what it is like to ache for the physical love of the man I once adored, until every mouthful of food stuck in my gullet and I could count every rib in my body?"

"Oh, Mum!" Debbie's eyes filled with tears as she flung herself into her mother's arms. They sobbed together for each others' sadness. Then the girl mopped her eyes with a soggy tissue and said, "Tell me about your first love."

So Sue told her all about David Morgan, the boy she had met in Wales at the age of fourteen. The boy who had helped fill the void left by the absence of parents and family during the five war years of exile. Then she went on to talk of the handsome ex-serviceman she fell in love with and married: their love, and the home and business they built together.

She spoke in a way, and with an openness, that Debbie had never heard before.

"You were fortunate, of course, that you were living back in the island again and able to talk to Grandma, like we are talking now," the girl observed.

Sue shook her head. "No way. Your grandmother would have been shocked out of her socks if I had tried to discuss the matter in this way. Certainly the sexual side was an unmentionable topic."

They talked on, for a while, till Sue looked at her watch and leapt to her feet. "Nobody will get any lunch today if I don't get down to the kitchen."

"Want a hand?"

"You might do the carrots for me while I turn the potatoes."

They exchanged warm, intimate smiles as they left the room and Sue only wished that things could be the same between herself and Stephanie.

Sarah was a wiry and agile baby, walking before she was a year old. Which didn't make looking after her any easier.

"No, Sarah, not out there!" Stephanie grabbed her in from the muddy yard, cursing the person who left the door open again, yet daring to say nothing. She was bruised enough. In fact everything was enough. Too much of enough. Too much work trying to make meals out of nothing. Too many swedes and carrots and no meat. Not enough eggs because the boys kept killing off too many chickens for the pot. Too much bread and cake from the local supermarket, going cheap because it had passed the sell-by date. Too much rain and mud. Too much cold. Too many arguments and fights. The nearest doctor or nurse was too far away when the little ones were sick. But what was the alternative? Thank God for Mum's food parcels: they'd scarcely survive without them. The only problem was keeping a fair share for the babies before the men got hold of it all. There had been six big bars of Cadbury's Milk Chocolate in one parcel, and the boys had knocked the lot off in one evening. It was so unfair. She kept a packet of chocolate digestives hidden in the nappy box under her bed, and was idiot enough to feel guilty about it. But Sarah's need was far greater than Griff's or Tony's, the two greedy gannets.

"No, Sarah. Don't cuddle that cat, she has an abcess from fighting off the tom." She picked up the baby who couldn't understand what she was saying, and blew a loving, explosive raspberry into her neck. Sarah squirmed and chortled with joy, unaware of the dirt that clogged her baby shoes and smeared her legs: not seeing her mother's concern at the fleabites on her arms.

Standing there at the kitchen sink, Stephanie's eyes wandered subconsciously to the ceiling, towards the bedroom above where money lay stitched into the lining of her jacket on the hook behind the door. Money sent by her mother to pay her fare back to the island for a holiday.

She bit her lip, took a deep breath and started counting out the wrinkled, sprouting potatoes that needed peeling for supper.

"Do you think I should try and force her to go to the doctor?" Sue asked. "Is there anything he might prescribe to help her?" Yet again she was at *Les Marettes*, the Banks's home at Bordeaux. And yet again she was consulting her cousin Sybil about her children, Debbie in particular at this moment.

"I don't know about medication, but what he might do is impress on her the seriousness of her condition. After all this time, her depression appears to have become endogenous," Sybil replied, gently. At fifty-five she remained a stunningly beautiful woman: her figure was good, muscle tone firm and only the glistening blonde hair had artificial assistance. "Have a word with him, first, and see what he thinks."

"I'll ring him in the morning when she's at work. See what he says."

"How is Roderick getting on, these days?"

"Splendidly, it would seem. He has bought the cutest little cottage near Cobo and is currently doing it up. He and Alex Grolinski have made a great success of their business. Stephen was very worried at first, you know. He did his best to dissuade the boy from giving up architecture. But now he's quite pleased he failed. I have to say that Roderick is a totally changed character. I don't know if it is Alex's influence, but he has joined the cocktail set, and started dating a variety of girls."

Sybil's elegant eyebrows shot up. "Wow! That's hard to believe. He was always such a quiet, serious boy."

Sue laughed. "So much so that I used to worry about him."

"I must admit there have been times when I've wished we'd had children. But then seeing the way they go on being a worry to one all their lives, not just as babies, I am thoroughly thankful we didn't!"

"It would be rather trying for poor Gordon, I imagine, to be coping with a teenager at . . . what age is he?"

"Coming up seventy-six this year. Yet I don't know. I think he'd cope better than I would. Know what he's doing at this moment? Lying underneath his car fiddling with the rear axle, or something. Says the garage man hasn't a clue!"

"If he's happy, why stop him? By the way, what's all this I hear about your mother and her next door neighbour?" Sue asked.

"Jim Mahy? Well, they play a lot of bridge together. Where did you hear the gossip?"

"From Dad. He says they are thick as thieves!"

"If you call trading help with their respective darning and their vegetable patches 'thick as thieves', yes. But as far as I can tell there is nothing wildly sexual in their relationship!"

"I should hope not. Otherwise you'll have to advise her on taking the pill."

"Sue, dear, Mother is the same age as Gordon. I hardly think that would be necessary." They both giggled, wickedly. "Talking of babies, how is Stephanie?"

"Not happy. Though she wouldn't dream of admitting it."

"Then how do you know?"

"By the number and length of her letters. She writes about the baby, and the vegetable garden, and her latest culinary achievements, but never says she is enjoying her life. I've told you how horrible I thought it all was each time I've visited her. I have the feeling my poor, uptight girl is stuck in an impossible situation."

"Would you let her come home to live?"

"I can't imagine she would want to. You know she and I could never hold a conversation without having a row." Sue screwed up her face, sadly. "But I have sent her the money to come back home for a visit. She may have spent it on food, of course."

Lady Sybil squeezed her cousin's arm. "Cheer up, old thing. Have another cup of tea."

Sue's and Stephen's social life took a very busy turn through the spring and summer of 1973. There were lots of new friends among his clients, as well as old friends from years back. There were dinners and dances, tennis and beach parties. Two of Stephen's clients had installed swimming pools which opened the way for enhanced barbecued lunches on summer Sundays. The Martels reciprocated with all-day tennis tournaments starting early on Sunday mornings through till evening, while Sue and and the solemn Debbie produced large meat casseroles, endless fresh fruit and cheese, and teas of gache, sandwiches and Victoria sponges. Debbie was occasionally talked into playing a set, but her obvious reluctance deterred all but the bravest from asking her. Nowadays beach picnics tended to happen in the evenings, after work, instead of being all day affairs. Sue loved the memory of those old days but one had to change with the times, and now she enjoyed the evening gatherings almost as much, swimming lazily in the path of setting sunlight then, snug in sweaters and slacks, settling down on rugs and cushions to enjoy a hot supper out of wide Thermos's, all washed down with paper cups of cheap wine, while the tide rose to lap at their feet. It was what island life was all about. Debbie would seek any excuse to duck out.

Greg, however, regretted the passing of the all-day Sunday beach picnics, when all branches of the family and all generations congregated for swims and lunch, followed by post-food snoozing for the oldies, and rock-pool shrimping for the young. There used to be beach cricket and more swimming before tea, after which sleepy children would be gathered up and hauled reluctantly home to bed. Those were the days, when all the generations were part of each other's lives, but where had those days gone? Why had the successive generations lost interest? Were they dumping the older and younger members of their families in favour of private pools and boats and a faster, more entertaining lifestyle?

"I'm glad you have retained the job of housewife," he told Sue. "So much more important to have someone building a happy home environment, being there for the young as they grow up, rather than this modern compulsion for young women to chase high-powered jobs."

"I was a working mother myself, remember, when Jonathan and I had the hotel."

"And you were thin as a wraith and looked awful, doing it."

"Well, Dad, there are so many more pressures, nowadays. The current working generations want to keep up a certain standard of living."

"Money! Practically all most people think about today is ways to make more money, or acquire it from the State. And most of it is spent on amusements and unnecessary luxuries."

Oh dear! Dad was on his hobby horse again! Sue tried not to grind her teeth. "There are certain improvements in life which are considered basic necessities, today."

"You mean cars and televisions and fancy gadgets. Well, fair enough if they can afford it, I suppose, and the children's family life doesn't suffer. But of course the lazy and the uneducated want the same advantages, and why should we, the taxpayers, pay for the entertainment of unemployed layabouts? So many of them could earn quite enough to live comfortably." Warming to his subject, he wagged a forefinger at her. "They don't put their money to improving their homes or family life, you know. The entertainment of the illiterate idiocracy has always been sex, booze and gambling. More money in their pockets has always meant more of those. Once upon a time a poor child's treat was a sticky bun. Now, they are fed so many sticky buns and iced lollies and chips they are grossly overweight; and all to keep them quiet while the parents sit watching endless TV, smoking and drinking too much and sleeping around. The kids are too often thoroughly neglected; they may have smart clothes and expensive toys, but their parents never bother to talk to them. Just like children of the upper ten, brought up by cheap nursemaids and so-called nannies. Never feeling their parents had any love or interest in them."

"Oh look! Here's Stephen home already. I must put the kettle on." Sue breathed a sigh of relief. It wasn't that she disagreed with much of what her father said. But once he got on his hobby horse there was no stopping him.

"Are you going to enter any flower arrangements in the North Show?" Coralie stood back to cast a critical eye over her latest creation.

"Me! I wouldn't dream of it. I'm not nearly good enough."

"Pity. I've put your name down."

"You haven't!" Debbie was horrified. "Honestly, I'm nowhere near your standard."

Coralie grunted. "Even my sister could do better than this with one hand tied behind her back." She glared with distaste at the arrangement in front of her.

"Why do you say that? It's lovely."

"Too much heavy foliage in the front, here. And I cannot get this altrameria to do the right thing. It keeps twisting."

"Are you putting in any entries?" Debbie asked.

"No. I can't because I'm professional. But I'm entering some of the riding events. Are you coming to the show?"

"I hadn't thought of it."

"Do. I'd love someone to go with. And you can shout encouragement or clap when I'm in the ring. There won't be anyone else to spur me on."

Which made Debbie feel she had to say yes, even while every bone in her body wanted to say no. She didn't want to mix with crowds of people, because inevitably she would catch herself seeking his face in that sea of faces, listening for his voice from the midst of passing snatches of conversation. After all this time she continued to ache for the dream of what might have been. People, including her mother, had tried to tell her that Amanda was only one in a list of infidelities – but she didn't want to know. She could not bear to face the thought that those years of loving, of lovemaking, of lying in each others arms giving all, body and soul, had been, for Justin, only a fake. That she could have been to him just another lay. So she told herself that Justin was a very sexual animal who needed more than one woman at a time to satisfy his needs . . . and she had to face the fact that he would never change. But though acceptance of that knowledge might be the first step on the road to understanding and forgiveness, it was not a situation she could live with: she loved him still, desperately. Although every hour of each day she suffered a painful lump in her stomach with yearning for the feel of his arms, she knew she was a one-man woman and needed a one-woman man . . . or none at all. And right now it was impossible to visualise any one ever taking Justin's place in her heart.

It had been a warm, misty summer and in Sausmarez Park the marquees were sweltering hot that August. Judges moved along the trestle tables tasting and comparing the scones and buns, Guernsey gache and Guernsey biscuits, fruit cakes and sponges. The entries were from all age groups from five-year-olds to great-grannies. Amongst the produce, wilting green vegetables vied for attention with huge pumpkins and onions: and in the Arts and Crafts, entries of knitted garments and framed tapestries, pretty handmade blouses and embroidered tablecloths, dressed dolls and quilted tea cosies had been submitted from the very young up to the very old.

Debbie was most impressed with many of the flower arrangements and glad she had entered after all when she saw she had placed third in her section. She loved the miniature gardens the children had made in tomato trays, tiny gravel paths leading between flower borders filled with minute flower heads, imitation lawns and hand mirrors for garden ponds. Three small children stood admiring their handiwork, and reminded Debbie of the children she and Justin would never have . . .

The two girls sat together in the tea tent eating huge wedges of coffee-iced walnut cake, then they wandered round the sales tents admiring shiny farm machinery, and the growers tents to see the boxes of dozens of different types of flowers prepared for Covent Garden market and trays of graded tomatoes.

"There aren't as many entries in the cattle sections, nowadays," Debbie remarked. "There used to be lots more cows and young heifers, bulls and goats."

"There seemed to be more competition in the animal sections at the West Show," Coralie replied. She looked quite splendid in her riding gear and won a rosette on Thursday afternoon. Then they both stayed on for the parade of flower-decked floats and the Battle of Flowers.

"I'm quite glad I made the effort to go," Debbie told her mother when she arrived home. "I really felt much better, most of the time. Part of the scene."

Sue and Stephen looked at each other. Might this be a turning point in Debbie's recovery?

After two or three abortive visits with feeble explanations and excuses, nothing more had been heard from Justin. Hilary relayed his whereabouts in England to Sue when the latter asked, and explained what he was doing – which seemed to be very little of any consequence. While Amanda continued her busy social life in the island, as well as in London. Being one to spread his favours around on his solo visits to England, Cy Blaydon was inclined to laugh off the 'incident', as he called it, and wonder what all the fuss was about. Not that he approved of his stepdaughter, or even liked her much, but he made no attempt to reprove or condemn her. Which did not improve his popularity in the Martel household, but of this he seemed blissfully unaware, continuing to seek their company, especially when his son Neal was on the island. He genuinely doted on the young man, now in his mid thirties, and was devastated when Neal's wife Annabel asked for a divorce.

"Why? What is the matter with the girl?" he demanded.

Devastated himself, Neal had no answer. Annabel had moved into a smart little terraced house with her cat, and he was allowed to visit her if he wished.

When he came over on holiday, it was immediately obvious to Sue that he was a lost soul going through the motions of a social life which had lost all meaning. "A very weird situation in the Blaydon household," she said to Stephen one night. "No one seems to talk to anyone else."

"Amazing, really," Stephen agreed. "Annabel staged her walkout months ago, and poor Neal doesn't seem to know yet what has hit him. He walks round in a daze, a bit like Debbie."

"Yes, I've noticed. He is a funny-looking chap, too much like his father in appearance to be attractive, but one has to feel sorry for him."

Sybil, Lady Banks, held a coffee morning that November for her mother Maureen, Sue, Richard's wife Anne and the latter's mother, Aunt Filly, for the sole purpose of them watching together the wedding of Princess Anne to Captain Mark Phillips. A trolley was loaded with cups and coffeepot, plus plates of hot, buttered Guernsey biscuits, and tiny savoury tartlets. Sybil had arranged the chesterfield and chairs to the best advantage round the big television screen and all the ladies were seated in good time to see the arrival of important heads of state, followed by members of the royal family in their respective carriages.

Princess Anne looked so lovely, walking up the aisle on the arm of her father, that everyone felt quite weepy.

"This must be a dream marriage, made in heaven," Maureen sniffed into her handkie. "Let's hope they look as adoringly at each other on their ruby anniversary as they do today."

Everyone "Mmmm,"d their agreement. They all knew what a very difficult marriage Maureen had had . . . and survived.

* * *

131

Cyril and Carol Blaydon gave a large New Year's Eve Party to welcome in 1974, and having established that Amanda Smith would be living it up in London that night, Debbie agreed to accompany her parents, plus Bobbie who was coming up thirteen and wearing a dark suit and bow tie for the first time, and Roderick, who was tending to team up nowadays with Jane Tetchworth, Justin's sister.

"It's time you had yourself a new look," Sue told Debbie, after checking through her wardrobe. "Come on, let's go into Town during your lunch hour and see what we can find."

Debbie acquiesced, not through any desire for a new dress, but rather because she lacked the will to argue, and they came away with a stunning number in green, a shoulder-strapped gown with matching bolero jacket which somehow managed to disguise her painfully thin frame. Added to which, Sue made an appointment at her hairdressers for Debbie at the same time as her own, from where they both emerged stiff-necked in headscarves, trying to protect their elegant coiffures from the south-easterly whipping up the High Street.

There was no lack of prospective partners for Debbie at the Blaydons that night: she danced politely but without enthusiasm with each gentleman who asked her and was greatly relieved when Neal took pity on her, led her to a corner of the conservatory and proceeded to question her on his stepsister Coralie's progress with the shop.

"I don't get to see the books, actually, but judging by the number of regular customers I would say the business is doing very nicely," she told him. "Coralie has tremendous artistic flair."

"Not the sort of girl to set the world on fire," Neal grinned, "But a genuinely nice, steady person."

Debbie warmed to him. "Yes. She has a heart of gold. She has been so kind to me." She smiled at the quiet, bald young man beside her, relieved to be under no pressure from a would-be ardent admirer.

132

Chapter Seven

Allegiances

Joe Mason withdrew his head and shoulders from the engine compartment below the deck of the cockpit and nodded at Richard. "Yes, well, she is obviously not new but seems to be in reasonable condition. What was the previous owner like? Did he know anything about marine engines?"

"I don't know anything about the man, except that he seems to have looked after her very well." Aware that Mason, their third prospective buyer for the boat, was trying to work a canny deal, Richard added. "He must have loved her like a mistress the way he lavished paint and oil on her."

"Hmm," Mason commented, running his hand along the smooth teak trim. "What do you think, dear?"

Monica Mason was grinning broadly. Fed up with the discomforts of their racing yacht on the Hamble, she had been trying to talk Joe into something like this for two years. "She is beautifully equipped below. Mr Gaudion says the crockery, cutlery and the saucepans in the galley are all part of the inventory. And I do like the layout of the master cabin."

"Fine. We are seeing another boat tomorrow," he said which judging by the expression on Mrs Mason's face Richard guessed was a lie. "And we will then discuss which we prefer. However, I think you will have to consider dropping your price for us to settle on this one. You are definitely asking more than I'd planned to spend."

When the Masons had gone, Richard crossed the road to George Schmit's house to report. "They are certainly hooked," he told his boss, "but trying to play hard-to-get."

George spread his hands. "They all do, my boy. Especially the ones who fancy themselves as businessmen. Where do they live?"

"Birmingham."

"Oh! So they'll want to purchase her through a locally registered company. Which almost certainly means they've got more money than they're letting on."

"I think you'd better handle the rest of the deal," Richard laughed. "You're obviously a harder nut to crack than I am."

Much to Billy's annoyance, his Uncle George did allow the Masons to knock him down the extra thousand he had added to the asking price, especially for the purpose. "You'd have got it, easily, if you'd hung on," he declared.

"Possibly. But this way I've not only got a happy, permanent customer in the repair yard, but also he is going back to Birmingham to tell his friends about this funny little halfwit dealer he found in Guernsey and how he knocked the price down. Then his friends will come over and buy some more boats from us."

"And they'll all want to knock us down," Billy grumbled.

"Don't you worry, lad. We've made a very fair profit on this boat. Richard's nearly finished the second one and she'll get a good price, too."

"Number three is a nice little cabin cruiser. When shall I fetch her?"

"Soon as you like," Richard told him. "We are taking on an another hand at the end of the month, to cope with the extra work."

"What's that new gadget you've got there?" Greg wanted to know as he sipped his coffee at Sue's kitchen table.

"This?" she patted a sleek white machine under the work counter. "This is my new dishwasher. An absolute godsend."

Her father shook his head and grinned. "I don't know what this world is coming to. Your mother never had any of these things and seemed to manage very well."

"Oh come on, Dad! With the help of a full time maid! I only have a lady coming in for three hours, twice a week."

"Is that all? I thought you had a girl called Sharon, every day."

"She left to get married years ago! And that was when the children were young and I had an old fashioned washing machine with a mangle. And no tumble dryer. I tell you, I needed her."

"They say that some young mothers nowadays use throw-away nappies. Can't be bothered to wash them."

Surreptitiously, Sue studied his grey head and noted the increasing lines round his eyes and mouth. He was still a fine figure of a man for his seventy-five years, broad shoulders showing no sign of a stoop, but mentally he seemed to be ageing. Maybe it was from being without Mum for so many years. "Well, I wish disposables had been around when my kids were babies. Though I don't know if I could have afforded them."

When Greg had gone, Sue continued her baking for the weekend, thinking about their conversation as she worked. How things had changed. She patted the over-worked Kenwood mixer which dominated the kitchen on baking days, knowing she couldn't produce half the cakes, pastry and homemade bread without it. She remembered the wet nappies strung out round the kitchen and round the sitting room fire on wet winter days; there were no nappies to worry about now but she was still grateful for the tumble dryer, and for the washing machine that did all the rinsing and spun the excess water from the clothes automatically. It saved so much time and energy, yet where did the saved time go? Years ago she travelled by bike or bus, now she flew everywhere in her own little Fiat: dashed to the shops, sped off to see friends and family, collected Bobbie from school and delivered and fetched him for all his extra-curricular activites like football, cricket and music. And there would be more of the latter now, since he had decided to learn the oboe as a second instrument, having reached grade five on the piano. He was growing into a strapping lad, way larger than Roderick had been at his age. And so like his father: he had Stephen's heavy black hair and grey eyes, and the same strong, square chin. He had lots of Stephen's mannerisms, too, like holding both hands behind his back while talking to one, and combing his hair back off his face with an impatient run of his fingers. He was good at sport, much to his grandfather Greg's delight, tennis figuring strongly as his favourite, probably because of the court in their back garden and the keenness for the sport throughout the family. He was fond of all types of music, from pop to classical, and it was not unusual to hear him switch over in his bedroom from Simon and Garfunkel to Gustav Holst.

Stephen was keen on classical music and he and Sue attended all the Guernsey Choral and Orchestral Society concerts which were of very high standard. Their friends Uhtred and Tilly Walgrave were enthusiastic members of the choir and often asked the Martels to their social functions which, added to Stephen's business associates and all their sporting friends, meant a very busy social life. "We really must leave a couple of evenings a week for just being at home," Stephen said, every few months, but it wasn't easy.

"Can't live, if living is without you," Sue crooned happily to herself as she drew the two quiches out of the oven. That was supper taken care of, which would leave her free to pop round to Aunt Filly this afternoon before picking up Bobbie and taking him to the football field. Then while he was playing she would run over to Uncle John and Edna to discuss the future of her vegetable patch which, at the moment, produced solely for the benefit of the bugs. From there she would fetch Bobbie, bring him home and feed him, and quickly get changed before Stephen came in for his meal prior to them both dashing off to tonight's concert. Maybe when Bobbie was a bit older and had the scooter he craved, life might ease up a bit. Or would the extra available time promptly fill up with more activities?

Poor, dear Stephen, he was such a home-lover. Such a lover, full-stop! He continued to be as deliciously romantic as that never-to-be-forgotten day, so many years ago, when they had met quite accidently, at the Buttes at L'Ancresse and on impulse, made love in the sea. She closed her eyes, smiling. And the memory made her tingle all over.

Roderick was very happy living in his little old Guernsey cottage. He was not an enthusiastic gardener so there were no roses round the door; the small area of garden between the lane and the front door was a neatly gravelled extension from the driveway down the side of the grey granite building. The only concession to floral adornment in the front was by way of a half barrel of soil either side of the white painted door, planted with azaleas into which, on dry days, he tipped a bucket of water while his breakfast kettle was boiling. There was a lean-to conservatory across the back of the cottage, which led out to a walled-in patio complete with a teak table, bench seat and chair, behind which, hanging on the wall was a terracotta flower pot containing a non-flowering plant which was also watered at breakfast time. A cleaning lady popped in two mornings a week to do laundry and hoovering, but as Roderick was a clean and tidy person, her tasks were not onerous. Of course he liked to entertain, keeping a small barbecue at the back of the garage for summer use, and an electric frying-pan for the winter. Whatever the season, the menu remained consistent: melon or grapefruit starter as available, barbecued or fried steaks with salad and French bread, followed by cheese and celery, coffee and mints. His guests always knew what to expect. In his quiet way Roderick discovered he enjoyed socialising; he loved to fill his one big cosy living room with friends, and they enjoyed examining the latest additions to the bookshelves that lined the walls, sinking into the leather settee and chairs, beers in hand, listening to Roderick's records. Most Sundays he went to *La Rocquette de Bas* for lunch with the family, and often dropped in during the week on the way home from work to sit in the kitchen with a cup of tea while his mother was fixing supper.

One Tuesday night just before Easter, Roderick and Stephen arrived at the same time. Sue had a pot of fresh tea waiting, and the two men automatically sprawled on kitchen chairs so that Sue might be included in their conversation.

"How well do you get on with Alex Grolinski?" Stephen asked.

"Much better now. I thought him a bit butterfly-brained in the beginning, but he has settled down very well. Funny really, the way you meet people at university, think you know them, and then later on when you meet them out in the big wide world they seem so different. Mind you, he always was a big talker! But why do you want to know?"

"We rather felt you had had your doubts about the venture soon after you first linked up with him."

"You're dead right I did! Some of his ideas seemed totally woolly – and I'd burned my boats!"

Sue swilled out a saucepan and left it on the drainboard, brushed the hair out of her eyes and sat down with the men. "Not entirely, you know. I suspect Stephen would have let you back into the firm if you'd asked him nicely. But what about the business side? You appear to be doing very well. Are you happy with the results?"

"Oh, very! And I hope Stephen is happy with the new clients we pass on to him. It is obviously a very good move to have a tie-in between the property business and the architectural firm. But I have to say that I think I'm in the better half, financially."

"Am I right in believing you and Alex are branching out abroad?" Stephen wanted to know.

"Correct. We are putting adverts in some of the big glossy magazines and brochures. It was Alex's uncle's idea. He already has an agent in the Caribbean, and now Alex is spending some time in Spain and Portugal. Quite a market there."

"What about here in the island? Heath's government made such a hash of the British economy, your trade must have been affected. I wonder if Harold Wilson can do any better?"

"Business has certainly slowed down in the past few months. I don't really know how much it has to do with the British economy or how much to do with this notorious property speculator we have here. He is getting somewhat tardier in completing his conveyancing."

"Really!" Stephen pushed his cup across the table towards Sue for a refill. "Are you worried?"

"Not so much for ourselves, though frankly he has been our proverbial golden goose, but we do have a few worried clients who have bought properties to move into, and now are stuck with both, plus a bridging loan. We simply have to keep our fingers crossed, and hope he doesn't default."

"Changing the subject, would you like to stay to supper?" Sue invited. It continued to feel strange asking her own son for a meal. She wasn't sure how much of a social life he had and was convinced he suffered from a lack of female company, even if the only company on offer tonight would be his mother and younger sister.

"Love to, but I can't tonight. A bunch of us are eating at the Marina."

"Lovely! Who are you going with?"

"Alex and his girlfriend, Tom and Alice and I'm taking Jane."

"Jane Tetchworth?"

"Yes. You don't think Debbie will mind, do you?"

"I'm sure she won't. She's a nice girl."

"A great deal nicer than her brother," Stephen muttered.

Sue also thought the girl rather pale and willowy, a true replica of her mother, Hilary, but maybe she was nearer Roderick's type than a more flamboyant girl, like Amanda Blaydon, for instance.

Sue was not prepared to worry about Roderick's love life, he was only just twenty-four and there was plenty time for him to select a prospective wife whilst playing the field, and she had more than enough to worry about with her two daughters. She planned to return to Wales to see Stephanie and little Sarah in the coming week, knowing that she would inevitably leave with tears in her eyes and a terrible ache in her middle. How could any normal mother fail to be devastated seeing her daughter and grandchild living in such circumstances.

Debbie meanwhile, was much improved but seemed positively off men. She was coming up to her twenty-first birthday on the second of June and Sue was determined to throw a really good party, alive with nice young people as well as family. She wanted to surround the girl with wholesome, decent boys her own age so that eventually memories of the misery caused by Justin might be eradicated, and he could be supplanted in her affections by someone infinitely more worthy. Debbie was starting to relax more, smile, laugh and join in family gatherings, but apart from Coralie, she socialised with too few friends.

Only four weeks before the party did Sue venture to tell Debbie of her plan.

"Oh!" the girl looked startled. "Who are you intending to invite?"

Sue read a list of suggestions from a spiral notebook on the kitchen counter, and Debbie expressed doubts about nearly all of them.

"I haven't seen Marjorie in yonks, or her brother," she complained.

"All the more reason to ask them," Sue retaliated. "And I thought of asking our friends Frank and Christine Jordan. Their son Ian finished his business course in England at Easter and is working over here, now, so he'll be included."

It was obvious to Debbie what her mother was trying to do, and, while on the one hand she appreciated the old girl's effort, on the other she wished she wouldn't interfere. She really did not want to be thrown into a pond full of prospective suitors and dearly longed to say so. Still, she didn't want to hurt Sue's feelings; her mother had been such a brick in the past couple of years, never once telling her to 'pull herself together' as other members of the family were wont to do, like Roderick had done till Debbie's redheaded temper reached flash point and she let fly at him. Muttering something about trying to help, he had retired hurt. So now, instead of making some adverse remark, Debbie merely said "That would be nice," and refrained from further comment, other than a sweet smile or a nod.

Sue was no fool. She had no doubt what was going on in Debbie's mind, but remained convinced she was doing

140

the right thing. "So, together with family, that should total thirty-five of us. How does that sound?"

Horrendous, Debbie thought. "Wonderful," she said, trying to force herself to feel grateful for having a caring parent. Then, on sudden inspiration added, "What chance, do you reckon, of getting Steps over for the event?"

Sue clasped the top of her head in mock despair. "Heaven alone knows. I don't. But I'm going over next week. I'll ask her. I'll say you have particularly requested she comes."

"I'm glad that she keeps up corresponding with me. Weird sort of letters, both ways. Neither of us mention touchy subjects, just relate our adventures in the world of vegetables, babies and flower arrangements. Funny really. She and I are only a year apart in age, yet in many respects we hardly know each other. If anything, I feel I know Roderick better than her."

"Interesting you should say that. She and I always had a rather strained relationship and I tended to blame myself, wondering what I had done to make her dislike me."

"I don't think it was a matter of liking or disliking anyone. She appeared to want to distance herself from everyone. Didn't like to feel tied or obligated, just hankered to be a totally free spirit."

"Well she is certainly all of that, though whether or not she is currently enjoying it is open to question." Sue sighed, staring into the middle distance. "Now let's talk about party food. We must get it all organised before I go away so that I can get straight on with preparations as soon as I return."

The river chortled over rocks and pebbles as Stephanie and Sarah lay on the bank blowing seed puffs off dandelion heads. A cotton sunhat was squashed down over the toddler's crown of soft brown curls, but she wore nothing else, bottom dimpled as she wriggled and laughed on her tummy in the long grass. Apart from the river, and the occasional raucous outbursts from the residents of a rookery in nearby trees, there was no sound on the still air. No mechanical rumble of cars, planes or trains hurrying people from offices to business meetings, or away on holidays to escape their personal stress: no thump of electronic music to relieve somebody's tensions. Stephanie smiled sadly and rolled over onto her back. Ironic, wasn't it, that she had chosen this laid-back existence to get away from the tensions and stress of mainstream life, only to find herself beset by more worries than she had imagined possible. Unless one got drugged out of one's mind, it was impossible to avoid the petty squabbles, jealousies and irritations of communal living. Maybe if some of the members were a little older, more mature, they would be more willing to share responsibilities rather than each others' supposed partners. Personally, she knew she was a far better artist than several of the other girls, yet she seldom had either time, energy or inclination to indulge her talent. Well, someone had to take charge of the catering or they would never eat at all, and Heaven knew their diet was far from satisfactory as it was.

Stephanie took deep breaths, sucking in the sweet scent of wild flowers together with the heady ambience of peaceful solitude, a rare enough commodity living in the commune. She thought about her mother's impending visit, about Debbie's letters, about . . . home. Her other home, *La Rocquette de Bas*. Were her nice clothes still hanging in her wardrobe where she had left them? The ones that were unsuitable for community living. Would Troilus and Cressida remember her if she went back? What a gorgeous pair they were, so gentle and loving . . . so different from the hungry, snarling curs around the farm.

She was suddenly swamped with an overwhelming sadness, an urgent desire to see *La Rocquette de Bas* again, and the dogs, and the people. Roddy and Debs. Granpa, Richard and Anne, and she thought yet again about the money sewn into her jacket behind the door of her room. How many times had she sat on the edge of her bed debating whether to hang on to it, or turn it into much needed food? Yet after all this time, over a year, the getaway money still survived.

"Wanna go fwishin'" Sarah declared, struggling to her feet and heading for the river.

"All right, I'll come and help you." Stephanie kicked off her sandals, tucked her skirt up into her briefs and crawled down the bank with the child into the shallow water. They waded barely ankle deep together, Sarah frequently slipping on the stones under foot and falling in, laughing. They spied tiny fish from time to time which got the child hugely excited, but they never came near enough to touch.

Sarah screamed with frustration when her mother finally dragged her out of the water. Their feet were frozen, skin wrinkled, and it was getting late. How late, Stephanie had no idea, someone had pinched her watch and flogged it for grass. She never did bother to find out who it was.

When Sue arrived three days later she found a much calmer and more smiling Stephanie. She is obviously much happier with her life now, Sue decided sadly. But she couldn't have been more wrong. The apparent happiness stemmed from her daughter's new resolve to visit the island again for the first time in four years. Nothing was said, however. Even when Sue passed on Debbie's message about the party, All Stephanie did was shrug and say she would think about it.

On the Saturday, the day before the party, Sue overslept. She was exhausted by the previous day's work, arranging tables and chairs, shopping, and preparing all possible food in advance. Deep in the throes of a nightmarish situation when double the number of anticipated guests turned up, obliging her to leave them while she chased round the island in her car trying to buy extra bread, she was startled awake by the phone. Dazed, she reached out to answer it, and was momentarily fazed by the caller. "Who are you? Where did you say you are phoning from? I can't hear you! All that noise in the background!" Then the fog cleared and the penny dropped. "Stephanie! Oh, darling, how wonderful! On the dock? I'll be there in ten minutes."

Seeing the girl at the farm, Sue had thought that, like her friends in the commune, she looked rather odd. Now, in long ethnic printed cottons and strings of beads, Sarah beside her looking quaint in a dress nearly to her ankles and their luggage not in a suitcase but tied up in a bundle, she stood out like a sore thumb alongside the horde of T-shirted

143

holidaymakers who had disembarked from the overnight boat. Positively weird. The need not to show any reaction helped overcome the emotion of Stephanie's return to the island. The girl allowed herself to be hugged, briefly, and Sarah let her grandmother carry her to the car.

They were sitting in the kitchen over the teapot when Debbie came downstairs for breakfast, and this time there was no stemming the tears.

"Steps!"

"Debs!"

And the sisters were in each others' arms, laughing and crying, watched in amazement by little Sarah. Debbie was introduced to her niece who adored her on sight, wanted to follow her every step and insisted on an identical bowl of cereal and slice of toast.

Stephen and Bobbie appeared and joined in the fray, delighted to welcome Stephanie home, Stephen thrilled for Sue's sake.

Upstairs in her old room, after Debbie and Stephen had left for work, Stephanie and Sarah explored every cupboard and corner, drawer and shelf. Nothing had changed, every item being in the old familiar place. Momentarily, the young woman was surprised, then assumed that as this was quite a large house her mother had not needed the room for visitors, or any other purpose so had simply left it alone. She took a dress out of the wardrobe and held it against herself in front of the mirror. It looked huge, but then she had been liberally coated in puppy fat before leaving the island, all of which had been worn off with hard work and poor diet.

Sarah fell in love with the old teddy, and with the wind toy which still dangled, tinkling, over the window. Her mother showed her pictures, photos of herself at Sarah's age, which the child could not fathom.

Four years! Stephanie lay back on the bed and stared at the ceiling. Four whole years! And yet nothing had changed. It was as though the intervening years had never happened. But no, that was not true: something had changed. She got up and went to the dressing table to gaze in the mirror.

And the person looking back at her was quite, quite different.

There was a chill easterly breeze blowing on the day of the party. Fortunately the garden was reasonably sheltered so the guests were able to spend most of the time out of doors, well wrapped in woolly cardigans. Older members of the family congregated on the verandah with Granpa Greg, except Sir Gordon who, although two years Greg's senior, considered himself to have mastered the art of perpetual youth, took command of the tennis rota and time off to play croquet and boules. Uncle John and Edna arrived and sat with Aunts Filly and Maureen, either side of Greg. Lady Sybil was proving her worth with a croquet mallet. Partnered by Uti Walgrave, she was soon roqueting Martin and Sheila Gillespie all over the garden.

Debbie found herself press-ganged on to the tennis court with Ian Jordan against her uncle Richard who was severely handicapped by his partner, Marjorie, whilst a gaggle of young people cheered and jeered from the sidelines.

Sue had pressed some of the young into service behind the temporary bar. Two at a time, they were kept busy as more and more people arrived. Debbie glanced through the tennis netting while changing ends and was convinced there was at least double the number her mother had originally told her. She saw the Blaydons turn up with Coralie and Neal: she did a quick scan of the area, failed to spot Amanda and just prayed she hadn't had the gall to show up. When her set was over, Ian led her across the lawn to the bar where they were joined by Neal.

"How did you get on?" he asked.

"We won," Ian told him. "Six games to one, no thanks to me."

"You played some excellent shots at net," Debbie commented.

"Perhaps you and I could have a set, later?" Neal suggested to Debbie.

But for the fact that she rather liked him, she would have made some excuse. She had never seen him on the tennis court and doubted if his shape was designed for the game. Instead she said, "Yes, love to. Now I really must circulate," and she left her two eager partners to talk amongst themselves.

Two complete buffets of food were laid out for lunch, one in the dining room and the other in the kitchen. It was simple and straightforward fare: bowls of prawns, trays of smoked salmon and huge ashets piled with Coronation Chicken, and sliced ham and beef. There were rice salads, tomato, onion and cucumber salads, lettuce, beetroot, pickles, and wicker baskets of French bread. Guests loaded their plates, carried it all off to the tables on the lawn and verandah, ate and came back for more. The bar boys circulated with trays of glasses of wine, and Sue thanked heaven that her help, Mrs Marquis, and her sister had agreed to give up their Sunday to help out. At a price.

Cheese and biscuits were followed by big bowls of strawberries, raspberries and logans, and jugs of fresh Guernsey cream, while in the background, Stephen was marshalling his bar troops with champagne flutes and bottles.

And then Roderick stood up. "Ladies and gentlemen," he called, ringing his dessert fork against an empty wine glass. "I feel that, as Deborah's big brother, it is my duty to draw your attention to the fact that she has, today, become of age. Age for what is open to speculation, but we won't go into that right now."

Debbie blushed scarlet and prayed the ground would swallow her up. Mummy hadn't said a word about speechifying. Neal put a comforting hand over hers on the table and squeezed.

Sue had agreed that Roderick should propose a toast before the cake was carried out for Debbie to cut, but she was totally unprepared for the speech that he proceeded to deliver. Unprepared both because she had no idea he was going to do it, and also because till that moment, she had no idea that her over-serious eldest child was capable of such wit. Without saying anything that could possibly hurt or embarrass his super-sensitive sister, he managed to reduce the company to eye-watering hysterics. Even Debbie herself was in a state of collapse as her half-brother, Bobbie, bore the massive cake, plus lit candles, out of the house and laid it on the hastily cleared table in front of her.

"Wish, wish," they all shouted.

Debbie closed her eyes, wished, took a deep breath and blew.

"Ladies and gentlemen, will you join me in wishing Debbie a very happy birthday!" Roderick raised his champagne glass, and everyone stood up to join him.

"Happy twenty-first, Debbie!"

Stephanie stayed for two weeks.

Sue had harboured a faint hope that she might decide against returning to Wales: the idea obviously crossed Stephanie's mind, especially as she watched little Sarah blossoming in the loving family atmosphere. Even Greg had fallen for the little scrappet, once he had got over the initial shock of her existence. "She looks so much like her great-grandmother," he kept saying.

"You know you are welcome to stay as long as you like," Sue told Stephanie.

"That's awfully sweet of you, Mum. But I think in all fairness I ought to go back. But I would like to visit again, next year, perhaps."

"Of course. This is your home from home. Use it whenever you want."

They managed not to get weepy when they said good-bye, and Sue was convinced that her granddaughter would miss the dogs far more than "Ganny".

Anne Gaudion was incredibly like her mother – everyone said so. Short, plump with blue eyes and blonde curls she was a naturally happy, contented soul with Felicity's bubbly characteristics. Greg, and George Schmit's wife Gelly, both of whom had known Filly in her twenties, never failed to laugh with incredulity at the amazing similarity between mother and daughter. And although Aunt Filly was now white-haired and in her seventies, even Sue, Stephen and the children remarked that there was no mistaking the relationship. Anne enjoyed life as it was, the way Richard did. They were only too willing to sacrifice the popular need for speed and affluence, for the sake of a gentler lifestyle. While their friends were dashing from tennis court to cocktail party and winging off to exotic locations for holidays, they were blissfully content with a day's boating, trailing lines for mackeral and dropping anchor in a bay to swim and lunch with their boys. And the highlight of their year was sleeping under canvas at the top of Herm Island, where they could watch the sun come up over Sark or a crescent moon poised over the distant lights of Guernsey as they returned to their camp from a late supper in the tiny island metropolis.

Therefore Sue was duly surprised to see the serious frown on Anne's face when she dropped in unannounced at *La Rocquette de Bas* with her children one afternoon in July. "Hello, sister-in-law! Hello Derek and George. Have you time for a cup of tea, Anne, or is this a lightning visit?"

"I'd love a cup," Anne responded. "Boys, you can go and play outside."

"Here you are, lads. Take these tennis balls out to throw for Cressida. She'll fetch them and bring them back to you over and over." Sue handed them a ball each from the string bag behind the kitchen door, then filled the kettle. "So tell me, Anne, what's on your mind?"

Anne looked startled. "What do you mean?"

"You look as though the end of the world is nigh!"

"Oh dear! Is it that obvious?"

Sue stared at her. "Oh dear," she echoed, "Is it that serious?"

Anne flopped onto a chair. "I don't know. I hope not."

Sue sat down opposite. "Tell me."

"I don't know whether or not I have anything to tell, to be honest. It's just that I'm so concerned about Richard."

Sue waited.

"You know what your brother is like. He is no great worrier. If I fret about something he is always the one to calm me down. 'Nine out of ten troubles will go away of their own accord,' he says, 'providing you leave them alone'. Well I've left this worry alone and it only seems to get worse."

"What worry?"

"That's the trouble. I don't know."

Sue sighed with exasperation as she made the tea. "Try telling me the symptoms."

"Richard isn't eating properly. He pushes the food round his plate and eventually gives half of it to the dog when he thinks I'm not looking."

Anne was looking so miserable Sue refrained from prompting.

"And he's not sleeping, either. Tosses the bed into a haystack by morning."

Sue put some milk in a jug and poured tea into the two cups. "Do you reckon it's a digestive problem or has he got something on his mind?"

"He doesn't complain of stomach ache or anything. And come to think of it, I have caught him gazing vaguely into space when he is in the middle of doing something. He dropped one of our dinner plates yesterday while he was helping with the drying up; one of our best set. Just didn't look what he was doing when he went to put it on the table." Anne added milk to her tea and took a gulp, blue eyes filled with worry as she stared at Sue over the rim of her cup. "What should I do?"

"Have you tried asking what's bothering him?"

"Oh yes, several times. And all he does is laugh, rumple my hair and tell me to stop fussing. I just don't know what I should do."

"There is nothing you can do at the moment. He is being a typical man!" Sue poured them another cup each. "Well, let me know if you find out any more, won't you?"

"Yes of course. You don't mind me dropping in for a moan, do you?"

"Of course not. A worry shared is a worry halved."

For the first time since arriving, Anne managed a wide smile. "Now I'd better drink up and go and rescue your dogs from my children."

*   *   *

Greg came round to watch the Wimbledon finals with Sue, Bobbie and Debbie, who had asked Coralie if she could take the afternoon off for the purpose. They drew the curtains to get a better picture, and sat glued to the television screen throughout both singles finals, as Chrissie Evert easily beat Olga Morozova, and her fiancé, Jimmy Connors defeated the old favourite Ken Rosewell, eighteen years his senior.

"Pity," said Greg. "I'd love to have seen Ken get it just the once."

Judging by his muttered comments during the game, the others guessed he was also backing the man with the old-fashioned manners and sense of good sportsmanship.

"Want a game before supper?" Debbie asked her brother.

"Yeah! Sure!"

The youngsters were both well satisfied by the outcome of both matches.

Sue re-opened the curtains. "Like to stay for supper, Dad? We've got mackeral, new potatoes, fried toms and mangetout."

"Sounds marvellous. Yes, I'd love to. Mrs Mahy said she'd leave me some cold ham in the fridge, but it'll keep. And I've been wanting to talk to you."

"Yes?" Sue sat on the arm of a chair. "What's on your mind."

"Richard. He doesn't really seem himself, lately."

Another member of the family worried about her brother! "What do you think is the problem?"

"I wish I knew. I wondered if you'd seen him recently."

She debated in her mind whether to tell him of her conversation with Anne, but decided against. No point in worrying the old chap unnecessarily. "No, I haven't. Do you think he might not be well?"

"I've a feeling it's more likely he has something on his mind. He has always had this habit of scratching his ear when he is worried. Just like your mother used to."

"I'll see if I can find out anything and let you know, Dad."

"Thanks." He shook his head. "Not a bit like Richard. Very odd."

*　　　*　　　*

150

"Hallo! Haven't seen you for weeks. How are you?" George Schmit emerged from the newsagent's on the Bridge and ran full tilt into Sue who was laden with shopping bags.

"Hallo, Uncle George! I suppose you want to read all about Nixon's resignation," she commented, eyeing his newspaper.

"About time, rotten beggar! Boy has he wriggled, like a fish on the end of a line. But they landed him in the end," he chortled.

"So how's business?"

"Excellent. Richard is doing marvels with those boats Billy has been buying in France. There is certainly more money in selling boats than just repairing them." He began walking beside her along the wide pavement. "It's great for me to see the yard doing so well, now that I'm semi-retired."

"I'd have thought you'd be sitting back with your feet up all the time, by now," Sue said, and laughed.

"You joke. Got to keep myself occupied or I'll be pushing up daisies in no time at all."

She would like to have talked to him a bit more about the business: probed a little to see if there could be anything there that was worrying Richard. But the old chap had obviously not noticed anything, and like her father she didn't want to worry him unnecessarily. But she did say, "I haven't seen Richard for weeks." And waited, hopefully.

"I'm glad you said that. Reminds me I must nip down here to Bougourd and Harry. I promised to get him another pound of brass screws while I'm out. Nice seeing you, Sue." And he limped off on his arthritic hip.

"Bye-bye, Uncle George," she called after him, cursing brass screws.

Debbie was cleaning out the flower buckets under an outside tap over a drain in the tiny yard behind the shop, when Coralie called her.

"There's someone to see you, Debs!"

151

It was the end of a long day, she was tired, her face was dirty and her hair all over the place. "Who is it?"

"A young gentleman."

Debbie's mind automatically flew to Justin, but she knew Coralie wouldn't do that to her, so she dried her hands, brushed the hair off her face and went through into the shop.

Coralie's step-brother, Neal Blaydon, was standing there. Thirteen years her senior, he wasn't exactly young, but compared with his father he could definitely be described as a gentleman.

"Hallo! What brings you back to the island again so soon?"

"You! I never had a chance to take you out to dinner last time I was over. So here I am. Would you like to go up to the Fregate tonight?"

"Wow!" Debbie giggled. "Well, yes I'd love to go to the Fregate," it was the best restaurant in the island, "but as for your reason for being here, I don't believe a word of it!"

"But it's true!" Neal protested. "Coralie, how late do you intend keeping Deborah's nose to the grindstone this evening?"

"Oh, take her away. She won't be any use to me now with the promise of a Fregate nosebag in the offing," she teased.

He turned to Debbie. "May I give you a lift home?"

"I'd make the most of the opportunity, Debs. It's not an offer he has ever made to me. Go on. I'll lock up."

Actually, Debbie wasn't at all sure that she wanted to go out to dinner with Neal, á deux. He was very nice, quiet and considerate, but not someone she wanted to encourage. In fact she didn't want to encourage anyone. Ever again.

He collected her again at seven-thirty, noting that her hair looked pretty but she hadn't smothered her face with make-up on his account, nor decked herself in some seductive outfit. And he was glad. Annabel always wore ultra slinky clothes, even to the office. He had been devastated when she walked out on him, but now he was beginning to view her departure with relief. And as for his step-sister

Amanda . . . she invariably looked like a third-rate tart. He never wanted to spend an evening sitting opposite a woman who looked like either of them, ever again.

He had managed to get a table alongside the window, overlooking the harbour and Castle Cornet. Conversation was very stilted at first, both rather shy, no sexual vibes prompting their tongues. Gradually the wine did its work and they both relaxed sufficiently for Debbie to question Neal about his work, and for him to ask about her tennis, her family and request details about the island of which he knew little.

When he delivered her home at eleven-thirty he planted a kiss on her cheek.

Debbie kissed him back, happy that Neal was interested in her company without wanting to get his hands on her body. That was nice.

Very nice.

"Hi, it's Sue here. Hope I haven't dragged you away from anything too vital?"

"No, not at all. I was just tackling some paperwork from which, I must admit, I am only too happy to be distracted," Richard said. "So, what can I do for you?"

"I was wondering if you could pop in for ten minutes or so on your way home to lunch today?"

Richard frowned at the receiver, mystified. "I could. Anything in particular on your mind?"

"Yes, actually. I'll tell you about it when you get here."

It was the first opportunity Sue had had, with the house to herself now that Bobbie was back at school and neither Stephen nor Debbie due home for lunch, to ask Richard round so that she could question him about his "problem". She had seen him a couple of times and given him an opening to speak, but he hadn't taken it up, just fielded her mild enquiries and changed the subject.

When he arrived she came straight to the point. "You are driving us all nuts, dear brother. When are you going to tell us what is bothering you? Why bottle it all up?"

He had guessed she would question him, but was totally

153

unprepared for her directness. "I don't see what possible business it is of anyone else's, if I choose to keep my own counsel," he said, obviously offended.

"Fair comment, as long as it doesn't affect anyone else."

"It doesn't affect you."

"Yes it does, when Dad comes and tells me how worried he is about you." She didn't want to mention Anne's visit for fear of creating trouble between them. "Anyway, I can tell there is something wrong. Are you nursing a secret illness or is it something to do with money?"

He crossed the carpet to the sitting room window to gaze out through the teaming rain. "It could all be a storm in a teacup, Sue. I could be imagining the whole thing. That's why I haven't said anything to anyone."

"So are you imagining that Anne is having an affair or something?"

"Good Lord, no!"

"Well, are you going to tell me, or not? Would a beer help?"

"I'd prefer a cup of tea."

"Then let's go into the kitchen. It's the best place for conferences, anyway."

Richard followed and watched her make the tea and pour it, before he began. "I'm seriously worried about these boat deals that Billy has set up. I won't bore you with all the details, but several little things, things Billy has said, apparently minor discrepancies in the paperwork, mix-ups over registrations for which Billy always has a perfectly good explanation, they are all building up to make me thoroughly suspicious. Possibly quite unjustifiably so."

"There was a rather unpleasant business years ago with Billy, wasn't there?"

"Yes, when we were in our teens. Very stupid. And as far as I know he hasn't put a foot wrong since. I mean, I shouldn't let the memory of that incident make me suspect him now, should I? Give a dog a bad name, and all that."

"Or, on the other hand, does a leopard ever change his spots? Look, you are not normally a suspicious type. Too easy-going, if anything. So if these little details are

154

bothering you, then I think it's worth talking them through with someone. I don't pretend to know the first thing about yacht brokerage, but if you want to go through it all with me I'll happily lend an ear. Otherwise, maybe you'd rather talk to an expert."

"No, not at all. I'd prefer to keep it in the family, if possible. You see, it all started with this document pertaining to the sale of the first yacht."

Sue listened carefully to all the details and guessed that Richard's main problem was in deciding where his allegiancies lay.

Chapter Eight

Balance of Power

"Heard the news?" Stephen shouted from the hallway. "Margaret Thatcher has won the Tory leadership battle."

"Yes. At last we may get some common sense prevailing in Westminster," Sue responded with glee.

"Dammit, I might have known you'd crow for Women's Lib."

"Come off it, you know I'm no bra burner. But this is nineteen seventy-five, International Women's Year, and I don't see why a woman can't be as good a Parliamentarian as any man!"

"Well, Thatcher can't hope to make a worse mess of things than Heath."

"I gather he's furious about her winning! Gone into deep sulks."

"Can't be funny for him being succeeded by a woman. Though it was actually poor Willie Whitelaw she beat. They say he was nearly in tears."

"Why? Because of coming second or because he was devastated that his beloved party would be in female hands?"

"The latter, I imagine! Now then, do I dare ask one of the winning species what she is giving me for supper tonight?"

A cushion whizzed past his head as he walked into the sitting room.

A freezing wind rattled the corregated iron roof and the huge gable doors at the north end of the boat shed. It whistled underneath the doors driving dirt and rubbish swirling under the boat cradle and into corners.

156

Richard and the electronics engineer, working in the saloon and helming station below decks, had made themselves quite snug with a little electric heater, and they didn't hear George calling till he climbed the ladder up the side of the hull.

"You two working in there or have you both gone to sleep?" he shouted.

"Trouble is your voice is failing, Uncle George. It's with all the yelling you do." Richard climbed out of the hatch to grin down at the older man over the gunwale.

"Trouble is having to employ young'uns like you who never listen," George growled. "I wanted to know if you've seen Billy today?"

"No. Nor yesterday. Not since before the weekend."

"Funny. He is meant to be here in the island at the moment, but I've tried telephoning him and there's no reply."

Richard drew the zip of his jacket up to the neck, shivering. "Want me to go round to his place at lunchtime and see if I can find him?"

"Might be as well. Someone in France has been trying to get him. I've got their telephone number for him to ring."

"Give it to me and I'll take it with me. It's nearly knocking off time, I might as well go now."

Billy Smart had a flat in a house in St Sampson's. Richard rang the bell, but without much hope of seeing the man, judging by the unclaimed cartons of milk on the doorstep.

A woman in a pinafore and curlers appeared as he returned down the stairs. "Oh! I thought perhaps you were Mr Smart," she said, sounding disappointed.

"I'm looking for him."

"You're not the only one. No one's seen him since last week."

"Seems like he must be away."

"Well, he'd better get back quickly if he wants to keep this place," with a tilt of her head she indicated the direction of the flat. "His rent is overdue."

The worrying knot in Richard's stomach which had been troubling him, on and off for the past several months, suddenly turned into a large granite stone. "Oh dear, I am sorry." He couldn't think what else to say. "When he gets back, if you see him would you tell him Richard wants to speak to him, please?"

The woman nodded. "If I see him."

He decided not to tell Uncle George of his encounter. No point in worrying the old chap, yet.

But by the end of the week George Schmit was worrying, anyway, on a slightly different score. "I hope that young idiot hasn't tried to bring a yacht through from Le Havre in this weather. He'll be in trouble if he has."

"I doubt it," Richard said. "He wouldn't set out without a professional skipper, who wouldn't leave port till this passes through." Then he frowned. "He isn't due to get another boat for a while, is he?"

"No. Not that I'm aware of. But he brought the previous one over before your father and I had agreed to it, if you remember. We don't want him acting on his own initiative again or we'll find the business over-capitalised."

"Yes," Richard nodded, thinking hard. "Quite."

After the freezing February, March had come in like a lamb and now it was going out like a lion. Sue imagined it was rain lashing against the bedroom windows that had disturbed her; she rolled over and curled her knees up under Stephen's rump, rousing him sufficiently for a warm hand to slide over the nightie on her thigh. She kissed the back of his neck and drifted down into a pleasant pre-dawn slumber.

The sound of voices brought her to the surface, footsteps, a child crying! Heart pounding she tumbled out of bed, into her slippers and dressing gown and out of the bedroom to the head of the stairs.

"What's going on down there?" Stephen had followed, calling over her shoulder.

"It's okay," Debbie's voice came from somewhere below. "We have a welcome visitor."

"Whatever time is it?" Sue asked.

Stephen peered at his watch. "Nearly seven," he replied.

"Stephanie!" she flew down the stairs, along the hallway

158

and into the kitchen. "Darling! What a lovely surprise!" She sank to her knees to gather the little one into her arms. "Sarah! You've come to see your Granma again!"

"Hallo, Mum. How are you?" Stephanie looked awful.

"I'm fine. What's more to the point, how are you?"

"Ghastly. We had a terrible crossing."

"Weren't you able to lie down?"

"Only on the floor with a number of other sick bodies throwing up all over the place." The weary traveller sank onto a chair. "Debs dear, I could kill for a cup of tea."

Debbie lifted the Aga cover and placed the kettle on the hotplate where it immediately began a comforting hiss.

Sue warmed some milk for Sarah, stripped off her wet, ill-fitting anorak and, sitting her on her knee held the glass while she drank. There were numerous questions she wanted to ask: what was Stephanie doing here? Why had she made this unscheduled trip? Where did she get the funds?

Sarah was tucked up in bed with a hot water bottle and Stephen and Debbie were upstairs getting dressed for work, when Stephanie finally explained her sudden arrival. "I felt I couldn't take any more of the commune. Not at the moment, anyway. I had to get out for Sarah's sake, if not for my own. Several of the original group have moved on and been replaced. A few of the new people are reasonable but others . . . well, I don't want to go into that. Enough to say it is right to be concerned about the wefare of other people, of animals, of our environment, but when folks get truly fanatical about 'rights' they seem to lose all touch with reality." She covered her face with her hands, slowly sweeping them back over her hair, scratching her fingers into her scalp. "What I want more than anything is a bath. Haven't had a decent hot bath for months."

"Of course. And where is your luggage? Perhaps you'd like to put some things in the machine . . ."

Stephanie held up her hand. "Forget it. We didn't bring any luggage, except Sarah's doll and a teddy bear."

No luggage! Had this been some quick getaway? Sue tried to look unfazed. "Fine. No problem. I dare say you'll find clothes in your room. If not you can borrow from Debbie and me. Ah, but what about the little one?"

"Perhaps we can wash out her dress for now, and then I'll have to buy her one or two things. If you don't mind lending me the money."

Stephanie hadn't been on top of the world when she came over for Debbie's birthday, but had shown no hesitation in returning to her weird communal life. Now, her mood was quite different: there were long silences when she seemed dazed and confused. Her words and actions were negative. Sad. "I did a really nice painting of the river, you know. I was very pleased with it."

"Good. I hope you have brought it with you."

"No. I sold it for just enough money to get us here." She leaned over the kitchen sink, looking out over the drenched garden. The lawn was strewn with twigs and dead leaves; tree branches bowed frantically at the gale's bidding. "Best price I ever got."

Sue wanted to weep for her. Heaven knew, the girl had asked for all the trouble she got, going off to live with a bunch of dropouts as she had. But now her regret was obvious in her tone of voice, the way she looked. Sue could not help but share her sadness; she felt desperately sorry that, as a mother, she had failed to protect Stephanie from all that had happened in the past few years. Yet what could she have done? She was the last person from whom the girl wanted to hear advice, let alone take it. "You'll do lots of others. Every view in the island is waiting to be transferred onto your canvases."

Stephanie turned with a slight lift of the eyebrows, and a half smile. "We will see. In the meantime it is nice to be home, Mum." And fearing that that sounded too emotional she added, "Nice and warm," as she held her hands towards the Aga.

Sue got the message.

"Remember that chap, Joe Mason, we sold a boat to last year?" George said, as he and Richard sipped flask coffee in the cubbyhole office in the corner of the boat shed.

160

"Yes. Hell-bent on knocking the price down."

"Right. Well, he rang me up this morning to see if he could bring a friend of his over to see us about getting a similar craft. He must have been impressed with Mason's bargain."

"I'm not surprised," Richard grunted. But he wasn't happy.

"This one," George indicated with his thumb the yacht on which Richard was currently working "is not what he is looking for. So we'll have to see if Billy can find something suitable. If we can find Billy."

"Mmm. If . . ."

George shot him a querying look.

Richard hurriedly drained his beaker and screwed it back onto the top of his flask. "I must get on with it or this job won't be out of the way before starting the next." He desperately needed time to think, to work out how to word his worries to his father and his boss without alarming them.

George watched him go, sensing what was on his mind.

Sue couldn't sleep that night. She tried to get Stephanie and her troubles off her mind and failed miserably. Her thoughts kept returning to those early months, and years, after the war when she had returned to the island, returned to home and family, only to find something drastically wrong. Something missing. Both she and her parents had been too close to their mutual problem to realise that the parent-child bond between them had been severed by their five-year separation. Each had blamed the other for the frictions that had arisen, failing to accept the basic fact that they were strangers from different backgrounds, coming together under one roof and attempting the impossible – a normal, loving and compatible family relationship full of sympathy and understanding for each other. Neither side had had the least understanding of the other's cares, worries, problems and peer pressures. Her mother and father had fully expected her to conform to the set of rules, standards of behaviour as existed pre-war. She on the other hand, had returned to the

161

island a self-sufficient teenager forced by circumstance to mature early. Not only had she deeply resented all attempts at parental authority but she had lost the art of living in an environment of mutual love and respect with others. She had often shared a billet with another girl whom she liked very much, and some of her billetors were very kind; but there had not been a solitary soul with whom to share love and affection, anyone for whom she might have felt deep concern.

So how did that situation compare with the relationship between herself and Stephanie? Had the parent-child affection between them been broken at some stage? And if so, how? Why? Sue's mind went back over the years, examining each incident involving Stephanie, looking for clues. The only possible answer that occurred and recurred, lay with the problems between herself and her first husband, Stephanie's father, Jonathan: the rows, the angry shouts . . . and the constant weariness. Instead of being there for her children, she had handed them over to a teenage maid to be looked after. Had Stephanie subconsciously felt abandoned? Or had the child thought her mother unsympathetic to her crippled father? Been deeply disturbed by the rows? There would be little point in asking her: she would have no idea and only be embarrassed by the question. However, in retrospect one could see how the little girl, "Daddy's girl", could have been deeply disturbed by the upsets and resented her mother's apparent unconcern for the man in the wheelchair. How could one so young have understood that her father's paralysis had turned him into a tyrant? And the biggest question of all was whether the damage could ever be repaired.

The unanswered problems continued to torment Sue's brain for hours. It was nearly dawn when she finally slept.

"Good morning. G and M Properties Limited," Mandy announced. "How may we help you?" She paused, ballpoint poised over a notepad. "I'll just see if he is in the office. Will you hold on please."

"Who is it?" Roderick was standing in his office doorway.

162

"Allan Fallaize for you," the secretary replied, hand over the mouthpiece. "Are you available?"

Roderick sighed. "Yes. Put him through." He returned to his desk and picked up the receiver. "Hallo, Allan. I suppose you are wanting some news."

"Desperately. I'm worried out of my mind."

"Let me make a couple of phone calls and I'll get right back to you. Are you at the office?"

"Yes. But I have to go out in half an hour."

"I won't need that long."

Alex Grolinski drifted in. "Another one?"

"Yes. Allan Fallaize bought that place in the Castel before the conveyance on his house had gone through. Naturally he thought the contract of sale had clinched the deal. And now our 'friend' has vanished leaving him the proud owner of two expensive properties and a bridging loan he can't afford."

"Well, at least he has the deposit on his place," Alex grunted.

"So what? That still leaves him nearly a hundred thousand in debt. He has a mortgage on his own place, remember." Roderick buzzed Mandy. "Try and get through to our elusive Mr B again, will you?"

She was not successful.

"Well, will you try Sergeant Burgess at the Police Station. We'll see if he has heard anything yet on the grapevine."

The sergeant had little to add, other than the fact that several people were wanting to know the man's whereabouts. "All we can tell you is that he does not appear to be in the island."

"I feel particularly bad about Allan," Roderick told Alex. "He's not just another client, we were friends together at school."

"What does he do?"

"He's an accountant with Moore and Whitehouse. When our dubious friend offered him and his wife such a crazy high price for the guest house his wife was running, they went a bit mad. The place at the Castel was really beyond

163

their range but . . . you know how housebuyers can get carried away."

"And may the Lord make us truly thankful!"

"Except when personal friends are involved!"

Sue stood at the kitchen sink, unseen, watching the game of tennis between Debbie and Neal Blaydon. Neal was spending a surprising amount of time in the island lately, and she couldn't help wondering if this was because he was doing more work in the island for his father, or whether, in fact, Debbie was the true attraction. The pair of them were certainly spending a great deal of time together and Sue was not entirely happy about it. In her opinion the family were neither good company nor socially acceptable, though admittedly Neal himself seemed quite reasonable and Coralie was very sweet in her way. But the parents! And that dreadful Amanda! Not that that was really the most worrying factor: she simply did not want Debbie to get involved with a divorcee so much older than herself. She longed for the girl to meet a handsome young Adonis who would sweep her off her feet and wipe the memory of Justin from her mind. Someone like the Jordan's boy, Ian. Now that would be a splendid match! Not only that, Neal was not an attractive man: plump and bald, he was far from Sue's vision of an ideal partner for her pretty young daughter. Debbie's bouncy red curls and shining green eyes, which so perfectly portrayed her personality up until the split with Justin, seemed so wasted on Neal. One had the feeling that she might deliberately throw herself away on Neal, imagining that the only true love of her life was lost and could never be replaced . . . and that would be too awful . . .

"I don't think your mother approves of me," Neal commented as they sat together on the bench putting their racquet covers back on.

"Whatever makes you say that?"

"Her cool politeness, mostly."

"You don't want to take any notice of that. She was like

164

that with Justin. I think she would be like that to anyone I associate with."

Neal's eyes slid sideways to study her. There was no doubt in his mind that he was heavily drawn to Debbie: she was so sweet and soft, so unsophisticated . . . so different from Annabel. The latter had impressed him so much when he was younger, with her sharp mind and air of confidence. Now, looking back, he could see that she had made up her mind that he would make a suitable partner for her, a man in the shadow of her ambitions. She had set out to woo him, ensnare him, dominate his life regardless of his own ambitions or feelings. And he had been fool enough to feel flattered by her attentions; fell for her line and married her without thinking through the forthcoming scenario. His euphoria had failed to outlast the honeymoon. Making love to Annabel had been equivalent to making love to a rubber dolly, he imagined, though not so bouncy on her almost anorexic frame. Her response, if any, had been a polite act. It was hard to imagine the same applying to Debbie . . . if they ever got round to it. If. Could she ever want to make love to anyone again, after finding his atrocious step-sister in bed with the beloved Justin? There was no doubt the poor kid was still hurting.

Zip cover fastened and tennis balls stowed in the tube, Debbie looked up and saw Neal's eyes on her. She smiled. "Penny for your thoughts?"

"I was just thinking what a kind and gentle creature you are."

Debbie's eyebrows shot up. He could say that when she had just given him one hell of a pounding on the court?

He laughed, reading her mind. "Yes, I mean it. Tennis apart!" He stroked her arm. "What shall we do now? Feel like a swim?"

"Mmm," she nodded. Anything to prolong their being together. Somehow, she felt so safe with Neal. This was no handsome and conceited Apollo with women galore falling at his feet: just a genuine person who seemed to enjoy her company. She tucked her hand into his as they left the court.

165

Sue watched them go, wondering.

"Dad? Can I bring Uncle George round for a chat after work?"

Greg frowned into the receiver. "Of course, Richard. But what's up? What's on your mind?"

"I'll explain to you both when we get there. See you later."

The line went dead and Greg drifted away from the phone with a deep frown on his forehead.

The three men sat round the kitchen table with mugs of tea.

"Hard to know where to begin," Richard said. "But I have to tell you I'm not happy about these boat deals of Billy's."

"In what way?" George asked.

"Well, I didn't pay too much attention when the first boat's registration didn't quite gel. These things happen. There were discrepancies on the second, too, but that could have been purely coincidence. But now that Billy's been missing for so long without telling anyone where he was going or why . . . well, I must admit the hairs on the back of my neck are beginning to rise."

"Billy's gone off like this before," George began.

"With his rent overdue and without even cancelling the milk?"

Greg cleared his throat. "Come on Richard, out with it. What are you suggesting?"

"I don't want to suggest anything . . ."

"Well, then tell us your suspicions. You've obviously got some or you wouldn't have called this meeting."

Richard ran a forefinger round inside the neck of his shirt, then scratched his ear. "What I'm wondering is how much we know, or don't know about the history of these boats? Can we be sure that there was no . . . foul play along the line?"

"Foul play?" George rubbed the whiskers on his bald head.

166

"He means, were they stolen?" Greg guessed.

"Stolen! Billy wouldn't . . ."

"No. No doubt he wouldn't." Richard agreed. "But just how scrupulous has he been in checking out where they came from before he bought them from the French yard?"

"You mean that the French yacht broker may have obtained them dishonestly?" George asked.

"Precisely. I mean, the man may be some kind of fence." Richard hated to see the alarmed expressions on the two elderly men. He felt responsible. After all, it was he who had put Billy's suggested deals to them in the first place. "Maybe he has returned to the Brittany yard, discovered the truth and, well, just been scared stiff and done a runner."

There was a long silence.

"Well, how are we going to find out?"

"Maybe we should take a closer look at the paperwork on the yacht we've got in hand at the moment. That might give us a clue."

"Haven't you done that already?" Greg asked with a half grin, having guessed the answer.

Richard nodded. "Yes, I have. Not that there was anything obviously wrong. But I wasn't entirely happy. That's why I wanted to warn you. And I think we ought to decide a plan of action in case the whole thing blows up in our faces."

The older men looked at each other, shrugged, and agreed. Suddenly they looked desperately worried. A plan of action!

The discussion went on for an hour, none realising that the whole matter would be taken right out of their hands within the week.

While Jane Tetchworth's fingers scampered over the keyboard of her electric typewriter there was a happy smile on her face. Having done all necessary research in the laboratories at university and made all relevant notes there, she was completing the final copy of her thesis in micro-biology before submitting it for, hopefully, a PhD. She had enjoyed the research, worked very hard, long hours and was now looking forward to relaxing with . . . Roderick?

She had never spent much time thinking about the opposite sex. They made her nervous. And it seemed that her brother Justin had more than a fair share of the family's sex hormones. His exploits made her shudder and she hoped never to get herself involved with anyone like him. Not that that was likely: his sort always finished up with girls with lashings of sex appeal, and she was intelligent enough to realise that that was not a commodity she oozed in abundance. In fact, boys at college had usually given her a wide berth, unless they were equally unattractive and covered in pimples. So it had come as quite a surprise when Roderick Martel, who's parents lived next door, asked her out for a drink, twice, which was nice, and to dinner with a group of friends at the Marina, which was fun, then suggested they play tennis together, which was not because she was hopeless at all sports except riding. And yesterday evening he had rung up to ask if she would like to go round to his place for supper tonight! She liked Roderick: he was sensible about things, not a bit flippant. He didn't waste conversation in trying to be clever with flashy repartee, but preferred intellectual discussion. He was a perfect example of the way she thought all men should be . . . as unlike her brother as humanly possible.

Rolling the last page out of the typewriter, Jane removed the carbon and copy, placed the pages on their appropriate piles and carefully lined up the separate stacks of foolscap sheets before stapling them. She tidied her desk, put the cover on her typewriter and slid the stapled papers into their respective folders. The pens and pencils were in a stone jar, reference papers filed in the cabinet drawers. She checked that that area of her bedroom was immaculate before moving over to the dressing-table.

The mirror image staring back at her was far from beautiful, but fortunately Roderick seemed to seek her company more for her brains and intelligence, than for her looks.

In fact, if she could be bothered to pluck her eyebrows a little and wear a bit of rouge and mascara, she could make herself really quite attractive. But she didn't want to create the wrong vibes. He mustn't get the idea that she wanted him for anything but his interesting company. However, she might try a little . . .

She heard his car wheels on the gravel sharp at seven-thirty.

"Ready?" he asked when she opened the door.

"Of course. Good-bye, Mummy," she called over her shoulder. "I may be late, so don't wait up."

Roderick steered her out to his car. He liked the sort of girl who was on time, and had her life under total control. "You don't mind me not wearing a tie, do you?" It was more of a statement than a question.

"Not in the least," she assured him, glad that she had decided not to change out of her cotton dress and cardigan. "Tell me, have you been toiling over a hot stove?"

"No! I've got a melon and a couple of steaks which have to be barbecued on the patio."

"Definitely my kind of food."

Richard had wanted to go straight to the police and voice his doubts. George had said no, it might go badly for Billy who had been in trouble with them years ago and police had long memories.

Greg suggested making a trip down the Brittany coast with George in the latter's boat. They could go into the yard where Billy bought the boats and try to find out more about their origins.

"If they were guilty they wouldn't admit to anything and all it would achieve would be to warn the yachtbroker to cover his tracks," Richard told the older men.

So in the end they had done nothing: decided nothing, and Richard was standing on the deck of a repaired local boat as she was lowered into the water, directing the operation, when he noticed a stranger wandering along the pier behind the crane, watching.

The yacht swayed perilously and Richard clung to the halliards as she broke the surface, then he bent to put a couple of reverse turns on the warps, fastening them to the cleats fore and aft. He had released the ring on one end of the thick, webbed forward strap which had circled under the hull bow and was making his way aft to undo the same on the stern, when a French voice called to him from above.

"Monsieur Schmit?"

Richard looked up at the stranger. "No. I am a business associate of his. Can I help you?" he called back.

"I telephone Monsieur Schmit because I wan' to speak wiv Billy Smart. You know 'im?"

Richard's feet were sweating in his Docksiders. "Yes. I know him."

"You tell me where I find him?"

"Just one moment." Unscrewing the bolt to release the stern strap gave him time to think, but it didn't help. Who was this guy? The French yachtbroker? Or some bloke who had lost a boat? He straightened. "Okay," he shouted to the workmen who were waiting. "Draw them up."

The crane driver thrust his gears and the straps slid up the side of the pier and were swung ashore to the men.

"Thanks, boys," Richard said as he climbed the vertical ladder. "I'll be in touch. See you." Then he walked up to the Frenchman. "I'm afraid Billy is away at the moment. Is there anything I can do?"

"For 'ow long 'e is away?" The man looked alarmed. He was short, thickset, and wearing a shiny blazer whose sole button was strained to the limit. He also looked angry.

"I don't know. Possibly a few weeks."

"But does 'e not work for Monsieur Schmit? Does Monsieur Schmit not know?"

"If you would care to come back to the boatyard with me you can ask him yourself." The dockside was rather too public for what might follow.

George was in his house, adjacent to the yard. He came out immediately, wiping cake crumbs out of his moustache. "Shall we go into the office?" he suggested. He didn't want Gelly to overhear what might be said. He led the way, indicated an ancient chair and the Frenchman sat down, none too willingly. "Now would you care to explain who you are and what your problem is?"

"Je suis Gaston le Sauvage. I am a vendor of boats, comprennez?"

George nodded. "Yes. And have you sold a boat to Billy?"

"Oui, oui! Many monfs past! And he does not give me ve monnaie!" He spread his arms wide in furious exasperation.

"What sort of boat was it?" Richard asked.

The waving of his hands did little to help the Frenchman's audience follow his description, but after a few minutes they agreed he could possibly be referring to the first boat they, or rather Billy, had purchased.

"Pour quelle prix? Er, what price? Dammit," Richard turned to George, "He's got me talking double Dutch, now!"

Neither of them could interpret the answer so they made their guest write it down.

George and Richard stared at the pad. The figure was not remotely near what they had paid.

George shook his head. "No. No idea what boat that is."

"You 'aven't seen 'her?"

"No. Did Billy pay you any of the money?"

"Oui, oui! Demi. 'Alf le prix. 'E say other 'alf after two monfs. Maintenant, is nearly six monfs!" The collection of papers, pens and miscellaneous objects bounced as his fist hit the desk.

Richard shook his head. "The deal you describe had nothing to do with this yard. Nothing to do with Monsieur Schmit."

The visitor flushed with anger. "But yes—"

"But no. We have not seen it here."

"Ven I go to ve police. Yes?" He was on his feet.

Richard stood, also, grateful for his several additional inches as he gazed down at Gaston le Sauvage, displaying a cool he did not feel. "Of course. If you feel it is necessary."

The Frenchman glanced at the phone, then changed his mind and stormed out.

Richard and George sat stood staring at each other.

"What do you reckon, Richard?"

"I reckon that Billy has been visiting more than one French yachtbroker. That chap never mentioned more that one yacht."

George slumped into a chair again and dropped his head into his hands. "Oh dear. Gelly is going to be so upset."

Sue parked her car in the front drive and opened the boot to collect all her shopping bags.

"Want a hand?" Stephanie called from the front door.

"Thanks. There is far more here than I'd expected. I got some extra meat, we can always put it in the freezer, but there seem to be so many people coming and going at the moment it's hard to anticipate what we will need." As she strung various plastic bags from her fingers, little Sarah appeared. "Hallo, sweetheart. Have you come to help Granny, too?"

"Me help Ganny."

Stephanie handed her a bag of bread rolls. "There you are. Put them on the kitchen table, please."

"Heaven knows what we will have for supper tonight," Sue groaned.

"Well I saw you had plenty of spaghetti so I've knocked up a nice thick bolognese sauce with the minced meat from the fridge. Would that do?"

"Wonderful. What a relief." And what a different Stephanie this was from a few years ago. "I didn't expect you to do that. I thought you and Sarah were going shopping this afternoon."

"We did. We found some nice pyjamas for both of us. Some socks and panties."

"An' a dress for me!" squealed her happy daughter.

They unpacked the shopping together while the kettle was coming to the boil, then sat down with their cups of tea to chat.

"Mum, I've been thinking. You and Stephen have been very kind to us since we returned to the island. You haven't complained once!"

"You have given us nothing to complain about!" Sue protested.

"Sweet of you to say so, but the fact remains we cannot sponge off you for all time. I have to get a job."

"No need to think about that yet, darling."

"Yes there is. We'll soon be into September and I want to sign up for some Further Education classes. At the moment I'm not qualified to do anything but scrub floors."

"Surely with your artistic talents you could get a job in an advertising agency?"

"No way. My art is totally undisciplined and self-indulgent. Sitting down in front of a view that appeals to one and transferring it to a canvas is comparatively easy. Producing something which will appeal to a certain section of the public, make them buy and please the client, is a different matter. For that I would need some serious training."

"I suppose you could be right," Sue acknowledged.

"The job I get will have to be sufficiently well paid to support Sarah and me in a rented flat or cottage."

"But surely you would stay here?"

Stephanie reached out to give her mother's arm an affectionate squeeze. "You are a dear, but we must not outstay our welcome. We will need to be here for quite a while yet, I'm afraid, until I can convince a prospective employer of my usefulness."

"You know you are welcome to remain here as long as you like. After all, it is still your home."

"Thank you. But do you realise I am going to have to ask you if you mind sitting-in in the evenings while I'm out on my courses."

"That's not a problem."

"I will try to help around the house as much as possible when I—"

"You do a tremendous lot already. I had hoped you were really going to take a long rest. You still don't look one hundred percent fit."

"You have been feeding me up so well I don't think I ever felt better. Now," Stephanie jumped up, "let's all go upstairs. I'll get Sarah bathed and ready for bed, while you have a wash and brush up before Stephen gets home."

"Fine. Let's go." Sue wanted to hug herself. It was so wonderful, not only to have Stephanie back home, but to wallow in this heartwarming new relationship.

"Don't you think we should notify the police that Billy is missing?" Gelly and George were sitting in front of a welcome autumn fire in their sitting room.

George stared at her. "I'm not sure that would be wise."

"Why not?"

"We don't know what he was up to before he left."

"Oh dear! You think he might have been involved in something . . . shady?"

Her husband nodded. "You know we had a chap from a French broker's yard over two or three months ago, asking why Billy hadn't paid what was owing on a boat he had purchased there."

"You mean one of the boats he got for you?"

"No. Richard and I didn't think the price matched up. Nor did he mention more than one deal, which we have had with someone. Someone of a different name."

"So you think that if we go to the police we might be getting Billy into trouble."

"I don't know, my love. All I do know is that he has disappeared leaving debts in the island. His landlady has had me collect all his gear so she could re-let the flat, and I have personally paid off his outstanding bills for milk and the like. Though why I should be roped in and not your sister, I don't know. After all, she is his mother."

"Yes. But of course she hasn't any money." Gelly sighed. "What does Richard think?"

"That we should go to the police to clear ourselves. This thing could blow up in our faces and it would look bad."

"You must do whatever you think right for yourselves. After all, you have given the boy two chances to behave himself."

Which was what George wanted her to say.

* * *

Debbie was concerned about her mother's reaction to Neal. She was not far wrong in her guess as to Sue's opinion and she wanted to talk about it. Square her own attitude with her parent before the matter became a serious issue.

It was a cold evening in late November when Neal was away in London and Debbie arrived home from work to find her mother curled up in a chair with *The Telegraph* spread over her knees.

"You are early," Sue commented.

"Nobody in Town so we shut up shop." She stood close to the fire, rubbing her hands. "Gosh, it's cold out." She sat down on the hearth rug at her mother's feet. "Are you about to dash off into the kitchen or somewhere?"

"No, why? Want to talk?"

"Yes. About Neal."

"Yes?" Sue waited, realising this was not easy for the girl.

"I'm worried you don't approve of him." Debbie sat staring into the fire, arms clutched round her knees, brooding.

"I'm sure he is a very nice person, dear . . . Oh, crumbs, that does sound trite, doesn't it? What I mean is . . ."

"What you mean is you think he's okay but not as a partner for me."

"Something like that," Sue admitted.

"Why?"

Sue sat up properly and folded *The Telegraph*. She took a deep breath and said, "I wouldn't want to think you were getting, well, emotionally involved . . ."

"Why?"

"Because . . . he is a lot older than you are, for one thing."

"And for another, he is not cast in the traditional 'Prince Charming' mould. Right?"

Sue hesitated. "He does not appear to be most young girls' dream hero."

"No. He is not. But then I've been through all that, haven't I, and look where it got me!"

"I know, darling, but that's not to say that all handsome young men are going to behave like Justin did!"

175

"You're probably right, mother dear. But I am not prepared to prove your point for you. Neal and I are very fond of each other. I feel happy, safe and confident in his company."

"But is that a good reason for making a commitment with him?" Sue argued.

"For me, yes. Honestly Mum. Please believe me!" Debbie's big green eyes gazed up imploringly.

Sue leaned over to kiss the top of her head. "Okay. I'll believe you. But thousands wouldn't!"

Debbie laughed happily. "You've been a very patient Mum. Now," she got up and went to switch on the television, "let's get the early evening news. I want to see if there are pictures of Juan Carlos's coronation in Spain."

It was typical November weather; freezing winds rattling the corrugated iron gable of the boatshed and whistling in under the great doors. The noise was deafening and it was some minutes before Richard realised that someone was actually knocking on the door. He dripped the excess varnish off the paintbrush on the rim of the tin before clambering down the ladder. "Hallo?" he shouted as he swung open the door. The light was very poor at that end of the shed and it was pitch dark outside, so he didn't see the face behind the fist. He reeled backwards from the blow to his mouth, tasting the blood from his split lip. Then another blow caught him in the solar plexus. He doubled up, totally winded, in time for the third blow to take him under the chin, driving his teeth through his tongue.

"Listen!" A knee was driven into his back as he lay face down on the concrete floor. "If Billy doesn't pay the money it will be worse next time!" The voice had a French accent.

Chapter Nine

Veering with the Tide

"Sergeant Burgess is here to see you, Mr Martel," Mandy's voice came through the intercom.

Roderick grimaced. If the sergeant had taken the trouble to visit the office the news must be serious. "Show him in please, Mandy."

The two men shook hands and Roderick raised a querying eyebrow.

With a sigh, Sergeant Burgess dropped into the chair in front of the desk. "Gone! Done a runner, it seems, leaving a whole heap of chaos and unfinished business behind him."

Roderick sat opposite him, glowering across the papers on his desk. "Hell and damnation!"

"Any idea how many properties floating on your books with his name attached?"

"Not exactly. I'll have to check with my partner. There may be some that he is handling that I don't know about."

"Are they impending sales or purchases?"

"Both. I am holding . . . let me see . . . four deposits for him on contracted sales, but I don't believe the conveyances have gone through for the prior purchase on at least two of them."

The sergeant frowned. "Are you telling me he is selling property he doesn't yet own?"

"Yes."

"Is that legal?"

"Let's just say it is a rather bad loophole in the law which invites property speculation on a grand scale. Several times he has had conveyances on a purchase through the Court on a Tuesday, then sold again on the Friday."

"Which means he must have re-marketed the properties at least before the ink was dry."

Roderick shook his head. "No. Before that. The conveyances couldn't have been prepared in two days! You know how long some of the local Advocates take." He sat back, running fingers through his thick, blond hair. "Naturally, I am not negotiating my local clients' cheques until and unless he reappears to honour the deals. But frankly, the ones I am most worried about are where my clients have already purchased a new property in anticipation of him completing on the sale of their original house. Admittedly they will ultimately be credited by the amount of the deposit, in a couple of cases, but in two others the man's cheques have bounced."

Sergeant Burgess flipped over a page of his notebook. "They are not the first rubber cheques, I'm afraid. Have you tried re-presenting them?"

"Not yet. They came back on Friday. Hasn't been a chance over the weekend. I'll do it today."

"This business is certainly going to leave a few people in queer street. He seems to have been offering such inflated prices for places."

"Yes. Encouraging the vendors to buy on, way above their means."

"Not good for business."

"Very good for business until the bubble bursts. Then the estate agent's reputation flies out of the window."

The visitor stood up. "We'll keep in touch. Let me know if you get any luck with those cheques. And perhaps you would let me have all the details of sales and purchases through G and M Properties Limited, pertaining to this character which have not been completed."

"This is all highly confidential information," Roderick pointed out.

"Of course. And we will respect that. As with all the data from the other agents, and some individuals who thought they were doing themselves a favour by cutting out the middle man," he grinned.

Roderick walked with him through the outer office.

178

"Speak to you again soon," he said. He returned to his desk worrying about Allan Fallaize and asked Mandy to get him on the phone.

He wasn't available but rang back later. "Good news, I hope?"

"No, sadly. I hate to tell you this but it seems the bugger's done a runner."

"Shit!"

"And there are several other people in the island in the same boat. I've just had the police here. Look," Roderick swallowed, "I feel very badly about this. You came to me because we are old mates and instead of protecting you I seem to have dropped you right in it."

"For Chrissake don't start blaming yourself. You weren't to know. Anyway, the situation has improved somewhat."

"Really? How's that?"

"The reason you couldn't get me when you called is because I've changed jobs. I was head-hunted and am feeling rather pleased with myself."

"Go on! Where are you?"

"With Goldberg Financial Services. A big step up in responsibility and also in salary, so things are not as bad as they were."

"Boy, am I relieved to hear that. And congratulations. In fact you are the third person I've heard about moving up in the finance industry in the past month."

"Well, you know the housing situation only too well. The banking houses can't get enough licences for overseas employees to occupy local market properties, so they are desperate to employ Guernsey people with local residential qualifications."

"I don't doubt your professional qualifications far out-weighed the other."

Allan laughed. "You are so kind. Anyway, let me know if there is any news on that so-and-so. If our deal with him does fall through it will mean delaying building our swimming pool for at least another year."

"My heart bleeds for you."

179

"Come off it. You estate agents have been creaming it in recently!"

"Did I say I was complaining?"

No one could possibly have described Jane Tetchworth as beautiful, or even pretty. But on the strength of Roderick's invitation to accompany him to a reception celebrating the opening of the extended offices at Goldberg Financial Services, she bought an elegant little coral silk suit, had an expensive new haircut and applied make-up with unusual care. Roderick watched her come down the stairs of her parents' house, next door to his own family's home, with increased interest: she was looking quite elegant and sophisticated. Jane wasn't feeling either of those things – she never would – but she did feel a little more confident than usual, once she noted the appreciative reaction on his face.

The reception was in full swing when they arrived. A waiter presented flutes of champagne on a silver salver; a waitress offered dainty canapés.

"Rodds, you old devil!" Allan Fallaize squeezed through the crush of bodies, his eyes lighting with interest as he realised Jane's presence. "Hallo! We haven't met!"

Trying not to betray his irritation at being called "Rodds", a form of address dropped when he moved up from the Lower School, Roderick made the introductions.

"Come over here, there's more room," Allan commanded. "I want you to meet my new boss, Malcolm Pennet."

The latter proved to be not much older than Allan and Roderick. Tall, heavy, with already thinning hair, he had piercing eyes which darted round the room constantly while he was talking, his mobile features no doubt mirroring his mental activity. Like so many others in the room, Roderick thought, looking round at the smart suits, hearing the slick chatter of his intellectually agile peers. These were not bank clerks with pens in their pockets who counted their tills and the minutes to clocking off time. These men and women didn't have tills, they handled portfolios worth hundreds of thousands of pounds. They didn't talk about weekend sport, they discussed money markets, the rises and falls on the FTSE, the Dax and the Dow Jones. They talked big money. They earned big money. They were happy to talk properties, especially abroad.

"Lot of money will be invested in Spain in the next few years, now old Franco has gone," someone speculated.

"In Portugal and Italy, too," another added.

"I've got a client dead keen on finding a few blocks of offices here in Guernsey. Got anything on your books, Roderick?"

"Yes. Two. One in the centre of Town, the other a little way out. I'll let you have the details in the morning. You don't happen to have anyone looking for a really beautiful Open Market property overlooking the West coast, do you?"

Jane was enormously impressed.

"I hope you weren't too bored," Roderick said as they drove off in the orange MG. "Afraid there wasn't much ordinary social chatter."

"I wasn't the least bit bored!" she responded indignantly. "I find the manipulation of money and markets quite fascinating. As a matter of fact I'm pretty hopeless at social gossip. I don't socialise enough to know who is sleeping with who, dying his or her hair or having their legs waxed."

He laughed. "You really are delicious. Talking of which, I've got a bite of supper laid on at my place. Could you face steaks again?"

Jane most certainly could. No one had ever before told her she was delicious.

Painfully, Richard dragged himself to his feet and clung to a tool rack near the open door. His mouth was full of blood, his tongue swelling by the minute. He was winded, his back agony. Worst of all he was shocked. The most unaggressive, inoffensive of characters, he had never been assaulted before in his life. He had made no attempt to defend himself, let alone retaliate. Slowly he regained control of his muscles and managed to close and lock the gable door before staggering to the rear door of the shed, peering cautiously through the darkness then crossing the yard to George's house.

George and Gelly were having their tea. The latter shrieked when she saw the battered face. "Richard! What has happened?"

It was difficult to explain, his tongue being several sizes too large for his mouth.

But they understood.

"That's it, then!" George announced angrily. "We've dilly-dallied long enough trying to protect Billy. But no more. I'm sorry, Gelly, but this is the boy's fault and he's got to take the consequences – if he ever dares set foot in the island again!"

Aunt Gelly agreed. "He has had his chances, but we can't be doing with this! Call the police, George. Right now. And the doctor."

"No, no," Richard protested. "I don't need a doctor. Just the poleesh."

"Well at least let me clean up your face."

George was already dialling. "Better let the police see him the way he is, first. They've got to know what we're up against!"

A police car drew up outside ten minutes later when Richard was trying to swallow a little tea.

"You've been in the wars, then," commented the plain clothes sergeant.

Richard attempted a smile. "You could shay that," he said, and painfully relayed the evening's events.

"A Frenchman, you say? Ernie, you'd better get through to the station and get a watch put on the harbour and airport. He might try to get on the hydrofoil to St Malo in the morning. Or a plane to Dinard or Cherbourg."

There followed a great many questions about Billy's business activities, much sighing and nodding of heads.

"Now may I clean him up?" Gelly asked when she reckoned they'd finished. "If he goes home looking like that his wife will have a fit!"

She was able to improve his face, somewhat, but his clothing remained shockingly bloodstained as he and George led the police officers into the boatshed so that Richard could show them exactly where and how it had all happened.

"Didn't realishe at first there wash anyone there. It's such a rough night. I shay night," he squinted at his watch, "but it's still only just past shicksh." He demonstrated the opening of the door, and the attack. Then shook his head, still disbelieving. "Right out of the blue!"

"Tell you what," the sergeant said, "You are looking pretty knocked up. I'll drive your car home for you with you directing the way, and Ernie will follow in our vehicle."

It was a very cold night, but Richard knew that was not the only reason he was shivering. He was in a state of shock and accepted gratefully.

"Would you like us to have our coffee by the fire?" Roderick asked her.

Jane eyed the cosy sofa in front of the burning logs, and nodded. "May I help?"

"You might bring in the tray. I'll get the coffee. Want milk?"

She shook her head. "Just sugar, thanks."

He let her pour, watching her long, slim fingers gently handling the cups which were placed on the little tables either end of the sofa. His arm slid along the back, a hand falling softly onto her shoulder. "Comfy?"

Her eyes gazed vacantly into the dancing flames. "Very."

His fingers strayed up into her hair, pressing her head gently towards him. "Happy?"

She turned her face and smiled. "Very."

Their lips touched, noses nuzzled and then they began some serious kissing.

Louis Brizzard was arrested as he boarded the St Malo hydrofoil in St Peter Port harbour, and charged with assault. He was a dumb giant of a man with a short forehead, half his teeth missing, obviously from a previous encounter, and blood on his shirt which would prove to be from the latest. He admitted being an acquaintance of Gaston le Sauvage. The court hearing was a few days later: the man was found guilty of the assault and sentenced to three months in prison.

183

After the hearing Richard asked the police sergeant if he could visit the man before he left prison. "I want to try to convince him that we have absolutely no idea where Billy is; that the latter owes us money and we are as anxious to track him down as Gaston is."

"I'm sure something can be arranged, providing we have your assurance that you won't try to get your revenge!"

Richard laughed. "What me? Against that hulking great brute? You have to be joking!"

"Surprising what some angry people will take on, you know. But are you so keen to find Billy Smart? Hasn't he caused enough problems?"

"It's old George Schmit, really. He is the one who has paid off all Billy's debts and arrears. I think he'd like to give him a piece of his mind."

"He wasn't obliged to pay off the debts."

"No. But Billy is his wife's nephew. Her sister hasn't any money and George did it out of kindness to them. He really is an old softy."

"I'll put in a word for you with the prison governor."

"Thanks. It's not that I ever wish to lay eyes on Billy again. He's nothing but an idle troublemaker, after easy money. I bet he's comfortably holed up, somewhere, living it up beyond his means."

The pale green Mercedes open sports car pulled up alongside the pavement. A young man climbed out and waited while his shapely blonde companion wrestled with her passenger door, a tight skirt and high heels. They wove through the pavement tables of the tapas bar to join a group of friends, shouting and waving.

"We kept you a couple of chairs but were beginning to think you weren't coming. You're nearly an hour late," complained a curly-haired man from behind sunglasses and beer-belly. "What you bin doing, Jason?"

Jason Smith, alias Billy Smart, dropped his dark glasses to the end of his nose and stared at his new friend over the top. His lips twitched as he said, "What the hell do you think I've bin doing, Kevin?"

Kevin's eyes strayed significantly over the blonde and he bellowed with laughter. "Miguel!" he shouted at the waiter. "*Dos cervezas, por favor*. And what are you having, darling?"

"The name's Sharon and I'll have a rum and coke, thanks," was the arch reply.

Benidorm was busy. As ever. Early tourists filled the cafés, cars ignored all traffic signs and pneumatic drills ploughed into rock and concrete as huge cranes swung over the tops of skyscrapers.

A long-haired, geriatric teenager at their table held his hands to his head. "How much longer is that racket going on? Had a heavy night last night."

Kevin studied the watch on his sunburnt wrist. "Half-an-hour. Then they'll stop for lunch and siesta. Where were you last night? Didn't see you at Dirty Dick's."

"Went up to Calpe with Ronnie's lot. Wound up in a place called *El Gato Negro*."

"Hell!" Kevin's girlfriend Annie laughed. "What a combination. Ronnie and the Black Cat. The *vino tinto* in that place is real gut rot." She made room for Billy's chair beside hers. "I like your car."

"Why don't you get Kev to buy it for you for your birthday?"

"Are you serious? Is it for sale?"

"All my cars are for sale."

"Huh! At a price, eh Corin?"

Corin swept a hand back over his black, oily hair and smiled. "I'm not complaining. I've had an offer for mine six hundred higher than I paid Billy."

Billy knew he was lying, but didn't say so. Corin had paid his asking price, which was far more than the car was worth. But the man was happy with the slinky yellow repaint. It suited his image.

In fact there was a very nice, lurative market down here on the Costa Blanca. And just think of all the other costas there were, as yet untapped. He was already building up a good trade in used cars, taking them to and fro through the French border with only one or two minor adjustments to the paperwork. Of course to really hit the big time he would need to take on a couple of extra drivers of which there were plenty around. What was difficult was finding ones with innocent faces. Take Kevin for instance. One look at him and the border guards would have him in irons, convinced he must be carrying contraband. Recently, however, he had had a brainwave. Girls. Really nice attractive, innocent-looking girls. And Sharon would start the ball rolling. Not that she could be classfied as exactly innocent! But the Spanish *aduana* were not to know that.

One day in March Roderick picked up another log from the wicker basket and placed it carefully at the back of the grate, withdrawing his hand quickly before burning himself. He checked he had not scattered ash on the hearth, then stood up, glanced in the mirror over the mantelpiece, pushing his hair back from his forehead with his fingers. The small family photograph on the mantelpiece was askew. He straightened it, then returned to the table at the far end of the room to double check that everything was exactly in place. But had he left everything ready in the kitchen? Hell, he wasn't yet twenty-eight and already he was becoming a fussing old woman!

Roderick Martel had been on edge for days. Weeks. Ever since that evening when they had kissed so long and passionately. But today had been the worst, so far. This was it. This was the day he had planned for so long. He always laid plans well in advance, it was all part of having a tidy mind. It used to drive his mother and siblings mad when he lived at home. He never let Mum put his clothes away – he couldn't be sure she would put the clean vests and pants at the bottom of the pile, or the clean socks at the back of the drawer. He had hated to join in some spur-of-the-moment family function because there hadn't been time to think it through. It wasn't possible to leave papers scattered over one's desk and just jump in the car and go . . . or dirty dishes piled on the drainboard . . .

He looked at the clock. Half an hour to wait. Too early to start drinking but he wanted something. A cup of tea?

He switched on the kettle and stood staring at the blackness beyond the kitchen window, seeing only his own reflection. So he drew the curtains, and went back into the living room to draw the ones in there . . . or would it look more welcoming to leave them open till she arrived? No. The light over the front door was welcoming enough.

He was standing in the kitchen sipping from his mug of tea when the doorbell rang. It made him jump and he nearly spilled tea down his shirt. He quickly tipped the remainder down the sink, swished the mug out under the tap and hurried through the living room to the door.

Jane was one of those people who could look immaculate in casual clothes. Removal of her overcoat revealed a high-necked tangerine jumper and a brown silk scarf knotted round her neck with studied carelessness, a brown skirt flecked with tangerine, and brown Hush Puppies.

Roderick almost purred with approval as he placed her coat over the back of the sofa, leaving his arms free to hold her. "You look even nicer tonight than last night," he said after kissing her, adding, "if that is possible." He took her coat and hung it on the row of hooks at the foot of the stairs.

"You have been saying some very nice things to me, lately. Do you feel all right?"

"Haven't I always said nice things?"

"Good Lord, no. Years ago when I was a pigtailed schoolgirl you were ever so high and mighty and disdainful. I used to be scared stiff of you!"

"Honestly?" He was shattered. "How can I make it up to you?"

"You could offer me a drink or a cup of tea?"

"Which?"

"Both, please, but I'll start with tea. It's been a hard day." She had recently got a temporary job as secretary to an Advocate.

"You too?" He returned to the kitchen to refill the kettle.

"We've been flat out from first thing this morning," she called after him. "I hate legal papers, especially all the French ones."

187

"It's fortunate you are so fluent in French."

"I thought so, once. Now I realise it only means I get stuck with all the interpreting."

He wondered if she would ever consider a job in real estate. Hardly a taxing position for a girl with a possible Phd, but Mandy had married last year and would soon be leaving to have a baby. There would be a vacancy . . . but there was another matter on his mind to be dealt with first. He carried in the cups and put them on the occasional tables. "Come and sit down," he said. His heart was pounding.

"You look terribly serious," she frowned.

"I am. There is something I want to . . . discuss with you before we start drinking."

"Before? Why?"

"Because I'd hate you to think what I have to say is alcohol induced."

Her grey eyes grew large as saucers, her mouth forming a small O. An onlooker might have thought she resembled a scared rabbit: "Go on," she whispered.

Roderick thought she looked utterly enchanting. His heart thumped so loud in his chest he thought she must hear it. "I was wondering if . . . Look, why don't you drink your tea?" He watched while she obeyed, took another breath and started again. "I was wondering if you might consider . . . the idea of er . . . marrying me?"

Her mouth twitched and his heart sank because he thought she was going to laugh at him. But she didn't. Her small mouth widened into a huge grin as she replaced her cup and hurled herself into his arms. "Oh Roderick! My own darling sweetheart!" She smothered his face with kisses.

He backed off. "Do I take this response to mean an affirmative?"

"Mmm! Oh yes. Mmm."

"Then let's forget this tea lark. I've got a bottle of Cordon Rouge in the fridge." He was glad he had got it over with early. Now they could relax and enjoy a really happy evening.

Roderick went through the formality of asking Johnny

Tetchworth's permission. Johnny went through the process of consulting Hilary but there was no doubt they were both delighted. So too were Stephen and Sue, though the latter had always thought Jane rather colourless. But then Roderick was so staid and straightlaced himself . . .

The young couple would have liked a small, quiet wedding but realised from the beginning that they didn't stand a chance. Johnny was determined to put an impressive show on the road and Hilary, for once, was happy to go along with him. The date was set for September, the setting was to be the Vale Church and the festivities were to be held at the Royal Hotel because it had the best car parking facilities and the largest reception rooms.

Sue was not required to do a thing, though she did offer. Still, she was quite happy to sit back, relax and watch her next door neighbours vacillate between joy and elation, annoyance and frustration and downright fury as their plans developed or were thwarted.

With a touch of regret Roderick came to a decision. "I do like my little cottage. It's a highly suitable batchelor pad," he told Jane, "but I don't think it is adequate for a married couple."

"Oh! But it is. It's lovely. You surely don't want to part with it!"

"Lovell's have got a rather nice place on their books at the moment which I want to take you to see tomorrow afternoon. Do you think you can take an hour off work?"

"Why Lovell's? Why not something on your own books?"

"Not ethical, my sweet," he said severely.

Set in lanes not far from Bordeaux, *Le Marais* was an old farmhouse with a long lawn in front and several outbuildings behind. "It's huge!" Jane exclaimed.

"Only five bedrooms."

"Five! What do we want five for?"

Roderick raised an eyebrow at her. "Hopefully we won't only be two of us forever!"

She grinned. "But at the moment . . ."

"At the moment we have a one-bedroomed one-reception-roomed cottage, suitable for one but not for two. Far too small. And now we must decide if we intend to keep on moving every time we swell our ranks, or make one move now, for life. Gradually we can develop this place to fulfil all our needs. We would have to transform at least one of the bedrooms into one or two bathrooms – there are none upstairs, and one of the downstairs rooms can be turned into a study."

"But it looks very expensive."

"It's not cheap but it is soundly built and the roof is in excellent condition. Come inside and see if you like it."

"I love it," she whispered out of the agent's hearing.

"Do you want to see some other houses?"

"I bet you've examined every property currently on the market and you've picked this out as best."

"True."

"Then you'd better open negotiations. I can't think of a better place to live. Though I'll be sorry not to have lived in the cottage at all."

Roderick gave her a discreet hug. "You may yet. We don't know how long it will be before this might be ready to move into. We only have five months in hand."

Meanwhile, Roderick was not the only one with marriage on his mind, but it was early May before Neal broached the subject with Debbie.

His step-sister, Coralie, had suspected he would for sometime, and was beginning to feel impatient that he wasn't getting on with it.

Sue had feared it for nearly a year, but had become resigned to the inevitable as Stephen tried to soothe her qualms.

Neal collected Debbie from work and drove her out to Vazon Point.

"Why are we coming out here?" she asked. "Are you wanting a walk and fresh air?"

"No. Just a chance to have you all to myself where we can talk without interruption." He parked high on the stony ground facing west across the bay, boisterous breakers

190

glistening in the early evening sunlight as they rolled up the beach below.

Debbie felt totally relaxed as she always did in Neal's company. He had a soothing effect on her soul.

He produced a stiff, manilla envelope from his pocket. "Guess what this is. My divorce absolute. My marriage to Annabel is now null and void."

"That must be a relief." He hadn't talked much about his marriage, or about his wife, but Debbie could think of nothing worse than being tied to someone who was nothing more than a irritation; someone whom one didn't even like, let alone love.

Neal laughed. "That's the understatement of the year. It's a great deal more than that. It means I am now free to get on with the rest of my life." He took her hands in his. "Our joint lives, I hope."

Debbie cocked her head on one side causing the sun to turn her red curls into a golden halo. "Joint?" She was smiling.

"You and I are a unit, are we not?"

"I certainly feel so," she whispered. Her green eyes were sparkling again, more intensely than they had done since that fateful day . . .

"Do you? I am so much older than you, and I don't kid myself I am God's gift—"

She withdrew a hand so that she might press a finger over his lips. "Stop denigrating yourself! Only thirteen years older: not so very much. And you are the dearest, sweetest person I have ever known, and I love you. You know that."

"More than you loved Justin?"

"That was lust. This is real love." At least, that was her newly developed conviction.

"Do you think it might ever be both?" he looked like a winsome schoolboy.

"The only reason I have never slept with you is because you have never asked. But of course I want to," she said determinedly. "You should have guessed that already."

"My darling Debbie! The only reason I didn't ask was

191

because I didn't feel it was fair to involve one so young in an adulterous relationship."

"You mean you were scared I would think you were a dirty old man!" she teased.

"Something like that," he agreed as he wrapped her in his arms.

Another car drew up alongside them and they realised the bunch of kids in the back were all giggling.

"Come on," he relinquished his hold. "I'll take you home and get Stephen's formal permission. And if your Ma isn't too appalled she might even ask me to stay for supper."

Sue guessed what had happened as soon as they walked into the house, so she was able to warn Stephen, adopt a happy smile and congratulate them as soon as they announced their news. "Wonderful," she said, "and not unexpected."

"Splendid," nodded Stephen. "You have our joint blessings, you know that."

Well aware how Sue had felt about the alliance, initially, Debbie blew her mother a kiss of gratitude.

"Where are you going to live?" Bobbie asked, being practically minded.

"I've been working for my father in the London office, up to now, flitting over here to see Debbie on the excuse of work and consultations in the island. But Dad hasn't enough work here to keep me going," Debbie's face fell, "so he has agreed to accept my resignation and I am now free to get a job in the local finance industry. Marriage to Debbie will give me local residential qualifications so it shouldn't be difficult to find one. I thought we might rent a small place till we find something we really like."

"And when do you plan to marry?" queried Stephen.

"As soon as possible," Debbie cut in.

"It will have to be a civil ceremony in the Greffier's office in the Court House," Sue pointed out.

"Of course," Debbie nodded. "As small and quiet as possible."

"We could walk on up the hill for a reception at Old Government House Hotel."

Debbie glanced at Neal for his approval.

"Great idea," he agreed.

And Sue's mind immediately got to work on the details.

Unlike Jane, whose mother went wild with raw silk, stiffened petticoats and antique lace veil and train, Debbie and Sue agreed that as an "experienced" woman, a gown of plain cream ankle-length satin and a pill-box hat trimmed with pink roses matching those in the small spray she would carry, seemed a far more suitable outfit for the Greffe. The doors to the hotel ballroom would be flanked by pedestal arrangements of pink roses, white freesias and ivory stephanotis, the simple, two-tier cake carrying a swathe of palest pink sugar roses from the base to circle the tiny silver vase filled with lilies-of-the-valley at the top.

Only closest family members attended the brief, formal ceremony, Roderick acting as best man and little Sarah, in cream net and minute ballet pumps, holding a posy of pink rosebuds, as an enthusiastic flowergirl. Seventy guests were hand-shaken and kissed when they arrived at the hotel shortly after the bride and groom. The hotel laid on a champagne reception and finger buffet, Stephen proposed the toast to the happy couple and Cyril and Carol Blaydon contrived to remain sober. Amanda had excused herself on the strength of a business commitment in New York. "Applying for a couch position" Stephanie speculated. Everyone was relieved by her absence, not least her step-brother.

Sue was delighted to see how relaxed and happy her sensitive, younger daughter appeared. The bride bubbled and glowed as she grasped her groom's arm possessively, waltzing him round the room showing him off to their family and friends, allowing herself to be kissed and congratulated, over and over. Barely taller than the girl, his bald head gleaming and stout frame encased in a morning suit, Neal too glowed with love and joy. He looked so supremely happy that, at last, Sue allowed herself to be convinced that this was indeed a true love match and her daughter had every chance of lasting contentment.

There was a guffaw of laughter from the far end of the room. Despite her in-laws, Sue thought.

The Blaydon's wedding present to their son and new daughter-in-law was a honeymoon in Hawaii.

Stephanie felt quite dazed at first by the new and different society of the business art world. Some fellow pupils in her art classes were school leavers, but a fair number were mature students with much the same ideas and intentions as herself. At first she found it extremely hard working to order, snipping away with scissors at shapes and colours, pasting together unrelated objects, blending them with her pen into what were intended to be eyecatching designs. She was disappointed and baffled when two of her favourite creations were met with bland and unenthusiastic comment, and totally bemused when the disaster she was about to screw up and hurl into the wastepaper basket, was hailed as a work of near genius. But the days she enjoyed most were those spent acting as dogsbody in offices and studios for "work experience". Though she stood more often at the coffee machine churning out cups for workers than at a drawing board, she loved the intensity of drive and direction, the camaraderie. These people were true artists, yet so capable applying their talents to business markets, relating mental images to customer requirements. A shaded wash of single colour, a reverse negative and half a dozen brush or pen strokes suddenly became a superb insert for a glossy magazine. The retail whizzkid about to set up in business who came in with a vague idea of presentation, within minutes was staring at inspirational logos, while someone else bounded into the room with crisp slogans. But more inspiring even than the products themselves were the people: lively, fun people with agile brains, mobile features, and hands full of expressive gestures. What was more, they seemed to like her, invited her to join them after work for drinks and even asked her to their homes.

Those homes in themselves were different. Different from *La Rocquette de Bas*, portraying a totally alternative concept of living, they tended to be open plan. Gone was the

194

formality of a dining room, kitchen suppers ruled. Barbecues were in, set on smart patios amid cascading flower pots and hanging baskets. Settees with throw rugs stood on pale polished floorboards under a tall bamboo palm or potted lemon tree. Clean, tidy, studied carelessness, an atmosphere in which to relax, laugh and exchange ideas . . . Stephanie couldn't stop herself thinking back to the commune, to the utter indiscipline of "waiting for inspiration", to the pretence of unity which did little to hide the petty jealousies, the irresponsible attitudes and irritabilities, the irrational arguments, the dirt, poverty and degradation . . . and nor could she stop herself from shuddering at the memory.

Time after time Stephanie wondered how her mother had managed to show so little reaction to the conditions in which her daughter and granddaughter were living, and still faced making return visits, keeping faith, smiling . . . and loving. And yet at the time she, Stephanie, perhaps because of her underlying guilt, had searched Sue's face for a hint of criticism on which to feed her antagonism and resentment. Why? Why had she resented her mother's very existence all these years?

In front of the cameras, Sarah was a natural. A flowergirl for the second time within months, on this occasion in a confection of pink taffeta with a mother-of-pearl headband which tended to slip forwards over one eye, she positively pranced up the path to the church alongside her mother, Stephanie, who had been invited to fill the role of her sister's bridesmaid.

Hilary was regal in her Paris couturier dress and three-quarter length coat, and a hat fit to grace the front cover of Vogue. Justin sat with his family, and Debbie was relieved to find she could look at him with scarcely a twinge of pain. Clinging to Neal, she was convinced that even that would pass in time.

Sue had not attempted to compete with the mother of the bride. She had found a very smart silk two-piece dress and jacket at Creasey's in High Street and, for once, quite admired herself in her chosen hat. She was delighted when

195

Stephen, who didn't usually notice these things, remarked that she looked stunning. Which was true. At forty-eight she had retained her figure, mainly thanks to the tennis court, not a single grey strand of hair was to be seen and only when she laughed did the deepening crow's feet betray the years. Both her daughters thought she looked marvellous, and said so.

The slightly ivory tone of raw silk did little for the bride's complexion. Jane had tried to oppose her mother's decision but the result was inevitable. Nevertheless, with her hair softly waved and after the judicious application of make-up, Roderick, waiting beside his best man Alex Grolinski, thought she looked fantastic as she approached him up the aisle. He spoke his vows boldly, and though hers were barely audible to the congregation, he heard them well enough, which was all that mattered.

The formal line-up at the Royal Hotel seemed to last forever as two hundred guests were greeted. Lord Hartwell, an old friend of the Tetchworths, had been invited to toast the bride and groom, his title intended to make up for his lack of gifted oratory.

Jane was longing for the opportunity to start married life in Roderick's tiny cottage, but instead allowed herself to be hustled up to the airport amidst a shower of confetti, en route to their honeymoon in Corfu.

Stephanie stood at the airport window with the crowd who had followed them up, waving till the plane was out of sight. She didn't feel the least twinge of envy. There was no man in her life, at present, with whom she particularly wanted to spend an evening, let alone a lifetime. She gathered her darling, sleepy daughter into her arms and bore her out to the waiting cars.

Chapter Ten

A United Family

"Solomon and Sheba are very lively for Golden Retrievers," Stephanie remarked. She was sitting in a comfortably
cushioned cane chair on the verandah at the back of *La
Rocquette de Bas*. There had been one or two changes to
the house in recent years. The verandah, had been extended
to nearly twice it's original width and glassed in, turning it
into a conservatory, though everyone still referred to it as "the
verandah".

Sue sat with her, a tray of tea between them on a glass-
topped table. "They are still only pups. I have no doubt that
within a couple of years they will turn into animated doormats
like Troilus and Cressida were." She sighed as she always did,
thinking about the two beautiful dogs who had been so much
a part of their family life for more than fourteen years.

Stephanie read her thoughts. "You'll grow to love these
two just as much, Mum."

"I do now, really. They are such bright, loving characters.
and they are so good with Sarah, aren't they?"

The two women watched as the five-year-old climbed
onto Solomon's back, trying to coax him into fulfilling the
role of pony. His response was to roll over onto his back
with his feet in the air, sending the child tumbling across
the grass, grumbling indignantly.

There were shouts of triumph from the tennis court.
Bobbie was over on vacation from university with three
pals, all equally keen on the sport; that and surfboarding
at Vazon where the rollers could be quite spectacular. The
gate to the court clicked and the tall, bronzed young men
crossed the lawn to the open conservatory.

"We'll just help ourselves to some juice and then be heading off to Vazon, if that's okay, Ma?"

"Of course, Bobbie. Have fun, all of you. Will you be in for supper?"

Tony, the chunkiest one, grinned. "That sounds good, Mrs M. If it's not too much hassle."

"No hassle at all, boys. See you later."

"Mum, you are a barefaced fibber!" Stephanie declared when they had gone.

"Why?"

"Feeding those four hulks three times a day, every day for a week! What on earth do you give them?"

"Food that is unimaginative but filling!" Sue laughed. "Sausages, mash and peas, tonight, followed by tons of bread, cheese and fruit."

"They look a nice bunch."

"They are. Bobbie is lucky to have met up with such a likely crowd so soon. Especially ones who are all keen on tennis."

Stephanie sipped her tea, watching Sarah throwing an old tennis ball for the enthusiastic dogs. "I suppose we would all describe our concept of the ideal friend quite differently."

Sue thought for a minute. "Perhaps. Yet on the other hand, wouldn't the universal requirement be loyalty and amiability?"

"Oh yes. But there is so much more. A sense of humour would be important to me, but I doubt if it would be Roderick's first priority."

Sue smiled. "True."

There was a pause, then Stephanie asked, "Do you think one should allow oneself to idolise people?"

"My mother considered idolatry to be dangerous. But I think that was through seeing it from a religious viewpoint. Not much difference in her eyes between worshipping a mere mortal or a graven image."

"Then what difference is there between worshipping and loving a person?" Stephanie was gazing into space, the palms of her hands cradling her cup.

A frown divided Sue's forehead as she considered the question. "Loving a person surely means warts and all. You know them, admire their strengths, understand and make allowances for their weaknesses, whilst not necessarily giving in to them. Worship, on the other hand, I see as a kind of blind faith. To worship God is good because he is immortal and perfect. But no mere mortal can be perfect; therefore if you worship one it is because you imagine quite wrongly that they are perfect. Blind to their faults, you may well turn them into atrocious tyrants." Sue paused, thinking she was getting a bit heavy. "Some parents idolise a child to the point of turning it into a fearful, precocious brat that no one else can stand." She laughed.

Sarah had mis-thrown the ball and Stephanie jumped up out of her chair to fetch it down from high in a bush which was threatened with destruction as the dogs scrambled to retrieve the missile. When she returned she asked, "Was I a fearful, precocious brat?"

Sue snorted. "Good Lord no! What makes you ask that?"

"The fact that I cannot remember Daddy ever scolding or correcting me."

"Jonathan? Really? Come to think of it I don't suppose he did. Not any of you."

"Did you know that I worshipped him?"

"You did? Are you sure that it is not more a matter of sanctifying his memory? You were very young when he died."

"Not too young to feel desperately sad for him, seeing him crippled and in a wheelchair."

Sue studied her daughter's face. It was as strong as ever, but her grandmother's big, amber eyes had softened in recent years: the obstinate contrariness had gone. And the long, wavy brown hair no longer hung down in strands over her eyes but was swept back either into a ponytail or a neat, Chinese style chignon on top of her head. "And I suppose you thought I was very cruel to him?"

Silently, Stephanie nodded.

"Perhaps I was."

"Why?"

"Do you really want to know? Do you want to hear about the constant tongue lashings I received from morning till night, often in front of hotel guests and staff? Do you want to know that I worked all hours God gave until I was down to skin and bone? But it was never enough. That try as I might I could never do a thing right? Not until he knew he had terminal cancer did he change, and then we had a most marvellous year together, of loving, caring and mutual respect, until he died. He was wonderful to me, to us all, during that year."

Stephanie kept her face averted from her mother so her swimming eyes would not betray her feelings. "What about Stephen?" she whispered. "When did he come into the picture?"

"During the very bad times. I think he saved my sanity. Mind you," she added, "The relationship we had had made me feel extremely guilty, later, when your father's attitude changed. When he became caring again."

Stephanie's sigh became a long, shuddering gasp. "And now it's my turn to feel guilty. Oh Mum! I am so sorry. I got it all wrong." And when she turned to offer a wan smile, Sue saw her lashes were wet, her eyes brimming over.

"Let's have another cup of tea."

"Yes. And you can tell me about Daddy and Stephen: the good things, but how they were different."

Tea freshly poured, Sue began. "It is so difficult to judge people. One can idolise a person one has never met . . . like President Jack Kennedy of the United States. Millions of people, worldwide, idolised him, followed his administration and his family life with close interest. And like so many of those people, I can clearly remember exactly where I was standing, near the television set, when the programme was interrupted with the announcement of his murder. And like millions of others I wept. Yet in the years since his death, and the death of his brother, Bobby, there has been so much sleaze written and said about him. He appears to have had the most awful downside to his character; to have been a shameless manipulator and adulterer. A thoroughly weak man, not the wonderful man of strength as his publicists portrayed."

"Perhaps he was a mixture of both – strength and weakness, good and bad," Stephanie suggested, thinking back over all the people in the commune, her old school associates, the new crowd who had become her friends in the business art world, here in the island.

"Stephen has none of the forcefulness and drive of your father, yet the strength of his gentleness and love is felt and remarked on by nearly everyone who knows him. Because of the war, Jonathan became a man before he was through his adolescence, yet looking back, I think much of the hail-fellow-well-met *bonhomie*, his driving force and laughter when we first met, were just a shell, a mask covering his actual deep sensitivity. No one was allowed to know how easily he could be hurt. But that hurt turned to such anger and resentment after his terrible accident that his character became almost unrecognisable."

"How sad, Mum. And how different things might have been if that kid hadn't lost control of his car that evening, so many years ago."

"Yes, so sad. Yet one cannot play the game backwards. But for that I would have had so much more time to spend with my children, instead of being tied to running an hotel. On the other hand I would never have had Bobbie. Obviously, for your father's sake I regret what happened, but I have no regrets for myself."

"Good. I should hate to think you had."

"Mummy! Granma! When is tea?" Little Sarah clambered up the steps to join them. "I'm hungry and Solomon and Sheba want some biscuits."

"Teatime is right now," Sue declared, pushing herself out of her chair. "Let's go into the kitchen and see what we have in Gran's cake tins."

The two octogenarians sat at a table in the window of the golf club, beer mugs in hand, complaining about the course, the club and the standards of behaviour of some of the newer membership: a well-worn theme, latterly.

"Standards are slipping all the time," George Schmit grumbled. "I actually saw someone walk into the bar last week not wearing a tie!"

"They think we are old-fashioned," Greg Gaudion snorted. "But in fact we know they are just slovenly. They'll be coming in here in shorts, next!" He drained his glass. "Want another?"

"Just the half," George pushed his mug across the table.

When Greg returned he asked, "Have you come to terms yet, with being retired?"

"Of course not. Never will, though I have to admit that your boy, Richard, is coping very well. He's selling a lot of fast boats to all these young money manipulators in the banking business. They must be earning huge salaries because the maintenance isn't cheap. None of them seem to do any work on their boats like we used to; it's straight to the yard for the least thing. I don't believe many of them could screw on a cleat!"

"I was down at the Town marina the other day watching some young fellow trying to put a reverse turn on a fender. He never did get it right."

They watched a fourball putt out on the eighteenth.

"You've never had any more trouble from those Frenchmen over the Billy Smart affair?"

"None at all. But I tell you what, your Richard has been doubly careful to check every last word on the registrations in our brokerage department."

"Has Gelly's sister heard anything of Billy?"

"She gets a card or letter from time to time, posted in various parts of England. Always says he is doing fine and means to bring his girlfriend over to meet her, but of course he never comes. Knows he'll be copped the minute he sets foot on the island."

"What for? You paid off all his debts."

"True. But he doesn't know that. Anyway, I doubt he would have the nerve to show his face."

"So you think Richard makes a good managing director of your business?" Greg prompted, loving to hear praise of his son.

"I have to say I didn't go along with some of his new-fangled ideas at first. But they seem to have worked. The shop he has added to the south side of the sheds brings in a lot of chandlery trade, and the smart new office has seen thousands of pounds worth of brokerage and insurance already."

"I don't suppose he has much time for physically working on the boats, now?"

"Not a lot. He has a good team of blokes working there, but he is always game to take his jacket off and show them how the job should be done, when necessary."

"He and Anne have a good life. Their boys are growing up. George is twelve, now and Derek is fourteen. Pity poor old Filly is so ill."

"Yes. Anne practically lives in her house at the moment, helping to nurse her, but I gather she is steadily going downhill."

Greg gazed down into his beer sadly. It was hard to think of young Felicity with her giggly blue eyes, yellow curls bouncing as she darted round the other side of the tennis net before he and Sarah were even married, now old, wrinkled, white-haired and dying. Was it a good thing, perhaps, that Sarah had been taken from him so many years ago, still in her fifties, so that she had been spared this awful ageing process? He sighed, knowing how much he would have preferred the opportunity to share their ageing together. He had missed her so dreadfully, the one and only love of his whole life. Of course, he was lucky to have a daughter like Sue and a son like Richard, along with their jolly families, to keep him young and alert. It was disappointing that young Stephanie was an unmarried mother, but she was a nice girl and hopefully would find a husband and respectability eventually.

"Better be getting home for lunch or Gelly will complain," George said, heaving his stout body up from his chair.

Greg drained his glass and unwound his lean frame to stand, towering, over his lifelong friend. "Yes. Sue likes to have lunch on the table sharp at one." He loved the routine of lunching with Sue and the family on Sundays.

* * *

203

"You are late today." Neal looked up from the Financial Times as Debbie came into the flat. "Is my step-sister overworking you?"

"Heaven's no! In fact I left the shop ages ago. I had one or two things to see to before coming home." She dropped her bags in an armchair and crossed to where he sat, planting a kiss among the few hairs left on the top of his head.

He twisted in his chair to find her mouth, kissed her long and hard. "So what things had to be seen to?"

"Well, we hadn't anything in the fridge for supper, for a start."

"So what did you get?"

"A couple of steaks, some French bread, salad, and a bottle of wine."

"Wow! A real feast! What's the celebration?"

"I have had an idea. You know Anne and Richard have decided to sell Great Aunt Filly's house, out on L'Ancresse Common?"

"I didn't. But go on."

"I wondered if we might consider buying it for ourselves?"

"We could consider it, I suppose," he said, doubtfully. "I can't even picture it. I've never set foot in the place."

"It's a lovely, old-fashioned bungalow with fabulous views."

"And equally old-fashioned plumbing and wiring, no doubt."

"Oh, Neal!" she pretended to pout. "Blow the plumbing! It's a place to die for! I've always loved it. Mummy used to take us there, visiting, when we were kids. It's a wonderful spot for children, being able to step out of the front door on to the Common to play. And perfectly safe."

"But what's brought this on? I thought we had agreed to stay here in Town until we started a family?"

"We did. And that's the other reason for a celebration dinner. I've just been to the doc and he has confirmed it.

I'm pregnant." She watched for his reaction, and wasn't disappointed.

A huge grin spread over Neal's face. "Yippee!" he bounced out of his chair, flinging sheets of the FT across the floor, and gathered her into his arms. "Oh my sweet! My darling, clever little girl!" At last he was going to be a father; he had begun to think it might never happen.

The late Felicity Warwick's bungalow was not yet officially on the market. Anne Gaudion had wandered through the rooms several times, but had not had the heart to begin the dismantling of her mother's treasures, which would have to be done before strangers were admitted for 'viewings'. There were so many precious ornaments, tiny silver replicas of tennis trophies she had won with Richard's mother, Sarah. Sepia photographs in silver-embossed frames. Mementos of holidays taken with Father, items of furniture which had belonged to generations of ancestors. It was impossible to know where to start. So sad. The end of an era.

Richard had apparently told his mother that the place would be sold, and Sue had mentioned it to Debbie. Hence the latter had telephoned the previous evening to ask if it might be possible to take Neal round to see it. Of course Anne had said yes – she didn't want to refuse and sound rude, but she wasn't at all sure she was ready for this move, yet, only two months after her mother's funeral.

"Debbie and Neal might be the very answer to the problem," Richard had said. "They might be interested to buy much of the furniture and fittings – you know how Debbie loves traditional things and antiques."

Anne had thought about it for a while, then agreed. "It would be nice to feel the place stayed in the family, along with some of Mummy's treasures. She would be heartbroken to think of everything being sold off to strangers."

So Anne had opened up the bungalow the following afternoon to air the rooms, and even put a vase of roses on the oak coffee table, waited till Debbie and Neal arrived and left them to wander at will and return the key to her at home when they left.

Neal was enormously enthusiastic, right from the beginning, quickly overcoming his reservations about the outdated bathroom and dilapidated electrical wiring. "That can all be dealt with in due course," he declared. "Just look at this view! And the lovely master bedroom built into the attic. We can lie in bed and look at the sea! I mean, it's not huge, but very cosy!"

"Our bed would fit in here very nicely, and Aunt Filly's single can go into a spare room. Don't you just love her dressing-table?"

"Do you think Anne would be willing to part with some of these pieces?" he asked, running a hand appreciatively over a pretty Victorian chair.

"I think she would love to feel that anything she can't take would stay *in situ.*"

"It will stretch our resources, I'm afraid, to the limit. We may not be able to do much by way of improvements for some time."

"So what? We have all the time in the world, haven't we?"

There was no question about the fact that they were both as keen as mustard to buy.

So after consultations with Roderick and Alex Grolinski with regard the true value, Anne and Richard came up with an asking price over which Neal haggled only slightly, hands were shaken and it was agreed they would pass contracts within the month.

"Cooee! Where are you?" Stephanie called as she hurried through the house.

"In the kitchen!" Sue and her granddaughter shouted in unison. They were both wearing pinafores and up to the elbows in flour.

"You're baking! What's cooking?"

"We've made a pie for tomorrow's lunch and this is for blackberry and apple crumble," Sarah told her mother.

"When Gran fetched me from school we went blackberrying. We got lots!"

"I see that. And ate lots, too, judging by the state of your face!" she stooped to kiss the child, then flopped into a kitchen chair. "Is this tea hot?" she indicated the pot sitting at her elbow, under a cosy.

"Made about ten minutes ago. There's a cup there for you. Help yourself. There, young lady, I think that crumble is about ready, don't you?"

"Can we cook it now?"

"We've got to get home, darling," Stephanie interrupted. "We both have things to do."

"Oh Mummy! *Please?*" Sarah wailed.

"Shh! No need to panic," her grandmother admonished. "I've put some of the fruit mixture into a plastic tub, and some of this crumble can go in a bag for you to take home and cook for your supper."

"Oh goodie!" the child squealed.

"Thanks, Mum," Stephanie acknowledged Sue's thoughtfulness. Which didn't start and finish with apple crumble! Her mother was such a brick, collecting Sarah from school every weekday, and having her here during the holidays, taking such a load off her mind, leaving her free to work and concentrate on her career. It remained hard going, forcing herself out of bed early every morning to make herself look neat and smart for the day, cook breakfast, make preparations for the evening meal and leave their home reasonably tidy. Then get Sarah ready for school and deliver her there, before hurrying into Town to hunt for a car park. However much she enjoyed her work, the extra chores at morning and evening made the days very long and tiring, so it was wonderful to know that Sarah was with her grandmother, and far happier than with a paid carer. That was another thing, the saving of money; for of course Sue flatly refused to be compensated financially, even for the petrol in her car.

"Having Sarah with me so much is all the reward I need. She keeps me young and feeling useful. You have no idea how redundant some women feel at my age."

Stephanie knew her mother wasn't exaggerating, though she guessed there were many times when she might have preferred the chance to relax, to do something more amusing. As for herself, Stephanie was aware that tiredness was the cue for the recurrence of memories of the commune, of the luxury of lying in bed till one felt inspired to get out, of drifting, undriven, through the hours of a day unhurried, unpressured by clocks and business hours, uninterrupted by beeping phones and appointment diaries, but those memories always ended with shuddering thoughts of the downside – the aimlessness and the endless dirt.

Her salary remained very modest but was sufficient to rent what had once been a holiday chalet near L'Islet, no great distance from *La Rocquette de Bas*. A roll of secondhand carpet, some discarded curtains from home and various pieces of redundant furniture from Mum's attic had turned the soulless four walls into a cosy home. Granpa Greg had supplied a bed and some old paintings and a few potted plants had completed the picture.

Of the pair, Sarah had most enjoyed the building of their new nest, installing her toys, favourite Rabbit taking pride of place on her bed.

"Long may your desire to fight redundancy continue!" Stephanie laughed. "Now we must away. Being Saturday tomorrow Sarah and I will be at home, so I doubt you will see us."

"But you will come for lunch on Sunday, won't you?" Sue insisted.

"Wouldn't miss it for the world!"

"Why, after nearly twenty years, do I still have this urgent desire to maul your body?" Stephen nuzzled under the curls in the back of Sue's neck while his hands moved over the front of her T-shirt.

"You always were a lecher!" She leaned against him, turning her face to rub the short stubble on his chin with her forehead.

"And I suppose the children would call me a dirty old man, if they saw us."

"Wouldn't they be right?" she stopped stirring the gravy, pulled the saucepan away from the heat and twisted in his arms, reaching up to draw his face down to hers.

"Really, you two! Must you carry on like that in public!" Bobbie exclaimed as he came in the backdoor.

"Why the hell not?" his father demanded. "You do!"

"I'm barely twenty!"

"So what? Do you imagine that gives you a priority on lust?"

The boy roared with laughter. "Lust! At your age!"

"Bobbie!" his mother complained. "I shall be very disappointed for you if you can no longer lust after your wife when you have been married a mere twenty years!"

"Honestly, Mum! You have to be joking!"

"Of course, darling," she said with a note of sarcasm. "Now I shall be dishing up in five minutes and I don't want you disappearing into the bathroom as soon as I put it on the table."

"Of course not, Mother," returning the sarcasm with interest. "As though I would."

Playfully, Sue pulled the ovencloth from her shoulder and flung it at his head.

"Lunch!" Stephen called across the lawn to the tennis court where Debbie and Neal were playing.

"Thank heavens for that. I'm starving!" Already there was a slight bulge under her tennis skirt, denoting she would be eating for two. "Anyway," she added as she came into the kitchen, "It's not much fun playing with Neal at the moment. He's so afraid I might over-stretch myself that he deliberately returns every ball to the centre of my racquet."

"Quite right too," said Greg from the doorway, remembering how taboo the subject of pregnancy had been when his Sarah was expecting Sue. When she had told her mother the glad tidings, the old lady hadn't spoken to her for weeks!

"Not many of us today for lunch," Sue complained as she carried in the roast pork.

"Uncle John and Edna not coming?" asked Stephanie, following with an ashet piled with roast potatoes.

"No. They've been invited out to friends in St Saviour's."

"And what about Roderick and Jane?" Stephen brought in the carrots and parsnips.

"She is still getting the most appalling morning sickness."

"Why?" Greg asked. "Is she pregnant again?"

"Oh Dad! You are becoming so forgetful! I've told you several times. She's nearly four months gone, now!"

"And I suppose Sir Gordon and Lady Sybil are still in Spain," Bobbie observed.

"Yes." Stephen picked up the carving knife and honed it up and down the steel. "I wonder how they are getting on."

Lady Sybil was stretching out on a sunbed on the *naya*, overlooking the little fishing port of Moraira on the east coast of Spain. They had seen scarcely a cloud since arriving at the villa nearly a month ago. General Sir Gordon Banks, now a youthful eighty-three, preferred a recliner chair where he could read yesterday's papers more comfortably until they dropped on to the *naya* tiles and he fell under the spell of the Spanish siesta hour. He enjoyed their annual trip to the sun; he felt truly invigorated by the drive south from St Malo, down the superb French autoroutes – even Spain was extending her autopistes, though Sybil who did all the navigating, complained bitterly that the signposting left too much to guess work. He thought this villa, the same one they rented every year, was delightful, with it's tosca stone arches, wide shady *nayas* with tosca balconies, decoratively curved iron *rejas* over the windows and colourfully tiled kitchen and bathrooms. Three times a day he plunged into the blue-tiled swimming pool to do the statutory ten lengths and showered away the clorine before changing into khaki shorts and sandals, North African desert gear as he remembered it. The only thing that got his goat, slightly, was the fact that the English papers were always one day late. Not that it really mattered nowadays – he was not in a position to influence national events any longer, though he did like to keep up with current affairs.

His eyes drifted over the stone balcony to the glistening horizon where two yachts were seeking, unsuccessfully, a breath of wind to fill their sails. Then he smiled as he watched his wife slumbering, her magazine on the floor beside her. She was so beautiful still, a mere girl of sixty-two. He knew she assisted her hair to remain as blonde as ever, but her figure in that skimpy two-piece bathing suit remained perfect, revealing how she had gently toasted her skin to a golden tan.

"Hmm!" he would need to get some sleep, ready for this evening. They were meeting up with some English friends who had settled out here, years ago. Not something he would care to do himself: nothing to do here all year round but drink till you dropped. No, he preferred living in the island amidst constant family and friends, where one had easy access to London's theatres and clubs.

Sybil wore a sleeveless, pale turquoise silk dress and matching stole, with gold-mounted ivory earrings and ivory bead necklet. Gordon was in a linen khaki suit, the jacket doubling as open-necked shirt and tunic.

Jean and Geoffrey Havers were waiting for them in the bar at the Parador in Javea, and the four settled down in a corner with gins and tonics.

"Lovely to see you both looking so fit and bronzed," Jean remarked. "You were quite pale when you arrived."

"Not a very bright start to the summer, this year, up north," Sybil responded. "In fact jolly frigid!"

"So the family tell us," Geoffrey nodded. "It's why we prefer to live out here." He turned to Gordon. "Doesn't the though ever cross your mind?"

"Not seriously. Too far from London and from the family."

"Personally, I think having the family out to stay for a fortnight each year is more than enough. Their visit always leaves us feeling totally washed out," Jean complained. "Can't think of anything worse than living within permanent hailing distance of them."

"Absolute hell," her husband nodded, laughing. "The women would end up never speaking to each other."

So much for family unity, Sybil thought, picturing the happy family lunches at the Martels' home. Of course she was in no position to make judgements, never having had any children herself. Gordon already had a family by his first wife and had had no desire to start again. They had a very different kind of lifestyle, enjoying each other, indulging their whims and fancies, travelling . . . but she would have considered herself a failed parent to have maintained such a miserable relationship with any progeny. Such antagonism and intolerance!

". . . bridge last night with friends who have a villa in near Orba," Geoffrey was saying. "We were talking cars: well, as you know ours is getting truly dilapidated and we want to get a new one. Trouble is bringing it into the country without paying phenomenal duty on it. So I pricked up my ears when they told us about this fellow who deals in really good quality secondhand cars. Brings 'em in duty free. So I asked them for an introduction."

"Are you sure it is legal?" Gordon asked.

"Seems to be all above board. The fellow swears they are clean, so who's to query it?"

"I imagine he is doing a roaring trade. Is he a Spaniard?"

"No, no. English. Name of Jason Smith. And by coincidence I believe he has some connection with one of the Channel Islands. He also deals in boats."

Brows slightly raised, Sybil caught Gordon's eye. They had both heard the full story of Billy Smart's dubious deals involving Richard Gaudion and George Schmit. "What is the fellow like?" she murmured casually into her drink.

"Short, chunky. A bit of a smart Alec if you ask me. But if he can supply any type of car I want at a good price, I'm not going to turn down the chance because I don't like the cut of his jib!"

Gordon had met Billy Smart once, at the boatyard, and he had to admit the description fitted to a T. But was it possible it could be the same chap?

Jean opened her handbag. "I can do better than that. We

all had lunch together, remember dear, at the *Los Amigos* restaurant and I took a photo. Look." She handed the rather blurred snapshot to Gordon.

Blurred it might have been, but there was no doubt left in Gordon's mind. His expression remained perfectly blank as he handed it back. "You seem to have had quite a jolly party," he said.

"We did. Oh, and by the way, you're going back next Monday, aren't you? He gave us some mail to be posted in the UK. No use posting anything out here: doesn't get sorted for weeks!" She took a packet of letters and cards from her bag and handed them to Sybil. "I told him we knew someone going back, soon. You might stick them in a box at Heathrow. They have English stamps on."

Gordon looked at his watch. "Great Scott, it's quarter to nine, The dining room must be open by now. Let's go and find a table."

"You didn't feel we should warn them?" Sybil asked as they drove back through the gorge at Gata.

"They didn't want to be warned," Gordon argued. "They knew well enough that they would be . . . skirting the law if they bought from him and they are prepared to take the risk." He paused, concentrating on the narrow, winding road. "Anyway, what could we say? That it was suggested he had been involved in some dubious deals a few years ago, but nothing was proved? And suppose their deal did go wrong and they were caught by the *Guardia*, do we want to be called as witnesses next time we come over?"

Sybil sighed. "I suppose not."

"Then let's forget it. The man was holding a beer mug in front of his face in the photo. Almost unrecognisable, eh?"

"Yes dear," she grinned into the darkness. "Now you had better slow down, this is our turning coming up, by that pile of stones." Then she added, "I tell you what, I think I might go down with a sore tummy next year when we are due to meet up with the Havers. Frankly, darling, I don't think I like them all that much."

"Good. Nor do I. Let's drop round to the Parsons' tomorrow and see if they'd like a trip down to the *Quo*

Vadis in Alicante, before we go? Now they seem very reasonable." He couldn't overcome the feeling that there were an awful lot of ex-patriots who had come out here for a geographical cure for their problems. The trouble was their problems always seemed to follow them.

"Are you happy, dear?" Sue asked Stephanie. They were sitting on the wooden bench at the court side, having just completed a set in which Sue had walloped her daughter.

"Good heavens yes, Mum. Why do you ask?"

"I sometimes feel you have a rather lonely life."

"Well, it might have been, a few months ago, but it is becoming less so."

Sue cocked her head. "Really? Tell me."

"There is a very nice crowd at work, you know. And I get asked out quite a lot."

"What do you do about babysitters?"

"Nothing. I take Sarah with me and put her to bed in the host's house. It's a very easy arrangement, then I take her home fast asleep and put her into her own bed."

"Excellent. And nobody minds?"

"No. Least of all Sarah! She thinks it all quite an adventure."

"Ever meet any nice men?"

Stephanie laughed. "I didn't think it would be long before you asked that. Yes. Several, and I have to admit there is one who is particularly nice. But it is very early days. We only met three weeks ago, but the vibes seem good."

Sue grinned. "I'll keep my fingers crossed." It would be lovely to think of Stephanie finally settling down in a happy partnership. And wasn't it wonderful to think that they could talk about such things so openly, now. Only a few years ago the girl would have deeply resented such an invasion of her privacy. "Let's go and see how Uncle Bobbie is getting on helping his niece with her homework."

Suzanne Martel looked down the length of her dining table with satisfaction. Although so many things had changed in the past twenty-five or so years, and not all for the better,

214

providing one was prepared to accept the changes – veer with the tide – much could remain constant. Her family were all here, all twenty of them, and nothing made her happier. Like any normal family they did have their squabbles from time to time, but generally it could be said that they were a very contented and aimiable crowd, sitting under the eagle eye of her father Gregory Gaudion, the family patriarch.

Her mother's brother, Uncle John, was still going strong. He had to be in his late eighties, but his dear Edna fed him so well he looked fit for at least another ten years. Then there was Dad's late brother's wife, Aunt Maureen, mother of the beautiful cousin Sybil who had married General Sir Gordon Banks. The latter was such a fun person, not the slightest bit pompous or stuffy, who had fitted into the family with the greatest of ease and showed Aunt Maureen so much affection.

Brother Richard was the shyest, quietest member of the family, happily married to Anne who, with her bouncy blonde curls, blue eyes and plump figure, was the reincarnation of her mother, dear Aunt Filly who had died earlier this year. Their two boys, Derek and George, now fourteen and twelve respectively, were proving to be a right couple of tearaways, but nice with it. She remembered when she was their age, away on the mainland during the war with no family, most of the time. How she had longed for a real home again, for the parents she had almost forgotten over the five years of separation. Yet it had been so hard to re-establish the parent-child relationship when she came back. Hard for both sides. As each of her children reached their tenth birthdays, she had felt deep sympathy for her own parents, waving good-bye to their then only child . . . though little had they realised that far from being for a matter of a few weeks, it was to be for five long years. Years in which she had grown up fast, to return as an independent young woman who would deeply resent interference with her decisions!

And now her own children were grown up, with families of their own. Roderick, blond hair and sharpening aquiline features like his father, her first husband, Jonathan, sitting down there next to the mouse-like Jane, who was spoon feeding young Gregory in his high chair, while attempting to fight down the nausea of her current pregnancy. Stephanie had sat herself next to Uncle John, but young Sarah was not to be separated from her idol, Uncle Bobbie. He was a handsome boy, the image of his father, Stephen, and studying architecture at university so that he might go into the family business.

Then there was her dear Debbie, the athletic, green-eyed redhead who still excelled so well on the tennis court. Despite her early misgivings, Sue had to admit that the girl's marriage to Neal Blaydon, a much older divorcee, showed every sign of being a huge success. Sitting next to her, he was ever attentive and enormously proud of her bulge, under the tablecloth. They had recently bought Aunt Filly's house on the Common, which was marvellous. It meant that they would be near so that she could see them and their children more frequently.

And finally, there at the opposite end of the table, was her beloved Stephen, his gentle grey eyes an everlasting source of comfort and contentment. They was an increasing amount of grey mixed with the jet black hair on his temples, but he was still gorgeously handsome. And what a wonderful husband he was: he had coaxed and soothed her through so many family crises, supported her when she was troubled and talked her out of battles and confrontations which her fiery temper had persuaded her to enjoin.

"What's on your mind, Sue?" Stephen asked, from the far end, always sensitive to her moods.

"I was just thinking how very lucky I am to have such a wonderful family. Forgive me, everyone, for being a bit maudlin today. It is just that this particular happiness is something I missed out on so dreadfully for a long period of my life. Which makes me appreciate it so much more, now."

Stephen thought she had never looked more beautiful, with her lovely dark hair and eyes as green as the sea had been, that day so many years ago when they had first made love. He smiled and raised his glass. "To happy, united families, my darling!"

And everyone joined in. "To happy families."

216